JESTER

JESTER

BRIELLE D. PORTER

CamCat Books

CamCat Publishing, LLC
Brentwood, Tennessee 37027
camcatpublishing.com

Hardcover ISBN 9780744305586
Paperback ISBN 9780744305906
Large-Print Paperback ISBN 9780744308853
eBook ISBN 9780744306651
Audiobook ISBN 9780744306491

Library of Congress Control Number: 2022930924

Book and cover design by Maryann Appel

5   3   1   2   4

To Johnny,
I know we don't believe in soul mates,
but baby, you're mine.

CHAPTER
1

A group of tourists has gathered to watch me throw knives at a shop-boy. They've come here for magic; I've kept them here with misdirection and lies. Maybe it's not magic exactly, but it is undeniably entertaining watching my unwilling assistant flinch every time the knife point gets too close to his groin.

I hold the knife steady, aiming, watching his limp hair flop as the wooden wheel he's strapped to slowly rotates.

Stefan lets out a whimper, and I toss him a smile. He was a lot braver in the shop where I'd found him, flirting as he bagged my books. It hadn't been hard to trick him into volunteering.

The crowd jeers.

"Aim lower!"

"Aim *higher*! Maim his ugly face!"

"Throw three at once!"

"Mirage, don't you dare!" Stefan shouts.

The nighttime crowd is always hungrier for violence. I hold up my hands placatingly.

"Obviously, I can't throw three knives at once. That would be dangerous and highly irresponsible . . ."

There are a couple of groans, but my reputation must precede me, because there are a few whoops and chuckles thrown in as well. With a sweep, I pull my deadliest knife from my belt, the one with the wicked serrated edge, brandishing it for the crowd.

"But I think we can spice things up a bit!"

I stab the knife into a vat of oil, the shimmering liquid sliding down the tang of the blade. Then, with a flourish, I sweep it through a nearby torch. Flame devours the knife. The crowd roars its approval. Stefan pales.

The hilt burns in my hand, throwing off sparks, as I wonder if perhaps I've gone too far. I've only tried this a few times. And the jackrabbit I had caught to practice with wasn't even good to eat after, blackened to an inedible crisp.

Either way, I'll give them a show.

Even though the knife feels like it's blistering my palm, I take a moment to pan the audience. This is always my favorite part. The tension is a palpable thing, visible in held gasps, wide eyes, and awe.

Magic.

And that's when I see him. Expression carefully neutral, almost bored, one eyebrow raised, arms folded across a suit that costs more than my father made in a year. A seeker.

My heart pounds, as I realize more than Stefan's crotch is at stake here now. If I nail this, that pretentious clown in a suit has the power to get my act in front of the queen. I could be the next Jester. It's the reason I've come here tonight, the same reason I've performed for thousands of crowds like this one.

Sucking in a breath, I hold the knife level.

Stefan thrashes, but the bindings pinning him to the wheel like a dead butterfly hold. Right as I pull back to throw, there's a shout.

"Kingkiller!"

The knife slips in my grip, but it's too late. I watch, horrified, as the blade wobbles in the air, the trajectory off. It clatters to the ground a few feet away from Stefan, flames smothered in the dirt. There's a moment of shocked silence, as though the crowd is waiting for me to do something.

Make a joke. Throw another knife. *Something*. I can still save this. Even Stefan gawps at me as I stare unseeing at the crowd. But I don't do anything. I just stand there, the word pounding in my head, over and over.

Kingkiller.

Even real magic couldn't save me now. It couldn't save my father— traitor to the throne and murderer of the king. Not that I have magic anyway, as my father's magic died with him when they executed him for treason. Leaving my family disgraced, leaving me to peddle illusion in a cheap imitation of the real thing.

The seeker is gone. I watch him leave, head shaking as if disappointed, the crowd swallowing him up again. My one big shot, gone as quickly as the smoke from my act.

I gather up my knives, suddenly too exhausted to even finish the show. There are a few shouted threats, but I hardly notice through the fog of disappointment. I can't believe it's over. Seventeen months I've waited for the opportunity to impress a seeker, and with just one word, it's over. And I didn't even make enough gold dust to buy myself dinner.

I loosen Stefan's bindings, my fingers slipping as a loud gasp from the nearby crowd steals my attention. Stefan drops with a thud and a curse, but I hardly hear his complaints. Most of my audience has wandered off, inflating the already bloated numbers of the show next to mine. The entire stretch of street, known fondly to those in the business as the Noose, is filled with performers clamoring to be seen. Nowhere else in the kingdom of Terraca is there a place so glutted with magic: everything from the mundane enchantments like the ones used to keep the hotels refreshingly cool inside—even here in the desert—to the spectacular.

Sandwiched between the most impressive hotels in Oasis—including the impressive Crown Hotel—the Noose is one of the best spots to snag wealthy patrons with too much gold in their wallets and too much liquor in their blood.

A bolt of lightning so bright it leaves a streak in my vision cracks the pavement several feet away. Applause and gold nuggets are thrown at the magician, who bows.

Ignoring Stefan's shouts, I wander over to see what has the tourists so hot. I've seen most of the shows in the Noose multiple times; after all, I've got to maintain a healthy edge over my competitors. So, I'm not surprised when I recognize the performer instantly. His name rises in my throat like bile.

Luc.

Long blond hair swept into a knot on top of his head and with a jawline that could cut glass, Luc is one of the most popular acts on the Noose, besides my own. Even with his face arranged in an arrogant sneer, he's still irritatingly handsome. A simple flourish of his long red coat sparks deafening applause. The crowds love him and he knows it. His gaze sweeps the crowd greedily, sucking in the cheers as though they physically sustain him. I know the feeling well.

I jolt when his eyes land on me, pick me out in the crowd. I want to shrink, to disappear, the same caught feeling as a mouse in the gaze of a hawk.

"Can I have a volunteer, please?"

The hand of every eligible woman in the crowd shoots up. He grins, cocky, surveying the desperate volunteers. He raises an eyebrow at me, intention clear. I cross my arms, unwilling to give him the satisfaction of a reaction. With a disappointed shake of his head so slight I could've imagined it, he selects a different young woman.

Even from where I stand near the back of the crowd, it's obvious she is heartbreakingly lovely and fantastically wealthy. Luc's smile broadens as he helps her onstage. Flowing blonde hair, full lips, flushed cheeks, and a garnet necklace like a collar of blood against her pale throat. I roll my eyes. Luc definitely has a type.

He takes her hand gently and leans in to whisper something in her ear. She titters, cheeks rosy. She's clearly enraptured, unaware of the fate that awaits her, a butterfly in a web. Even if she did know, I doubt she'd care. Half the women in this audience have seen Luc's show before, and in spite of its macabre ending, they still keep coming in droves. He ignores her fluttering lashes, his eyes finding me again in the crowd. A chill runs down my spine.

Without breaking eye contact, he stabs the girl onstage. And even though I've seen his show hundreds of times, know exactly how it ends, a gasp breaks free from my tight lips as she crumples to the ground. Blood stains the wood around her, a stage that has seen its fair share of death. Seeing my reaction, he actually has the nerve to smile as she bleeds out on the ground beside him.

He steps away from the blood before it can reach his expensive snakeskin boots, ignoring the paunchy man who clambers onstage with him, pawing frantically at the bloody maiden.

"Olivia! What have you done to her? Olivia, wake up!"

Olivia's father, I assume, if his age and resemblance to the girl are any indicator. Luc smiles down benevolently at the man, whose face is blotchy and panicked. Tears run down his cheek as he blubbers, and my gut clenches both in shame for him and pity.

"Who will pay the debt for this maiden?" Luc asks. He doesn't extend a hand to the man, who grasps at his trousers, unaware of the blood that stains his fine clothes.

"I will," the man cries, wiping the snot from his face. "Please, I'll do anything! Just bring back my daughter."

Luc has chosen wisely; it's obvious this man will pay anything for his jewel of a daughter. Luc eyes him as though weighing a handful of gold dust and then glances at the ropes of garnets choking the woman's fragile neck. The desperate father seizes upon his meaning, and with shaking fingers unclasps the heavy necklace and passes it to Luc. Holding it up for the crowd first, Luc pockets the jewels with a satisfied smile.

"The debt has been paid. Arise, fair maiden!"

For a moment nothing happens. Everyone's eyes are on the girl, whose lips have turned a faint blue. But my eyes are on Luc. I can see the strain as he tries to bring her back from Beyond. The sweat that runs, neglected, down his temple. The clenched fists. Watching for any kind of rise in her lungs. But they stay still.

I've only seen Luc fail once. That girl's family was desolate but could do nothing, because that's what these wealthy fools come here for. To be thrilled. To be entertained, no matter the cost. And Luc never fails to give them a show.

Heart pounding, I watch Luc cross the stage, jaw tight. To anyone else he looks collected, but I can see the way his teeth grind. *She's not coming back*, I think, and before I can register the thought, Luc lifts the dead girl up and kisses her passionately. The man, her father, I remember numbly, lets out a startled cluck like a chicken on a chopping block.

For a minute it's deathly silent. Then the girl gasps for air, hands scrabbling at Luc's neck. I let out a gust of air, then feel my lungs inflate as hers do. Luc bows to riotous applause as gold nuggets rain on the stage. No one sees the girl, whose lips are still blue, whose lungs struggle to reset, her father crying into her hair. She'll likely suffer brain damage, being without oxygen for as long as she was. That's the price of magic, true magic. Luc's show is cruel but effective. There's a reason he's known on the Noose as the devil. Sell him your soul, and he'll give you a show.

And although I'm loath to admit it, he's my biggest competition for the position of Jester.

Sure enough, not one, but two seekers have joined him onstage. I watch as they fight for his attention, eager to claim the commission that comes with finding a worthy act. As though he can feel my eyes on him, Luc lifts his gaze from the seekers. I can read the words on his lips as clearly as if he spoke:

"Kingkiller."

CHAPTER
2

I whirl away, the anger so hot I can feel it pounding in my blood. How did that idiot find out about my father? For not the first time in my life, I curse my father for his murderous impulses. I don't care if he killed the king. But I do care that he left me alone, disgraced, the daughter of a traitor, and without magic.

There's no point in performing my last show of the evening now, not after Luc reminded half the Noose of my father's wretched legacy. I reach the doors to the Shipwreck. I grasp for the mother-of-pearl inlaid handle, ignoring the valet rushing to open it for me. The hotel is nothing short of magnificent, despite the name. Marble floors gleam. Everywhere, jeweled sea life frolics, creeps, and slithers.

The opulent chandelier is even a pearl-and-diamond jellyfish, long tentacles swaying. But the true jewel of the Shipwreck is the huge wall-to-wall aquarium, which boasts a large array of sharks, a shy cave octopus, and mermaids.

The mermaids aren't real, of course. Like everything else here, they're a carefully crafted illusion, not truly sirens of the deep but show-girls wearing fake tails, spelled to breathe underwater. Even knowing that, I find myself captivated. Their long, powerful tails flash as they swim elegantly through clouds of jellyfish. They are nude on top, only the barest sprinkling of glitter. One of the mermaids catches my eye through the glass, long azure hair floating, framing her heart-shaped face. I notice her eyes are bloodshot, no doubt from hours of exposure to tank water and exhaustion. The sympathy in her gaze shakes me, as if from a dream.

Turning away from the mermaids, I make my way to the front desk, praying Bale, manager of the Shipwreck, is off duty. Unfortunately for me, I haven't had good luck for longer than I can remember, so I steel myself for the worst.

But the woman at the desk is new, dark hair pulled back into a shining clamshell clip and a worried look on her pretty face. I force a haughty expression, the kind most of the patrons here are wearing, and slam my hand on the heavy gold bell, even though she's right in front of me.

She jumps and eyes me, taking in my worn and filthy costume and unkempt hair.

"I'd like to check into my suite early," I say, drumming my fingers on the gleaming countertop, scanning the room as if everything in it displeases me. Still, the receptionist hesitates, not buying either my look or my tone. Time to seal the deal.

"After suffering a wretched bout of motion sickness through the canyon, I certainly hope your establishment proves itself worthy of my husband, John Ellington's, patronage."

This gets her attention.

"Of course, madam. We've been expecting you both."

I cover my mouth as if yawning, hiding the relief that gusts out of me. The name was a crapshoot; John Ellington, oil baron and notorious gambling addict, visits Oasis often and always seems to have a reserved room. Thanks to the many holes pockmarking the desert from his drills, he has neither a shortage of gold nor new wives.

She riffles through the guest book and scratches a neat checkmark next to John Ellington's name. I watch, hardly daring to breathe, as she pulls two tiny brass keys from a drawer. Just as she reaches to hand them to me, a shout turns my blood to ice.

I turn, groaning inwardly, as a short, sweaty man makes his way across the shining floors. Even in a hurry, he keeps his head high, as if to bely the fact that he physically can't look down on anyone, not even me.

"Hello, Bale," I say, resigned, when he finally reaches the desk. He daubs at his high forehead with an intricately embroidered handkerchief. Even Bale's sweat is worth more than I am.

"Elizabeth, darling," he begins, once he's caught his breath, "this girl has a lifetime ban from the Shipwreck."

"Come on, Bale," I break in, as Elizabeth's gaze darts in my direction in shock.

"I can't believe you made it past the valets," he mutters, wiping his brow again. "What's the story this time, Mirage? Traveling royalty? A lady-in-waiting sent early to prepare the queen's rooms?"

"She said she was the wife of Mr. Ellington, sir," Elizabeth says, twin points of red on her cheeks. I curtsy.

"Ah, of course," Bale says, shaking his head. "Get out of my hotel."

"Please, Bale," I say, hating the pleading tone that's crept into my voice. I'd really prefer to do this the easy way tonight. "I'll give you all the dust I make tomorrow."

It's a lie and we both know it.

"Shoo," he repeats, stubborn. Out of the corner of my eye, I see one of the guards glide in. To anyone else, he's just a very big, well-dressed man. But I see the copper stains on one cuff, the one that he self-consciously folds into his suit sleeve. Bale is clearly not going to change his mind, so I make my way to the doors, shame curdling in my stomach.

I'm so focused on the floor, I almost run headfirst into another patron.

"Watch it!" I cry.

"Begging your pardon, *madam,*" the patron says, smirking, and that's when I realize I know him. Tall, lithe frame cloaked all in red. Luc.

"Get out of my way," I snap, but he just stands there, barring the door. A heavy gold snake winds its way across his shoulders, a scaled stole. I ignore the way its slitted eyes follow my every move.

"I didn't know you were married," Luc says, a lazy smile on his lips. "And to John Ellington, no less. That makes you his fifth wife in six months. Lucky man."

So, he saw everything then.

"Move before I disembowel you," I say, meeting his arrogant gaze, making sure he sees the glint of the knife in my hand.

"Such a lady," he chuckles. "How did you like my show?"

"Getting a bit predictable," I bite out, finally shoving past him. To my great annoyance, he follows me out into the street.

"We can't all be wizards with a knife, can we?" he calls after me. "Pity you can't do any real magic though."

I whip around to face him, pleased when he almost stumbles.

"Even so, I did notice you still had to resort to name-calling to steal away my audience," I say, trying not to wince when the snake lets out a low hiss.

Luc strokes the snake on his shoulder, enjoying my evident disgust.

"I'll be honest, not my finest moment, but it worked better than I could've imagined. Headliner at the Panther now, thanks to you."

I scowl. That should have been me.

"Soon to be Jester," he murmurs near my ear, and it's then I realize how close he is. The snake on his shoulder sways, half its body suspended in the air. I stumble backward quickly, as I realize it's bridging the gap between us.

"Oh, I do apologize," Luc says, letting the snake slide down his arm and twine around his fingers. "Do you not like my snake?"

"I have no interest whatsoever in your *snake*," I reply scathingly.

"Shame," he says, white teeth glinting.

I turn away, disgusted.

"Come now, *Lisette*, don't be like that. I'm only teasing."

I freeze at the mention of my name, my real name, not the stage name I don like a mask. I whirl around, but he's gone, nothing to indicate he was even there, other than a few wisps of smoke and the smell of oranges.

I always swear that I won't come back. That each night will be my last. And yet, every twilight finds me here again, returned like a dog to its vomit.

The place certainly smells like vomit. I wrinkle my nose against the assortment of foul odors assaulting my senses: cheap alcohol, the spicy musk of body odor and bad breath, years of mold . . . I'm fairly certain that if despair had a smell, this would be it.

I peel off my Noose costume regretfully—black corset, black cape with embroidered gold stars in the lining, black trousers that lace up the sides, black boots. It's a simple outfit compared to Luc's, but I like to think my show stands on its own. Trading one disguise for another, I fold my clothes neatly, careful to ensure nothing comes in contact with the grimy vanity or stained carpets. The server getup, like everything else in the Bird of Paradise Casino, is gaudy. Bright, unnaturally colored feathers adorn the corset, which is sequined, and the headdress, which is heavy. Fake gold bangles, chipped and worn, line my wrists and arms. The headdress is studded with large plastic jewels. I eye the faux gemstones balefully. Once upon a time, the jewels I wore were real.

Everything was real, once.

I cringe as I slide on the bottom half of the costume, little more than a pair of panties adorned with a sweeping tail of feathers. Half the feathers are missing, no thanks to the wandering hands of patrons. Given the more than fifty servers working the casino floors and a less than adequately staffed laundry, there's never any telling whether or not the girl before me bothered to wash the costume.

I sit in one of the stained wardrobe chairs and unbraid my hair, shaking out the long rose-gold waves, hating the feel of them against my exposed back. The shoes are always last, painful stilettos that I'm not allowed to kick off no matter how much they pinch. I take a shallow breath, as deep as the corset will allow, eyeing myself in the cracked gilt mirror of the vanity. One of the girls told me when I first started working, in scandalized whispers, that Louie, the owner, had a black-market magician spell the mirrors to be two-way. I squint at my reflection, wondering if he's watching right now.

I cared once.

Now I pretend not to know, like the rest of the girls.

"Last night," I promise the girl in the reflection. I've only said it a million times before.

The dressing room door bangs open, and Pearl, one of the servers, collapses into the chair next to mine in a heap of feathers. She peels her shoes off, groaning.

"Long day?" I ask, patting a glittery balm onto my lips.

"One of the patrons won the jackpot," Pearl says, without even opening her eyes, still slumped in the chair.

Now it's my turn to groan. Most of the time the bouncers, Louie's carefully trained enforcers, can sniff out even the faintest magic, ensuring there are never any cheaters. Not coincidentally, most of the bigger winners end up accused of magical manipulation, but even the bouncers can't prevent all wins.

"Louie's been a nightmare," Pearl adds, although that part is obvious. Louie hates winners, even though a big win usually means more patrons, all hoping the luck is contagious. I steel myself for the long night ahead.

Adjusting my headdress, I head out onto the casino floor, grabbing a tray of drinks. All around, dead-eyed patrons drink and gamble. Faded palm trees adorn the worn and scuffed carpets. Being one of the lower-end casinos on Oasis, Louie doesn't have it in the budget to use much magic to keep patrons willingly imprisoned here, so he has to resort to more ordinary techniques. There are no windows, no clocks, nothing to distract players from their own self-destruction. Even without the added allure of magic, I've seen players spend days in the casino, unaware of anything but the whir, spin, and lights of the games.

"Over here, darling," a voice drawls, shaking me from my thoughts. I dutifully make my way to the Hanged Man table, where a group of elderly women are tossing dice. Free liquor is another tactic Louie employs to keep his patrons happy and stupid enough to keep losing money. I set down the drinks wordlessly. I've learned better than to engage the patrons. Louie likes us to flirt a little, to tease, but he has showgirls for that, and anyway, I don't get paid nearly enough to endure more torture than I already do.

"Fill 'em up," the woman says, not even looking my way. She's clearly on a winning streak; a stack of crystal chips sits in a pile next to her heavily adorned wrists. It's obvious she had money, once. Maybe her husband died. Maybe she lost it gambling. No one worth anything gambles at Bird of Paradise. Likely all these women are disgraced in some way, hoping to clamber back into society's good graces with someone else's money. I know the feeling.

I take the shot glasses, filled to three-quarters with a garish purple liquor, and with a snap, light them on fire. It's just a cheap bit of theatrics and carefully placed chemistry, but the patrons love it. A few of the ladies ooh, although most are focused on the woman who summoned me. From across the room, Louie's heavy brow darkens into a scowl. I'm not supposed to perform while on the clock, just fill drinks and clean, like a good little waitress.

"Beautiful," the woman says, downing the whole glass without even looking up. I'm dismissed. I collect the spent glasses as the women chatter and murmur, pretending I don't exist.

"Did you hear Raster is holding one of his parties tomorrow?" One of the women says, fanning her florid face. It is abnormally hot tonight; Louie's clearly tight-fisting money after his loss, skimping on air-conditioning.

"The seeker? I heard he's still sore about losing that headliner from the Panther..."

I stop, gripping one of the glasses, still warm from the pyrotechnics. I hadn't expected the news about Luc to travel so quickly. He might actually have a shot at Jester.

"I heard he spent more gold on his new menagerie than the queen spent on the princess's christening."

"Such a show-off," one of the women sighs. "Isn't he single?"

"Now, now, Cecilia, the party is by invitation only, very exclusive, you know..."

The woman named Cecilia, who must be pushing seventy, waggles thick eyebrows. "Like that's ever stopped me."

I manage to choke back my surprised laugh just in time, although the noise catches the attention of one of the other women.

"That will be all," she says pointedly, casting a disdainful look at my costume. All hopes of a tip vanish. I take the hint. Hurrying, I pick up the tray and gracefully make my exit.

"Maybe if I wore something like that," Cecilia says as I swish away, and the table erupts into hoots and catcalls. I barely hear them; my mind is racing. Raster can ignore me all he likes on the streets, but if I were able to go to his party, I could make him pay attention to me. Unfortunately, there's no way I can secure an invitation to a party as exclusive as Raster's.

Which means I need Del.

I'm so focused, I barely see the man stumbling from a chair in front of me, and we collide head-on. My tray falls, glasses shattering. I let out a cry of dismay, but hardly anyone looks up at the sound.

"Stupid girl," the man grumbles, wiping at his suit, a worn thing that does him no favors. I kneel to pick up the broken tumblers, ignoring the bite of glass in my fingers and palm. As long as I can get this cleaned up before Louie sees—

"What's all this?"

I grip the handful of shards, cringing.

"Your idiot server ran into me," the man slurs, swaying on his feet.

"Shoulda known it'd be you," Louie grumbles behind me. I stand up on wobbling knees, still clutching the broken tumblers.

"It was an accident—"

"Sir, I do apologize," Louie says, talking right over me, using the stuffy voice he saves for patrons. "Allow me to assist you in cleaning that up."

He snaps his fingers at me, and confused, I hand him the sodden rag I've used to wipe up the mess. Bits of glass cling to it, and it's stained purple.

Louie's eyes roll heavenward, as though I'm the biggest fool there ever was. "A clean one, if you please?"

I scramble to the bar, dumping the tray of broken glass at the bartender, who casts me a bewildered look. Grabbing a pile of clean cloths, I hand them to Louie, who snatches them away without even looking at me. He daubs uselessly at the man's lapels, the giant blotch of purple refusing to budge.

"It's ruined," the man says, lamenting. "My best suit."

I can see the way Louie's teeth grind as he wipes so hard at the stain, bits of cloth scrape off.

"There's a laundress in town," I pipe in, tentatively. "Magical stain removal—"

"Quiet, you," Louie growls. His face smooths, as he turns to the patron. "We'll replace the suit."

The man's face grows shrewd. "And you'll throw in a free round of Dead Man's Bluff?"

Louie's jaw works. "Of course."

The man shambles off, pleased. I know better than to be relieved though, and sure enough, as soon as he's out of sight, Louie turns on me.

"Third offense in less than a month," he snaps, shoving the cloth back at me. "You know what that means."

I do know what that means. Louie has been threatening to fire me for months. Outrage blooms in my chest. "It wasn't my fault!"

This time, anyway.

"Not my problem," Louie says, bustling off in the direction of the game machines. I follow him, limping, a shard of glass burrowed deep in one toe.

"What about my room?" I get half my meager salary in dust, and the other half pays for one of Louie's dingy rooms. Without that, I'd be homeless.

"Every bit of dust you earned tonight is going towards damages," Louie growls, then plasters on a large, fake smile for a table of patrons. "Who's feeling lucky tonight?"

"We had a deal!"

Louie's faux smile becomes bared teeth as he turns to face me. "A deal that was conditional on you remaining an employee."

With a snap, one of the bouncers slides in between us. The man is large, brutish, lacking the subtlety of the Shipwreck's bouncers. Two meaty hands clasp in front of a garish suit covered in flamingos.

"Escort her out."

I shrug away from the bouncer's reach. "I'll walk myself out, thanks."

"Leave the costume in the laundry room."

Cheap pig.

"Fine," I snap, although I have no intention of doing so. I stomp back to the dressing room, livid. Thankfully, it's empty, and there are no witnesses as I throw the headdress as hard as I can at the mirror. To my great disappointment, the glass stays stubbornly whole, although the headdress cracks. I flop into one of the chairs, listening to the throbbing of my own heart in my ears.

This is the fourth job I've lost in three months. As bosses go, Louie isn't even the worst around. Girls younger than me have been forced into showgirl jobs at other, seedier casinos, and although Louie is far from perfect, the only thing he allows underage girls to do is serve. I'm not going to find a better job than this one.

I stare at my red-rimmed eyes, my face lined with exhaustion too great for my seventeen years. If my father hadn't killed the king, I'd be training to inherit his magic right now, not slaving away at a minimum wage job.

My father's magic should've been mine. But my father was as selfish in death as he was in life, and when they took his head, he took his magic with him to wherever comes after.

There's only one way to get back everything I've lost. I have to win the position of Jester. As the queen's hand-selected entertainer, I'll be the most sought-after show in the kingdom, magic or no. The highest-ranked magician in the world. With fame like that, no one, not even Luc, will be able to use my past against me again.

I've wasted enough time in jobs like this, going nowhere. I stare at the girl in the reflection, the one I've lied to so many times.

"Last night," I tell her, and this time I mean it.

I've got a party to go to.

CHAPTER
3

The high judge is tired. More than tired, he is exhausted, bone deep. The current case appears beyond even his abilities. He knows that somewhere there's an answer, if only he could find it. If only he wasn't so bloody tired . . .

He is facedown in his book, drool blossoming on the last words he read when the door creaks open. The high judge awakens with a jolt.

"What is it?"

The girl, his second wife's daughter, peers in at him.

"Were you sleeping, my lord?"

"What is it?" he repeats, using a handkerchief to blot at the spit-smeared words. "Quickly now, I'm very busy."

"I learned a trick. A special one, for you, Papa."

The high judge doesn't bother suppressing the sigh that whooshes out of him. "Where is Hattie?"

The girl's nursemaid seemed to lose track of her charge more often than not. He would have to fire her.

The girl shrugs, undeterred. Eager, she rocks on her heels, back and forth. The high judge can feel the beginnings of a migraine throbbing at his temples.

"I don't have time for tricks," the high judge growls, quickly losing patience at the interruption. There is so much that must be done and yet, here he is playing nursemaid.

"Hattie! Where is that infernal woman?"

"I'll take care of her, Father."

His oldest son, his pride, kneels at the girl's side. "Father is busy. Let's show Hattie your trick."

The girl's face dissolves into a pout. "Hattie is stupid."

"Now, now," his son croons, taking the girl's hand. The high judge has always felt that his son is too soft with the girl. He shoots a warning look at the boy, who straightens instantly, still holding the girl's hand.

"Come, Lisette. Father is too busy, and that is that."

"But it's for Papa!"

The girl's sobs trail after her into the hallway. The high judge rubs at his temples until the door finally shuts with a blessed click.

The son wipes tears from his half sister's face.

"Show me your trick, Miss Lis. You know how much I love seeing your magic."

The girl brightens at the word magic despite the snot smeared across her face.

"It's not real magic," she confides, in a whisper.

"That's okay," the boy whispers back. "As long as it makes people happy, it's real."

Giving him a watery smile, the girl takes a deep breath. Little face creased in concentration, she pulls a marble from one of the pockets of her pinafore; one of his, the boy realizes with amusement. Spinning in her palm, the glass orb catches the light from the hall sconces. The boy finds himself leaning in. It spins until she claps one tiny palm on top.

"Now say the magic word," she instructs him.

"Hattie's bloomers."

"Not that one," the little girl says, dissolving into giggles. "It's Roland."

Their father's name.

"Roland," the boy repeats obediently.

"Now, watch."

Lifting her palm, the girl reveals not a marble but a gold coin. One from their father's prized collection.

"That is a wonderful trick," the boy says solemnly, applauding. "But does Father know you took one of his special coins for your trick?"

The girl's eyes drop. "I wanted to surprise him."

"You know, Lis..." The boy searches for the right words. "Papa..doesn't appreciate magic like you and I do. Perhaps you should just show Hattie and I your tricks from now on."

The girl's lower lip juts out, the way it always does before she does something she's not supposed to. Stubborn as a baby goat, the boy thinks fondly.

"I'll find a trick that impresses him," she vows, and the boy can't help but laugh.

"If anyone can, it's you, Miss Lis. Now, let's get that coin back in Father's study before he realizes it's missing."

CHAPTER
4

After spending the night on the floor of the shared room of four showgirls who took pity on me, my neck aches and my eyes are gritty, but my resolve has never been clearer.

It's not hard to find Del. Even though it's only midmorning, his bottom is already firmly planted in front of one of the gambling machines at the Palm, frittering away his inheritance. He doesn't even look up when I tap him on the shoulder.

"Yes, I'll take two more," he says absently, eyes glazed.

"Get ahold of yourself, Del," I respond, disgusted. He blinks, taking me in.

"Lisette! Why, how lovely to see you. To what do I owe the pleasure?"

I ignore his eyes raking over my outfit. I've foregone my usual all-black ensemble for something I knew Del would appreciate. The emerald-colored dress is tight at the bodice, flowing in the skirts. Although I enjoy pretty dresses as much as the next girl, it seems a waste to use this one on Del.

I try not to cringe as his gaze stops at my cleavage.

"I need your help," I say, hating the bitter taste of the words in my mouth. That gets his attention. The game behind him is forgotten.

"You have no idea how long I've waited to hear you say those words." He sighs, standing up and embracing me. I stiffen as he buries his head into my shoulder. Del is a good foot shorter than I am, although he tries to cover up the fact with heeled boots and pomposity.

I shove him away as gently as I can.

"Do you know Raster MacMillan?" I ask, trying in vain to steal his attention away from my décolletage.

Del preens. "Of course. Esteemed seeker, heir to a fortune, debonair playboy . . . we have a lot in common."

It's a struggle not to roll my eyes.

"Then surely, you know about his party tonight?" I hold my breath. The odds are fifty-fifty that Del's family money is enough to score him an automatic invite, his reputation as a bona fide idiot notwithstanding.

He casts me a wounded look. "How can you even ask? Of course I'm invited," he says, offended.

Now, I don't even have to force a smile. "Can you get me in?"

The gleam in Del's eye turns appraising. For once in his life, he has the upper hand.

"Well, well, little Lisette is finally chasing me. What an interesting turn of events."

I have no interest in playing this game. "Will you bring me or not?"

Del smirks. "Perhaps. What's in it for me?

I spread my arms wide, letting him take me in. I even did my hair the way he likes it, tied low in a chignon. "Me. As your . . . date." I choke a little on the word and hope he doesn't notice.

He does. His expression sours.

"I have plenty of women interested in being my date," he says, peevish, brushing invisible lint from his pressed suit. Everything about Del screams new money, from his boorish attitude down to his constant overdressing. No one wears a suit that nice this early in the morning, unless they're on their way to a party. I reconsider; as Oasis's premier party boy, he very well could be on his way to a party.

I bite back the snarky response that lingers on my tongue. Hating myself, I lean in, running a finger along his opal cufflinks. His eyes track my every move, pupils dilated.

"Del..." I breathe, watching his own breath hitch. "I'll do anything."

I won't. But he doesn't know that. I go in for the kill, let my lips brush his ear. He shudders.

"Please. Take me."

He doesn't miss the double meaning.

"Yes, yes, of course, yes," he babbles. I smile, pleased.

"Wonderful," I say, pushing him away. He leans against the machine as if dazed. "Pick me up at eight forty-five sharp."

I leave him there, glassy-eyed.

The only problem with going to a party I'm too poor to be invited to is that I have nothing proper to wear. I pick through my meager collection of clothes, currently stuffed in a beat-up suitcase: the worn costume I don for performances; my regular day clothes (all black); and a few day dresses (cheap and gaudy). The dress I wore to seduce Del is the nicest thing I own, and it's far too tame for a party thrown by Raster. I tap my teeth with a finger.

The costume is just as important as the show, and I have nothing fitting to wear. Which is how I find myself backstage at the Bleached Skull, a cirque-style show.

I wander through the knot of performers hastily preparing for the next show, passing several girls in leotards and a woman with her legs wrapped around her head. No one looks twice at me. Costumes are everywhere; tossed over chairs, thrown in heaps on the floor. Adopting the stressed-out expression of the other performers, I rifle through a wardrobe rack, looking for anything suitable. The costumes are lavish, extraordinary. I find one dress pinned with delicate, translucent wings taller than me. I'm sorely tempted, but then I picture getting caught in a doorway and reluctantly set it back with the rest. Fur, jewels, feathers, scales, gilt . . . there are a million different outfits, but none of them are quite right. I need something unforgettable. I pull out a stiff velvet dress, hold it to myself in front of the mirror.

I look like a dead duchess. And the entire atrocity is covered in cat hair. Sneezing, I replace the velvet dress and pull out a heavy lace one instead. For a moment, I'm excited. The gown is gorgeous—intricate flowers worked into the luxurious red lace. It even has pockets. Unfortunately, it's more than a little too big for me and would drape like a wilted rose on my frame.

I'm about to put it back, when something in the pockets shifts, clinking. Reaching in, I remove a tiny glass vial. Inside, pearlescent pink beads knock gently against one another, and my eyes widen. If I'm not mistaken, it's a powerful love imitator known as Euphoria. I've seen tourists with vials of the stuff, eager to enchant their intended for an evening. It's illegal everywhere but Oasis, after a high-profile case where a count's daughter turned up murdered, Euphoria in her blood. It's also very expensive, and I have no doubt it'll come in handy. Pocketing the little vial, I reach back into the waves of fabric on the rack.

My fingers snag on a strand of gold. Pushing aside curtains of silk and crushed velvet, I reach for the dress, so slight it's almost hidden. When I finally see it, I can't help the gasp that escapes; it's easily the most beautiful dress I've ever seen. It looks like molten gold, shimmering strands melted into the form of a gown. And, I realize belatedly, holding it up, it shows quite a lot of skin. Grimacing, I recall the promises I made to Del this morning. Not that I'm going to let him ruin this dress.

Shedding my own clothes, I slide the dress on, relieved by how well it fits, clinging and molding to my body. The metal curves down my spine, framing the flawless skin beneath. There is no way Raster is going to forget who I am after seeing me in this dress.

"I can't bleeding stand aristocrats," Del mutters from my elbow. "Tell me again why we're here?"

"Aren't you considered an aristocrat?" I ask, barely listening to his griping as I take in the opulence around me.

"Hardly," Del says, "I've got better blood than these inbred fools. And you'd never catch me throwing one of these ridiculous garden parties, just for the chance to show off my wealth."

It's a surprising amount of scorn from someone who is wearing not one, but three diamond-encrusted pocket watches dripping from his Radolfi-tailored suit.

He's not wrong though; Raster certainly does know how to throw a party. Everywhere, lush, exotic flowers are in full bloom, even though we're in the middle of the desert. No doubt the exorbitant work of garden magicians. The air is heady with their scents; it's pleasant, but after a while, my head spins with the richness.

"A drink, Mr. Fredrickson? . . . madam?"

A shimmering platter appears near my elbow, foisted by a straight-backed waiter. He's young, handsome, and bland, like most of the guests at these parties. I clear my throat.

"Mirage."

I don't know why I bother correcting him. To him, I am no one.

To everyone here, I am no one, other than Del's date for the night. I'd give anything for them to know my name.

"No, no, unfortunately, the lady must decline," Del chuckles, reaching past me for one of the thimble-sized glasses. I smile tightly at the waiter, who betrays only the barest of curiosity in his light eyes before bowing and edging away.

Del pinches the tiny glass between his forefinger and thumb and tosses back the contents, hardly more than a swallow. Elation lights up his features as the drink takes effect.

"Bet you're glad you're of age," I say, trying not to let the hint of bitterness at the back of my throat creep into my tone. Del smirks.

"Thirsty, dear?"

"Shut up."

"Why are we here?" Del asks again, tapping his long nails against the glass, resuming his usual bored expression.

I ignore him and pretend to be fascinated with my surroundings. It's not difficult; new wonders glitter everywhere I turn. There, a devastatingly lovely woman draped in nothing but jewels spins lazily in the air, suspended from a palm. Here, a group laughs as the flowers they feast on turn their heads into bubbles that pop with a shower of sparkles, only to grow back in an instant. Everywhere, more wealth than I've been around in years.

Although this dress is one of the finest I've ever worn and I'm on the arm of one of the wealthiest men in Oasis, I forget it all in an instant at the sight of so much affluence and finery. All I want, although I'd never tell Del, is to be accepted by these rich fools. To be one of them. And for one night, I can pretend to. Even if it means Del is my date for the evening.

"What are these?" I ask, picking up what appears to be a glass orb at my feet, more in an effort to distract Del than actual curiosity. Del shrugs, nibbling at a platter of cheeses and berries. I half expect it to pop at my touch; the glass is thin, delicate, and shimmers just like the surface of a soap bubble.

"Del, look, there's something inside—"

Del sets down his cheese with a great sigh and takes the bubble from me, leaving greasy fingerprints on the surface.

"Typical," he says, handing the orb back.

"Is it real?" I ask, staring in disbelief at the glittering sapphire ring with a stone the size of my knuckle winking in the light of the moon.

"What did I tell you?" Del asks, around a mouthful of cheese. "Any excuse for these opulent wastrels to show off—"

"Can we take it?" I hardly dare to ask. Around me, the rest of the guests ignore the hundreds of glass orbs dotting the lawns, unaware of, or simply unimpressed with, the offerings inside.

"I expect that's Raster's idea of a party favor," Del says, rolling his eyes. "You'd offend him if you didn't take one."

"But no one else is taking them . . . I don't want to be the only one . . ." I trail off, trying hard to ignore the gem twinkling up at me.

"Suit yourself." Del shrugs, snatching a tart of some kind from another waiter.

"Maybe I'll just hold on to it," I say. I don't know what kind of etiquette applies to something like this, and I'd rather not be the first one to try. Faint strains of string music drift across the lawn. Around us, couples swirl in sweeping circles. I watch, entranced. From his partner's arms, an elegant silver-haired boy, probably old money, catches my eye. I feel my breath hitch as the faintest of smiles flashes across his face. Please come ask me to dance, please, please, please—

"Try some of this," Del says, holding out what looks like a giant shrimp garnished with a slice of lime, effectively ruining the spell between me and the beautiful boy. He dances away with hardly another glance in my direction.

Another reminder that I'll never be one of them.

Suppressing a sigh, I wave Del's offering away. A tinkling of glass jerks me out of my spell.

"What was that?" I ask, but I already know the answer. Glittering shards of glass reflect the moonlight from near the feet of a handsome couple. Smiling, the man lifts a heavy gold-and-emerald necklace from the sparkling shattered orb and fastens it around his maiden's neck. Several of the other guests whistle and cheer as the maiden preens, the necklace a magnificent collar on her waspish neck.

Crashes shatter the dreamy night, as more gentlemen follow the initiative of the first, gifting their ladies with everything from raw rubies the size of my fist, to thick strands of creamy pearls, to handfuls of tiny, perfect diamonds.

My fingers tighten around my own orb, still whole. I glance at it, admiring the gleam of its surface, the dark, almost black, of the sapphire inside.

Now it won't seem odd if I break it, I'll just be another reveler—

The smashing of glass is almost continuous now, as more and more of the guests expose the glittering contents of the orbs. A waiter is shoved to the side as the orb near his feet is discovered, the guest who found it knocking the server over in his haste to grab it before someone else does. The plates on the server's tray fall and smash in quick succession. One woman lets out a cry as the delicate glass from a broken orb slices her fingers.

Suddenly, my orb is snatched from my hands.

"Hey—" I manage to grab the arm of the thief, a petite woman in a poofy ballgown that seems to swallow her up.

"How dare you! Unhand me at once, thief!" the woman cries out loudly, attracting the attention of everyone around us. I drop her arm, surprised.

"Now, this seems a little more like something that Raster might like," Del says, surveying the chaos unfolding before us.

"My ring!" I cry, as the woman is swallowed into the throngs of revelers.

Del waves a hand, lazily. "I can get you much better than that cheap trinket."

I grit my teeth at his nonchalance. That ring could have paid for room and board for several months, at least.

That's why you're here, I remind myself. If I can impress Raster, I won't need to pawn off valuables to find a cheap place to sleep. I gust a sigh; the party has lost some of its enchantment for me.

"Could we meet the host now?"

Del's face closes off. "There's plenty to do with me; what do you need to meet that scoundrel for?"

"Don't tell me you're jealous," I say, groaning.

"It just feels like you're using me is all," Del pouts. "For my good looks and my connections."

It takes every ounce of patience I have not to throttle Del. "You forgot your money."

Del's outraged look is almost worth it.

"I'm joking, I'm joking," I say, looping my arm through his, which seems to placate him more than my words do. "I'm just curious about the man behind the party is all." Del calms, but I do catch a muttered "gaudy prat" and I know better than to push the subject. Although I'm desperate to meet Raster and convince him to see my show, I can't risk upsetting Del. Without him, I'm nothing more than a homeless showgirl in a borrowed dress. I can only hope we run into Raster by chance. After all, it is his party.

I steer Del toward the menagerie. Raster owns an impressive number of exotic animals, including three elephants, a jaguar, and a thirty-foot boa constrictor. But the true jewel of his collection is the rare albino winter grizzly. It's rumored to be both blind and lethal. The menagerie is designed to be an immersive experience; cages are cleverly concealed using magic, so that the stroll through the humid forest habitat feels like an actual stroll through the jungles of Sumuran. We pass an open tank of piranhas, low enough that a careless partygoer could lose an arm leaning too closely to look. They swarm and thrash as we pass, mouths agape. I jump as the boa makes its appearance: bands of bright yellow wrapped around the thick trunk of a tree. Without meaning to I think of Luc. No matter how important he thinks he is, I'm the one at Raster's party, while he's devil knows where. But being here means nothing if I don't find Raster.

It's hot in the menagerie; my hair sticks to my neck. It's almost a relief to enter the next exhibit, although the temperature drops at an alarming rate. Bits of snow gust into my eyes, which I blink away in surprise. I haven't seen snow on Oasis ever. The magical upkeep of the menagerie must cost Raster a fortune. Whereas the rest of the menagerie is built to imitate a jungle clime more suited to the desert of Oasis, this room is a frozen tundra. My skimpy dress is highly inadequate against the freezing wind and snow, and I shiver uncontrollably. Del finally tears his eyes away from the wasteland and notices my state.

"Good heavens, you're freezing. Come, the elephants are just past this room—"

He tugs on my arm, but I've stopped, frozen, not because of the cold, but because of the man standing several feet away from us. He's holding court with a lively group. Even from where we are, I don't miss the glint of the seeker pin on his lapel.

"Is that him? Raster?" I ask Del in an undertone. He follows my gaze and rolls his eyes.

"The very same."

"Let's go meet him!" I say, suddenly ignorant of the fact that I can't feel my own face anymore.

"You can't just 'meet' him," Del says, grabbing hold of my arm. I almost stumble in a snowdrift, my feet two frozen stumps. "He doesn't let just anyone into his inner circle. He has to talk to *you*; you don't talk to him."

I gape helplessly at the man who has been my target all night. So close I could shout and he'd look up, only I'm not allowed to speak to him?

Unacceptable.

"Lisette! How charming."

I scowl as Luc, cloaked in furs and the tightest leather trousers I have ever seen, breaks away from Raster's group and strides toward us.

"It's Mirage," I grit out.

"Right, my apologies," Luc says, brushing a speck of snow off his fine coat. I shiver as the snow layers into my hair, as fine as powdered sugar. "A fitting stage name. The only thing more disappointing than finding hot sand when you're dying of thirst might be your show."

I bristle, but it's Del who steps in, eager to be my champion.

"Tight enough pants, mate?"

"Like what you see?" Luc asks, not even bothering to look up from his heavy gold pocket watch. Del splutters something incoherent in response as I try not to roll my eyes.

Luc tucks his hands into his pants and takes me in. Blood heats my cheeks.

"Why, Lis, you look good enough to eat."

I open my mouth to retort but it's Del's voice that responds yet again.

"Do not address the woman so informally, my good man."

One arm snakes around my shoulders, drawing me possessively toward him. I really wish he'd stop doing that. I duck out from under his claustrophobic grip, only regretting the loss of warmth from his heavy overcoat.

"I rather think she liked it," Luc says lightly, one eyebrow raised in challenge. Del's hand goes to his sword, a fancy, useless thing more suited to ceremony than actual combat. Oh devils, if Del decides to challenge him for my honor—

"Of course she didn't," Del snaps, glancing towards me for reassurance. "Right, Lisette?"

"I can speak for myself, thank you."

Both men look at me as though they'd forgotten I was there. I suck in a breath. As usual, Luc has distracted me from my true purpose. I turn back to Raster's group, now clustered in front of the empty habitat.

Luc follows my gaze. "You'll never get his attention."

He's standing so close, I can feel the heat coming off his body in waves. I tighten my grip on the frozen wall.

"Where's your pet, Ras?" one of the men drawls. Raster surveys the tundra carelessly.

"Must be hunting."

Several of the partygoers let out disappointed murmurs.

"However," Raster says, reaching into one of his trouser pockets and pulling out what looks like a tiny gold dog whistle. "I think I can get his attention."

Holding my breath, I watch as he places the whistle to his lips, the gold winking in the swirling snow. Three sharp notes pierce the empty wasteland. For a moment, it's completely silent, all the guests watching the horizon expectantly as the snow blankets the ground. But nothing appears.

Raster shrugs and replaces the whistle. "Who knows where the beast is off to? Perhaps we'll see him later."

He and the group amble forward as if to leave. Luc smirks and throws a mock salute at me, close behind the others. Del's hand on my arm is a reminder of the cost I've paid to get here tonight. And after all that, I can't very well just let Raster walk away. The vial of Euphoria burns against my hip, the only warm spot on my body.

The vial.

If I can get the grizzly over here, and do it in style, I'm certain I'll finally have Raster's undivided attention. And with a spell as powerful as Euphoria, what have I to fear from a blind bear?

Staggering on frozen legs, very aware that I could lose my toes or worse tonight, I make my way to the glass separating us from the bear's habitat. I can just make out the edges of the enchanted glass, blurred unless I stare at them exactly right. The top is barely a foot above my head, low enough that I can reach. Thanking the stars, I wrap my numb and clumsy fingers around it.

From behind me, Del lets out a cry of shock.

More people have started shouting, but I hardly hear them as I scramble up the glass wall, slipping on the icy surface. It's a struggle to pull myself up over the wall, but once I do, it's an easy drop into the habitat below. I come down on a patch of ice and my ankle crumples beneath me. I chide myself for not sticking the landing. Pulling myself up, hoping to regain some semblance of grace, I realize the entire habitat has gone deathly silent. Only the wind speaks, muttering as it unravels my fine updo, casting tendrils of hair about my face.

A huffing from my left startles me. Hot, stinking breath washes over my face. I look up, shaking all over, the breath catching in my throat. Covered in shaggy white fur, the beast stares at me, unseeing, with colorless eyes. Panting, jaws agape, rows of teeth glint dully in the light reflected off the snow. Ropes of saliva glisten as they dangle from its mouth.

So fast. And so *quiet*. I never even heard it coming. Whatever abilities sight might have granted it, the great bear more than makes up for in speed and stealth. There's no way I can outrun this creature if things get dicey.

It occurs to me then that it's highly likely I've made a huge mistake.

"Stay still," Raster's voice breaks through the silence. The bear's head jerks toward the sound, nose twitching. "If you run, you're dead."

My heart feels like it's throbbing inside me.

Straightening my back, I hold out a hand, willing my heart to calm, steadying my breath.

The bear sniffs my extended fingers and then roars, a sound that nearly knocks me off my feet. Letting loose a growl that sends my entire body quaking, the bear pulls itself up on its hind legs, towering over me.

I need the vial, but my fingers are numb, clumsy. *It was right here*, I think. But my fingers grasp only my frozen dress.

The vial is gone. I'm going to die.

But before I can process the thought, someone knocks into me, hard. The wind gusts from my lungs as I hit the ice. I scramble to my feet, only to see someone between me and the bear. Luc.

"Never fear, madam!" Luc says, ducking right as the bear swipes an enormous paw in his direction. He even has the nerve to smirk at me; one quick quirk of his lips before the bear snaps its jaws right near his ear and he's off again.

He and the bear dance, slipping and dodging on the ice. The bear is fast, but Luc is smaller and lighter on his feet. The bear lets out a frustrated roar as Luc slips out of arm's reach again. He twists right into the bear's face, and to everyone's horror, pats it on the nose.

"Sleep," he croons, and the big thing blinks once, as if bemused, and then topples, the impact shaking the ground like a fallen tree. Luc stands there, chest heaving. The sound of clapping makes me jump. I turn to see Raster, slamming his hands together as though he's never seen anything better in his life. One by one, the other guests join him, until the sound is deafening. Like a flower turned toward the sun, Luc basks in the applause, even allowing himself a silly bow. I can't believe my eyes. That idiot stole my show again.

Before I can stop him, he scoops me into his arms. I hiss as the ice on my dress presses against my frozen skin. With hardly any effort, he carries me through the habitat door Raster has unlocked for us both.

"Are you all right?" he asks loudly, for the crowd's benefit. Always a showman. But two can play that game.

"I'm fine," I say, forcing a saccharin smile.

Wrapping my arms around his neck, batting my eyes up at him, I tug him down to me. He leans in.

"And I'll be sure to repay the favor."

Luc doesn't miss the threat in my tone. He straightens up, all traces of congeniality gone, and drops me. I land in a heap, a startled *oof* escaping me.

"Oh dear, clumsy me," he says, smirking as he extends a hand. "Not the gratitude I expected for saving your life."

I swat his hand away, pushing myself to my feet. "I had it under control."

"Did you?" Luc asks, eyebrow raised. "Because from where I was standing, you were seconds away from being eaten by a giant blind bear."

"I had a plan," I grumble, jamming my frozen fingertips into my armpits. My entire body feels like a block of ice.

Luc considers me, and with a whirl of red, drapes his coat over my shoulders. I start to protest, but it's deliciously warm, and I'm dangerously close to hypothermia.

"Oh, you mean this?" Luc says, inspecting a tiny, glinting vial he seemed to pull from midair. The Euphoria. "I did wonder who you planned to use it on, although I have to say, I never expected you to choose a bear for your paramour."

I lunge, but he dangles it just out of reach. Curse his long legs.

"I'll hold on to this, I think," he says, tucking it neatly into a tiny pocket of his impossibly tight trousers. "You're welcome to try to get it back, of course."

He smirks at the flush that heats my numb cheeks.

"Not that it would have done you much good in the face of a winter grizzly. You're lucky I came when I did."

"Are you really that afraid of a little competition?" I ask, unable to stop myself.

"Maybe I just can't stand the thought of a bear defeating you," he says, leaning down to brush the ice crystals from my lashes. I shiver at the contact. "That's my job. Ah, your boyfriend is here."

Before I can correct him, Del huffs over to us.

"Excuse you!" he says, jabbing Luc in the chest. Luc, who is a good foot or so taller than Del, looks down, surprised. "I was on my way to rescue the maiden, *my* date for the evening, when you interjected yourself most impolitely—"

"That's funny," Luc says, leaning back, the cocky grin never leaving his lips. He has the amused look of a lion being scolded by a mouse. "I'm fairly certain I saw you cowering behind the Delacorte twins during the incident."

Del splutters like a hot teapot. "The sheer impunity! Of all the nerve!"

"Luc, you old devil!"

I stiffen as Raster himself approaches our little group and gives Luc a hearty slap on the back. "Can't even help being brilliant, can you? Still wish I'd gotten to you before Aurora did, devils be hanged."

Luc ducks his head in a show of false modesty. I roll my eyes.

"I've an admitted weakness for a damsel in distress," Luc says, holding my gaze. I bare my teeth in response. This should have been my moment with Raster, and I've lost it once again to Luc.

"Ah, yes," Raster turns to me, concerned. "Are you all right, my dear? We should probably get you warmed up."

Del puts a belated arm around me and rubs my arms emphatically, the fabric of Luc's coat bunching against my skin. I shrug him away.

"I'm quite all right," I say, and realize it's true. Luc's coat must be enchanted, because I'm warm all over, all the way down to my exposed toes. Arrogant show-off.

Raster nods, already turning his attention back to Luc.

"Of course, I'd be better if I'd had the chance to try my latest trick on your pet," I say, hoping Raster doesn't hear the obvious desperation in my tone. I hold up the tiny bottle of Euphoria I managed to steal back when Raster joined us, allowing myself one tiny wink at Luc. His eyes narrow. Raster stares at it for a moment, then at me.

"And what, exactly, did you hope would happen once you used that on my grizzly?" Raster asks slowly.

"I rather hoped he'd find me enchanting enough not to eat," I say honestly.

Raster bursts into laughter, startling Del.

"That's very amusing," he says, wiping away tears. "I should have liked to see that very much. That old bear could use an admirer. Who did you say you are again?"

"Lisette Schopfer," I say, curtsying prettily, even though I'm practically drowning in Luc's coat. "I perform as Mirage on the Hangman's Noose."

Raster's expression turns shrewd. "Ah, yes, I've heard of you. Street performer, right?"

My heart throbs even harder than when I was staring down the bear. "I'm performing tomorrow evening, if you'd like to come."

"I'm sure you'd rather not waste your time," Luc says lightly, grabbing Raster's arm in an attempt to divert him. "Lis performs mainly for low-class tourists. Drunkards, criminals, the like."

It's all I can do not to strangle him in front of Raster.

"I'll see if I can wander by sometime. Let's get back to the party, shall we? I'm positively frigid!" Raster says, rubbing his hands together briskly. "Come now, Luc, show me that trick with the drinks you did earlier—"

In one elegant motion, Luc tugs the coat from my shoulders as he passes. The cold envelopes me instantly, but it's nowhere near as chilly as the smile Luc gives me, as sharp and cold as an icicle to the heart.

CHAPTER
5

"*Show me again.*"

Edward almost laughs out loud at the sight of his sister's little lips pursed in concentration. Taking the coin, he waves it for the girl to see.

"*Watch carefully, now.*"

Tossed into the air in a flash of gold, the coin lands with a heavy sound in the palm of his hand. With a simple maneuver, he lets the coin slide up into his sleeve.

"*And . . . it's gone!*"

"*You forgot the magic word!*"

Smothering his smile, Edward slaps his forehead in mock consternation. "So I did. Can you say it for me?"

"*Terrificus Majesticus,*" *the little girl intones seriously. With a flourish, Edward reveals his empty palms. Awe lights up the little girl's face. Then, just as soon, it turns to despair.*

"*I wish I had magic, like you and Papa . . .*"

Pity overwhelms the boy as he stares down at his half sister's forlorn expression. Kneeling, he takes her tiny hand in his.

"I don't have magic yet," he confides. "Papa won't give it to me until I pass a test."

Her hazel eyes are round. "Then how did you do that?"

"That's a different kind of magic. A very special magic indeed," he says seriously. "Would you like me to teach you?"

The bow pinned in her gold curls bounces as she nods eagerly, in very real danger of dislodging it. Depositing the coin into her hands, he folds her palm over it.

"The most important thing to remember, Miss Lis, is to make sure your audience only sees what you want them to see."

When he unfolds her fingers again, the coin is gone. Using deft fingers, he plucks the coin from behind the girl's ear, as if from thin air.

"Show me!"

Laughing, he obliges, doing the trick again slowly so she can follow the coin.

"You see, Lisette, when you distract them well enough, even very smart people will miss the trick happening right under their nose."

CHAPTER
6

I'm enjoying a drink in the Panther Hotel lobby, when a man takes the seat next to me. I recognize him instantly as Luc's second-act shill; I've been expecting him. He, however, is not expecting me. I engage him in conversation easily, and he does not notice when I slip the vial of sleeping powder into his drink. He knocks back his scorpion water without even so much as a glance at the contents. He has no reason to fear being poisoned; he's only a shill.

The potion is fast-acting. Within minutes, he slumps onto the bar and begins snoring, loud and wet. A few nearby customers chuckle, but otherwise, no one pays much attention to the poor sop.

I wave over the bouncer, who drags the lug outside.

"Going to make sure he's still conscious," I tell the bouncer when he returns inside. "He always drinks too much."

I find the man in the alleyway next to a trash can, still snoring. It only takes a few minutes to undress him, leaving him in his grungy underthings. I cringe as I replace my own clothes with his, a flannel shirt and trousers, still uncomfortably warm. I'm grateful for his slender build, at least. The clothes are baggy but not enough to draw undue attention. Doffing his cap, I stuff my long hair up under the brim and tug it low, over my eyes. I check the man's gold pocket watch: 7:47 p.m. Tucking the watch back into a shirt pocket, I make my way to the Panther's theater.

Luc is about halfway through his show, in the middle of his snakebite act, which means I'm right on time. Flashing the shill's badge at the ticket taker for the Panther, I shove my way into the packed audience to the seat Luc left open for the shill, duck under the gaudy "Reserved" sign, and make myself comfortable.

Onstage, Luc fondles a snake, the very same one he taunted me with.

"As I'm sure you're all aware, the Yanpur cobra is the most venomous snake in the world," Luc says lazily as the snake twines up his arm. His eyes are lidded, and he looks half reptile himself. "A single drop of Yanpur venom is enough to kill a grown man seventy times over."

With a snap of his fingers, the snake lashes, sinking two glinting fangs right into Luc's carotid artery.

His body seizes. Frothing and convulsing, he collapses. Forgotten, the snake drops and slithers offstage, where one of the handlers shuts it tight in a cage.

"Oh my!" One of the ladies next to me fans herself rapidly. "Do you think it's real?"

It's real, all right. Every performance, just for the sake of a few extra claps, Luc allows a snake to inject him with one of the deadliest poisons known to man. Checking the pocket watch, I stifle a yawn. Luc may seem flashy, but he's kind of a one-trick pony, once you know what to look for.

A man, another of Luc's shills, hops on stage, feigning concern. Placing a hand on Luc's chest, the man feels for a beat.

"Sir?" he says, tentatively. "Are you all right?"

Luc's tremor stills.

The man's face goes pale. "Someone help, I think he's dead!"

The audience gasps, collectively. But of course, no one moves to help. They're still waiting for the ending, the big reveal. I think of Harrison Montgomery, who died onstage to riotous applause after his act went wrong.

Nobody knew his death was real until hours later, when he was found facedown in a puddle of his own blood.

Luc shudders violently and then jolts upright, the veins in his neck straining. As he holds up a glass vial in one shaking hand, the two puncture marks on his neck begin to weep a hissing green liquid. Sweat beads on his face as he forces the venom out of his body. A final quivering drop lands in the vial, and with a great effort he corks it and holds it up to the audience in triumph.

The clapping is deafening.

His face is wan and he looks on the verge of collapsing again, but the applause seems to sustain him.

"I have died onstage once already tonight, and now, I will face death yet again."

From his pocket, he removes a tiny silver pistol. This next act seems dramatic, but it's mostly filler while Luc recovers from the snake venom. There's no magic involved, only some clever sleight of hand. Which, as it just so happens, is my specialty.

"Could I have a volunteer, please?"

I raise a hand, ducking my head so he can't see my face. The pheasant feather placed jauntily in the brim is more than a fashion accessory. It stands out in a crowd, making it easy for Luc to find his prearranged plants. Not all performers use plants or stagehands disguised as regular audience members, but Luc's show depends on them.

"Yes, you, in the hat."

I make my way onstage, careful not to make eye contact, head down. Luc doesn't pay me any attention anyway, he's far too focused on his audience.

"Would you please inspect this pistol, my good man, make sure it's in working order?"

Pretending to inspect the pistol, I pop several of the rounds out and show them to the audience, per Luc's normal routine. After a good sweep, I replace the rounds. They're heavy in my hand, no fakes here.

"Now, just to make sure everything's working as it should, why don't you take a shot at the target, just over there."

Aiming carefully at the target, I pop off a shot. It hits just left of the bull's-eye, and I don't miss the raise of Luc's eyebrow. His normal shill is something of a wild shot, and it usually makes for a good bit of comedy in the routine. Before he can scrutinize me too closely, I wave to the audience, turning away from him.

"Well done, what a lucky shot," Luc says, doing his best to disguise his surprise. "As you can see, the pistol is real and in fine working order. For as long as man has existed, he has feared death . . ."

That's my cue. While the audience's attention is on Luc, I eject the remaining rounds into my pocket, and reload the gun with the blanks. Even blanks can be harmful if mismanaged, but they won't kill him. At least, I don't think they will. Anyway, the point isn't to kill Luc. The point is to steal the spotlight back, the way he stole it from me at Raster's party.

Humiliate him, the way he humiliated me.

". . . and tonight, I shall face death, not once, but twice! As I allow this man to shoot me, right in the mouth."

The bullet catch is an old trick, although every magician does it a little bit differently. After being tied up to ensure he won't have any second thoughts, Luc has his man stand twenty feet away and shoot. Once the gun has gone off, Luc reveals the hidden round in his mouth. It's a bit cheap, but it buys him the time he needs to recover for his next act.

I stand at the mark Luc has drawn onstage and consider the gun in my hand. It's a pretty thing with whorls of silver embellishments that look like roses on the grip and slide. It's clearly an antique. I hope Luc's trust in it is not misplaced.

"Go ahead then!" Luc calls from across the stage. "Shoot!"

Luc has his method for the bullet catch, and I have mine. Removing the hat, I shake out my rose-gold hair, watching with satisfaction at the way Luc's eyes bug from across the stage as he finally sees me.

"Sorry everyone, but this is not your usual bullet catch! This is a good old-fashioned shootout."

Strolling past Luc's mark, a streak of charcoal on the stage, I stride right up to where he's bound. He struggles against his bindings, but his assistant—excuse me, *my* assistant—made sure the ropes were tied good and tight. Luc stares up at me, completely at my mercy. His amber eyes are wary, but to his credit, he doesn't say a word.

"Look at that, he's sweating bullets!" I jeer, to the crowd's delight. Luc's eyes dart to the gun I'm twirling.

"Oh, don't worry," I say, winking at him. "I made sure *all* the rounds were live, just as you asked."

Turning back to the audience, I survey the gun as though displeased. "The bullet catch is so dull though, isn't it? Hardly impressive, catching a bullet from twenty feet away. Where's the thrill in that?"

Luc shakes his head at me, almost imperceptibly. I throw him my most dangerous smile in return.

"And since the devil here is a world-class magician, I've no doubt he can handle the danger."

Running a finger along his full lower lip, I gently pry open his mouth and wrap it around the end of the gun. His eyes are desperate, pleading.

I lean in close, so only he can hear.

"Don't ever interrupt my show again."

And then I shoot.

Luc's head snaps back. The cartridge is only a blank, but the force from the gun is still enough to give him a good bit of whiplash. The explosion would be lethal to anyone else, bullet or no; with Luc, it's just a loud annoyance, thanks to his ability to heal himself.

Slapping his head forward, I watch as he spits the concealed cartridge into the metal cup I have outstretched. It lands with a satisfying plink, spattered with Luc's blood. He glowers up at me, lips blackened from the gunpowder.

I hold the cup up in triumph. The crowd roars. I live for that sound. And it's somehow even more delicious when stolen from someone else. Luc's eyes glitter as I pass, malevolent, and I know without him even saying it that he will make me pay for this little trick. But at least he knows now that if he does, I will bite back. And I have venom too. Leaving him bound, I hop lightly off the stage as stagehands rush to free him.

Hands grasp at me, praise washing over me like honey, as I make my way through the crowd.

"Well done, young lady!"

"Fine execution of the bullet catch, never seen anything like it."

"Excuse me!" A man struggles up the aisle, trying to reach me. "Mirage!"

I can just make out the emerald tie and charcoal suit, a head of short, dark hair. For a moment, I'm positive it's Raster, until I realize it's a woman, not a man.

"Roseanne, call me Rose," she says, sticking out a hand, standing in front of me with a wad of tacco seeds stuffed in her cheek, spitting. "Owner and manager of the theater at the Saguaro."

I ignore her extended hand, looking over her shoulder, scanning the audience for Raster. A seeker. Anyone else. There is no one but Roseanne-call-me-Rose. My heart sinks. I know the Saguaro. It's a mid-range hotel, nowhere near as grand as the Crown or Panther. Granted, it wasn't my greatest work, and I did sneak into the theater, but I still hoped it would be enough to get Raster's attention anyway.

"That was quite a show," Rose says, nodding at Luc, whose stagehands are still struggling with the knots in his bindings.

"Thank you." The words are bitter in my mouth. It's never good enough.

"I'm a sucker for a good rivalry," Rose admits, brushing off her suit. "And I've been dying to take ol' Millie at the Crown down a notch or two. If I were to offer you a spot in our show lineup, I expect there would be more shows like that?"

"I'm really not interested—"

"Of course, you'd have a shot at Jester too."

My head jerks up. "I thought only luxury hotel performances were considered—"

Rose waves away the idea. "Any act is considered, even if those nepotistic fools at the Crown are given preference. So long as you can snag a seeker, you'll get to that final show."

Hope struggles inside of me, thrashing like a wet cat. Onstage, Luc has finally managed to free himself and is rubbing at his chafed wrists. His wrathful expression is all the convincing I need.

"I could destroy him," I say. "And I'd make the whole thing wildly entertaining."

Rose studies me. She's older than I first realized, streaks of gray in the wiry dark hair tucked behind her ears. She breaks into a smile.

"I daresay you would," she says, sticking out her hand again. This time I take it.

"The shows are nightly. You'll be given a room at the Saguaro for the duration of your employment and have full access to the Saguaro's world-famous stage while there, as well as all the Saguaro Hotel's numerous amenities. I suggest you avoid the gambling tables though."

Her eyes twinkle.

"Of course." I'm quick to agree.

"Most important, don't make me regret my choice." Her voice is stern, belied by her bright smile. "It's not just your reputation on the line now; it's mine too."

"I won't disappoint you," I promise. Rose nods, wide smile returning. Her teeth are yellow, stained by years of pipe smoke or coffee.

"Welcome to the Saguaro."

CHAPTER
7

Edward closes his eyes, searches his memories for the right bylaw. His father watches him expectantly. It does not matter that he is the firstborn son; nothing less than a perfect score on the Apprentice's Exam will secure his position as heir to his father's magic. And with less than twelve hours left until the exam, Edward cannot seem to cram enough knowledge into his brain.

"Section seventy-three," he begins triumphantly, when the door to the study bursts open, followed by wailing. Like a bullet, his sister launches herself at him, nearly knocking him into the bookshelves.

"Edward, tell her I won't do it," his little sister says, not so little anymore at twelve, her splotchy face buried in his robes.

"What is the meaning of this?" his father snaps at the nursemaid, who always trails his sister just a little too slowly.

"I tried to stop her," the nursemaid says, panting.

"Hey now," Edward says, patting his sister's heaving back. He can feel his father's gaze like lead weighing on him. "What's wrong?"

She looks up at him, eyes watery. "They've assigned me to Madam Luelle."

The smile on his lips feels suddenly false, too cheery. "The seamstress?"

She nods, squaring her shoulders, even though her wet lashes still threaten to spill over.

"I won't do it, Edward. I won't be apprenticed to a seamstress!"

"You ungrateful child," their father says, rounding on her. "After everything we've done to secure you such a prestigious apprenticeship—"

"But Papa, I want to apprentice with you," his sister breaks in. "Please, just give me a chance—"

Before their father can purple any deeper, Edward catches his sister's arm gently. "Lisette, you know Papa can only take on one apprentice."

He doesn't add what they both know, that he was chosen long before she was born, that their father's blood magic can be passed on only to a single heir. That she'd never even had a chance.

At his touch, all the fight goes out of her. She slumps in one of the high-backed leather chairs, eyes red.

"Madam Luelle is a renowned seamstress," Edward adds. "You really are lucky, you know."

The lie tastes like ashes on his tongue. He tries not to think of his sister's messy attempts at embroidery, her inability to sit still. Surely though, she will grow into her apprenticeship, just as he has grown into his.

"But I want magic like you!" Lisette bursts out. Edward's heart twists at the raw emotion on her face.

"Enough!" Their father slams a hand against his desk, startling Lisette. "Hattie, kindly remove the child so we can return to Edward's studies."

Hattie scurries in to obey, grasping Lisette by the arm. "Come now, Lisette—"

Lisette wrenches her arm free but follows Hattie reluctantly from the room. Edward tries to catch her eye as she leaves, throws her one last encouraging smile, but she does not look at him again, the door gliding shut behind her.

CHAPTER
8

The Saguaro squats, like the cactus it was named for, in the Sagebrush district of Oasis. It's still on the main strip but farther down, at a respectful distance from its luxury cousins. The designer boutiques have faded into kitschy souvenir shops and liquor stores. A towering cactus stands in front of the entrance, which would be impressive, if not for the tacky cowboy hat someone has stuck on top. The landscape would best be described as "manicured desert," although "manicured" is a stretch. Sweeps of red rock and smaller versions of the cactus out front dot the sparse grounds. I wrinkle my nose. Rock means scorpions.

The hotel itself is faded, beaten by years of sun and desert wind, but still majestic. Everything is as well-maintained as an aging whore. I squint up at the sparkling letters that spell out "Welcome to the Fabulous Saguaro Hotel and Casino!" and wonder if it doubles as a brothel, like many of the lower-end hotels. All in all though, it's a decent hotel. Miles above Bird of Paradise. Miles beneath the Crown.

I grit my teeth and clutch my meager belongings. *It's a journey*, I remind myself, picking through the scattered rock to the entrance. *You're farther than you were yesterday.* But the truth pricks at me like a bundle of cactus needles—still not good enough. The door attendant is as faded as the hotel itself, his wrinkled uniform dusty. He opens the doors for me without a word, and my heart sinks even further. Any hotel willing to let someone like myself in without question is not exactly a classy establishment. Resigned, I make my way up to the front desk, which is made of sandstone. A bleached bison skull stares sightlessly from the heavy wooden beam above the lobby. The receptionist, a plump girl with the thickest eyelashes I've ever seen, smiles at me.

Another bad sign.

"Welcome to the Saguaro! Are we checking in today?"

I look around to see if perhaps I was followed in by another patron, but it's just me. The receptionist's name badge reads "Ellie Mae."

"I'm the new headliner for the Saguaro. Rose said to talk to you about a room?"

"Of course!" the receptionist chirps, pulling out the guest list. It's a faded ledger with so many blots and cross-outs, I wince. Her pen tracks the page, leaving behind a faint black line, until it hits my name with an excited smudge.

"Oh, a magician! How exciting! What sorts of magic tricks do you perform?"

I've never met someone who talked solely in exclamation marks before. It's exhausting just listening to her. However, I can never pass up the opportunity to talk about my show.

"Oh, you know, knives, fire, death-defying feats, revenge," I say airily, as though discussing the weather. Nobody likes a braggart, after all. "The usual."

Ellie Mae's eyes are round. "Well, it sounds extraordinary. Perhaps I can check it out after one of my shifts."

"I'd be honored," I say, and this time I mean it. Ellie Mae hands me two scratched keys shaped like cacti, one for theater access and one for my room.

"There's also an all-day buffet," she says, puffing out her chest. "It's one of the big attractions around here."

The smile fades from my face. The Crown Hotel boasts an in-house restaurant catered by a world-class chef, but here, I can have all the shrimp cocktails I want. Food poisoning too, no doubt.

"Thanks," I say grimly, and Ellie Mae points me to the stairs, because of course the elevator is broken. I'm on the fourth floor, so after a bit of huffing and puffing, I reach my room. There's a cigarette burn in the carpet, which is dotted with tired-looking coyotes, but other than that, it's not bad. A crisp, clean white bed, a clawfoot tub, and even my very own cactus. I sit on the bed, well-worn springs giving at my weight. It really is a vast improvement over Bird of Paradise, I think absently, tapping the end of a particularly menacing cactus needle. No bedbugs, at least.

It's a stepping-stone is all. A temporary stop. The queen will be here in two days. Which means I have only two days to make sure my name is as well-known as Luc's.

The next morning, after a bath in the tepid water that never seems to get cold enough despite the extensive groaning from the pipes, I make my way down to the Saguaro theater. My theater.

A framed advertisement next to the doors showcases the Saguaro's past headliner, Cassidy Belle. Cactus needles protrude from every inch of available flesh on her body, even her eyeballs. I wince. Apparently, Cassidy's magical ability was extreme pain tolerance. It's not difficult to figure out why she was fired. With only one ability, most magicians lack the versatility needed to stay fresh and keep up ticket sales. Which, as it happens, is my strength.

Pushing open the garish teal doors, eyes still adjusting to the dimness of the theater, I take in the space. Candelabras, more suited to a haunted house than a theater, hang over a cluster of tables, offering a meager halo of yellowish light. The tables are small, designed to house only four audience members each.

The stage itself is only a few paces long, two steps above the rest of the theater. I finger the tasseled ropes tying back moth-eaten velvet curtains. Staring out at the tables, I quickly calculate how many guests the tiny theater can manage. The number is grim: fifty, at full capacity. My heart sinks. The Panther's theater can seat at least five hundred, the Crown as many as one thousand.

Smaller is not always worse, I remind myself. It's a different setup than I expected, but it allows a level of intimacy between the performers and the audience. I make a mental note to work the tables into my next show. A moth beats itself against the light of one of the candelabras, casting frenetic shadows across the room. I sit on the stage, which isn't even high enough for my legs to dangle off the edge, my boots scuffing the stained carpet. I have a theater, dingy and cramped though it may be.

Now all I need is a show.

I need an act good enough to get the queen to the Saguaro. It's not hard to see why the Jester is almost always chosen from the Crown acts. For you to be considered for Jester, the queen must attend one of your performances. Only those lucky few will be allowed to perform in the final show, when the queen selects the next Jester.

The queen rarely deigns to leave the Crown during her visits to Oasis. Rumor has it, she hardly even leaves her rooms, much less the hotel itself, so competitors get creative trying to attract her attention. I need to get in front of her somehow, find a way to stand out from a sea of other performers. After bribing a Crown housekeeper, I find out the queen's exact arrival time to Oasis.

I pass not one, but two monstrous billboards featuring Luc as the Panther's Jester act, not including the massive one hulking next to the Crown. I plant myself as far away from his leer as possible, trying hard to ignore the way his eyes track me, even on an advertisement.

A small crowd has gathered when the queen's motorcar pulls up, despite all attempts to be discreet. The car is nondescript, the sort of bland luxury car every courtier drives in Oasis. If it weren't for my tip, I'd never have guessed this was the queen.

A large man in a dark suit stands mute, holding open the door as the queen exits. I've never seen the queen in person, so it's strange at first to see the woman whose image graces the giant painting in the lobby of the Crown Hotel. She is pale, almost translucent. Gold hair catches the sunlight, which she squints against. Before she can even raise a hand to block the sun, an umbrella is deployed, shielding her fragile complexion. Here is a woman who has never had to open a single door for herself. Her heavy velvet dress hangs on her, wilting in the heat. She looks like a relic, a traveler from a different time, and she is as out of place here in Oasis as feathers on a tarantula.

Turning, she plucks a tiny girl from the car. The girl is just as preposterously dressed as the queen, in a dress dripping with so many bows she looks like a cake topper. This must be the crown princess. Instead of the pallor of her mother, red blooms on her cheeks, and her little rosebud lips purse in disapproval at the sweltering heat. The queen anxiously fusses, brushing away the child's sweaty curls, then passes her to a nearby attendant.

Swaying on her feet, the queen pays no heed to the assortment of curious onlookers. She takes the proffered arm of a bodyguard, her thin arms as frail as an eighty-year-old woman, and ducks into the hotel without a word. It's a disappointment after waiting so long, and rather than sating my curiosity about the mysterious woman I'll be competing for, it does nothing but stoke it.

"Just can't stay away from me, can you?"

I jump when I realize the real-life version of Luc is standing just beneath his billboard counterpart, an identical sneer on his lips.

"I was hoping I might get the chance to shoot you again," I retort, praying he didn't see how badly he startled me. My heart gallops like a runaway horse. Luc smiles, revealing gleaming teeth. Even though I know his ability better than anyone else, it's still jarring to see how quickly he managed to heal himself. His mouth should be ruined after what I did to him. And yet, there's not a trace of the blast that ripped through him, not so much as a smudge of gunpowder on his full lower lip . . .

"It's a pity this is as close to the queen as you'll ever get," Luc muses, stepping closer. Without meaning to, I instinctively step back. His smile turns predatory. "Her Majesty can't be subjected to the sort of drivel the Saguaro turns out, of course," he continues, running a hand through his long hair. How he found out about the Saguaro so fast is a mystery.

"Maybe I'll just come to her then." I'm mesmerized against my will, a trembling sparrow in the presence of a rattlesnake. Luc lets out a loud laugh.

"I'd be disappointed if you didn't, little Lis."

I freeze at the nickname, trying hard not to remember the other boy who called me that name once, long ago. It's enough to break the hold Luc has over me, at least. I cross the remainder of the distance between us, so close I can feel his breath on my lips. He smells like oranges and lies.

"There are worse things than being shot, you know," I remind him, softly.

His answering smile is grim. "I have known more of hell than you could ever dream."

I pause, disarmed. Those golden eyes track my lips hungrily, as gravity, and something else, pulls me ever closer. Like a dreamer falling out of sleep, I wrench myself away.

"Hell has nothing on me," I respond, and leave him there, beneath his billboard.

How does Luc always manage to get under my skin? I stomp away from the Crown, teeth grinding. I'm so distracted, I almost walk straight into a shimmering wall of heat. Acrid smoke blooms from flames, which are rapidly eating the façade of a blazing theater. I stare, brain blank, trying to figure out if I should look for water or call for help, when the front door opens. Although there's hardly a front door left to open, most of it charred beyond recognition, the person takes their time, shutting the blackened door carefully. My eyes water as I squint at the person, blurred around the edges from the heat of the blaze but seemingly uninjured.

"Hello?" I call, because I have no idea what else to say. "Are you okay?"

"Bugger." A tall, gangly young man, in his mid-twenties or so, marches resigned from the inferno to meet me. He looks as if he were born from the fire itself, soot streaked on both high cheekbones. Ash floats from the sky, settling on his hair and shoulders, flakes of gray snow against his messy black hair. "The one time I commit arson and someone catches me in the act. Just my luck."

He pulls off a pair of filthy spectacles, absently wiping them on his sooty shirt, streaking even more grime on them in the process. I goggle at him, at the inferno raging behind him.

"How did you do that?"

Grabbing my arm, the boy steers me away from the burning building, his footsteps purposeful.

"I don't know what you're referring to," he says as he pulls me along, lips thin. Behind us, there's a splintering crash as the building marquee topples to the ground. It occurs to me then that I may have just been taken hostage. Snapping my arm out of his grasp, I yank the vial of Euphoria from my pocket and hold it in front of me like a shield.

"Don't you dare try anything," I warn. "Or I'll throw this hex right in your face."

The boy's face is pleasantly confused.

"What on the beard of a goat skull would I try? I'm just getting away from the scene of the crime. You asked a question, and I thought it would only be polite to bring you along so I could answer."

I gape at him, the vial in my hand wavering. Fire magicians are rare, and I've never seen one that could walk *through* fire, completely impervious.

"How did you do that?" I demand, shaking the vial at him for good measure.

The boy's eyes grow shifty. "I haven't the slightest idea what you're talking about—"

Speechless, I gesture wildly in the direction of the building, billowing black clouds visible even from where we stand, a good mile away.

He sighs. "Oh, that. It's quite a long story, I'm sure you don't have the time—"

"Show me how."

The boy stares at me, mouth slightly agape.

"Excuse me?"

"I want you to show me how you did that. Teach me," I repeat. If I could learn magic like that, there's nothing that would stop me from becoming Jester.

"I can't just teach you—"

"Sure you can." I'm breathing hard, my throat burns from the fire. "Because you're going to make me your heir."

The boy's eyes widen. "I don't think so."

"I do." I can hardly believe the words escaping my lips, words formed from desperation and smoke. "Because I have evidence that could land you a quick execution. Intentional arson, statute 67b."

The boy stares at me. I memorized the heavy *Book of Laws* the year I turned eight. That was before I'd understood my father would never want me for an apprentice.

"I could kill you right here, right now, you know." Flames spark in his hands.

"I have no doubt you could," I respond, pretending the sight of both his hands bursting into flame doesn't unsettle me. "But something tells me you won't."

I'm betting an awful lot on my gut feelings about a stranger. His hands clench and unclench as he considers me.

"Oh, very well. But not here." Looking around, as though expecting a squadron of guards at any second, he darts down an alleyway, and I have no choice but to follow him. He ducks and twists down nooks and crannies in such a bizarre, illogical pattern that I wonder if he's trying to lose me. A quick, disappointed look over his shoulder when he spots me keeping pace confirms my suspicions. I hurry my steps so I match his stride, even though his legs are far longer than my own. My lungs burn hotter than the flames eating the theater behind us, but there's no way I'm letting him get away now.

Finally, the boy huffs to a stop in front of a bookshop. I stare up at the faded sign over the door: The Book Emporium. Below the hours is a large "Closed" notice, hanging crookedly. I honestly didn't even know we had a bookshop in Oasis, let alone one for used books. The boy makes an impatient noise, and it's then I realize he has been standing there, holding the door open for me. I hurry past him into the cramped store, which is tiny but pristine. Orderly rows of book spines peer out, organized neatly by author and category.

"Tea?"

I jump as the boy nudges me with a dainty ivory teacup. The handle is shaped like a carp, I realize with some amusement.

"Do you work here or something?" I ask, taking the cup from him, more out of surprise than actual need. Peppermint-scented steam wafts from the tea, tickling my nose.

"No. I own it."

Folding himself neatly into a large armchair that looks as though it's older than Oasis itself, the boy balances his own teacup on his knee and takes a leisurely sip.

I gape around the shop.

"Please, sit down." The boy motions me toward another armchair, this one covered in gaudy pink roses. I hesitate, unsure if we should even bother with pleasantries.

"Come now, I've even given you the good chair."

I sit reluctantly.

"I lied." The boy picks at a bit of emerald fuzz on the arm of his chair. It matches his own startlingly green eyes. "I gave you the chair with the saggy middle."

It's clear he's going to make this as difficult as possible. I can't say I blame him.

Conceding the loss, I settle into the saggy chair. The springs are tired, but it's surprisingly comfortable, the worn velvet cool against my skin. There's a soft thud as a scowling gray cat lands on my knee, startling me. Its face is squashy, and it eyes me disdainfully before curling into my lap.

"George likes you," the boy says, sipping his tea. "He's usually right about people."

I smile.

"But obviously not about you," he adds. My smile falters.

"Who are you?" is all I can manage.

The boy slaps a palm to his head. "Oh, how dreadfully embarrassing! All the blackmailing made me forget basic etiquette, it appears. I'm Cillian Forge. I specialize in rare and occult books."

"And arson?" I throw him a wry smile, stroking George's long matted fur.

"You really must stop bringing that up," Cillian says, shaking his head. "You're a witness. I've never committed a crime before, I have no idea what to do with a witness. Kill you, perhaps?"

I throw up my hands, upsetting George, who casts me an irritable look.

"You wouldn't dare—"

"Perhaps. Perhaps not."

George settles back on my lap once he's certain I'll stay good and still. I have no idea what to make of Cillian. He's like an eighty-year-old dowager stuck in a young man's body.

"Why did you set the theater on fire anyway?" I ask, sneaking a cookie from the plate between us.

"None of your business," Cillian says, sniffing. He gestures to my tea. "You'd better drink that before it gets cold."

I lift the cup to my lips, and the smell of mint with an acrid undertone wrinkles my nose. I set the cup down and raise an eyebrow at Cillian.

"Poison? Really?"

Cillian throws a hand to his heart, in mock offense. "I would never!"

"Then that was the worst-smelling cup of tea I've ever been offered."

This seems to offend him more than my accusation. Dumping the contents of both cups down the drain, he refills them both from the same kettle and takes a sip, keeping his eyes on me the entire time.

It could still be a trick, but I'm parched. I decide to risk it. This cup smells delicious, with notes of cool mint and rose. It soothes my dry throat.

"Attempted murder and arson, all in one day. You're a busy fellow," I note.

Cillian scowls. "Don't be dramatic. I wasn't trying to *murder* you. Let's just say you would've suffered severe intestinal distress for several hours afterward, nothing more."

I roll my eyes skyward.

"Let's get this over with. In order for you to keep your mouth shut about . . . what you saw that had absolutely nothing to do with me, you want me to make you my heir?" Cillian goes on.

I nod once, swirling the cup. Mint leaves and rose petals spiral.

"Fine. But I plan to live forever, you know."

"Oh, I don't intend on waiting for you to die," I say lightly. This is the part that might get me killed, so I need to play my cards right.

"Excuse me?"

"Well, that's an awful lot of risk for me, isn't it?" I give him a bland smile. "After all, we've only known each other for an hour or so, and you've already tried to poison me."

It takes a moment for my words to sink in, as though he's either unable or unwilling to understand. But catch on he does, and his rage sparks instantly.

"You can't have it now, you horrible little wretch—"

"Well, you did just burn down a building, so I really don't think that's your call, now, is it?"

No mock outrage now. Cillian looks as if he's ready to shove my head down the drain and force me to lick up whatever remains of the poisoned tea.

I can see him processing my words, trying, like a caged thing, to find a way out.

"Listen, you seem like a nice guy," I say, patting his hand. The gesture clearly infuriates him. "But I was the high judge's apprentice. Don't even bother trying to find a loophole."

It's not exactly true, but I know as much as if I had been, so why bother with technicalities? Cillian's shoulders slump. It's a temporary defeat however, and I know it. This boy does not seem like the type to give up easily.

"I take it you have no family ability?" Cillian finally asks, eyes narrowed.

"My father won't tell me his gift until I'm of age," I say finally. It's both true and not true. I never knew what my father's gift was, but only because it wasn't meant for me.

"So, you have no magic." Cillian concludes.

"Not yet."

"Well then, you know as well as anyone that magic cannot be taught. It must be passed down, bestowed as a gift upon an heir, usually a blood relative—"

"Which is what you're going to make me," I interject. Cillian scowls.

"Fine. But we're doing this on my terms. If you're going to steal my magic, you'll have to learn how to use it properly first. I refuse to pass such a dangerous gift down to someone unprepared for it."

"How long will that take?" I ask.

Cillian considers. "Six weeks, at least."

"I don't have six weeks!" I burst out, wanting more than anything to smack him across his smug face. "I need it now."

"Unfortunately, this is the same process all magicians must go through." His face is serene, the face of someone who knows they have the winning hand. "I'm afraid it's nonnegotiable."

"You're hardly in a place to make demands," I return. He's right though. If I don't learn the magic first, I could end up killing myself. If I can just get his magic before the final show, which is in two months, I'll be fine.

I cross my arms over my chest. I'll let him have this one. "All right, I'll let you have four weeks in which to teach me."

"Six."

"Five."

"Six."

He's infuriating.

"You'll give it to me whenever I'm ready," I snarl, to which he only smirks.

"All right," he amends, like a saint bestowing a blessing. "I'll give you my magic as soon as you've proved you can pass the Apprentice's Exam. Come back tomorrow and we'll start your lessons."

It's too easy. I don't trust him.

"I want it in blood."

Cillian stares. Blood pacts are binding, and no amount of magic or hesitation can undo a deal sealed in blood.

"No." The word breathes out of him, so quiet I almost don't hear.

"It's that or death," I shrug. "Your choice."

"Who's going to believe you?" Cillian growls. "The high judge is dead, and you have no evidence."

"The word of a witness can be confirmed, especially once the crime has been investigated thoroughly." I let my words sink in like hooks. "Of course, I'm sure you covered your tracks completely though, and absolutely no damning evidence will come to light during the investigation, thorough arsonist that you seem to be."

I lean back, pretending to pick at my fingernails, but secretly watch Cillian closely through my eyelashes. His face is gray as he processes my threat, no doubt going through every last step of the crime in his head, exactly as I'd hoped.

"Fine," he snarls finally. I try not to let my relief show, though it courses through me like a wave.

Unfolding a dainty penknife, he slices the palm of his hand, careful to catch the blood that spills from the wound before it can stain the carpet. Delicately, he wipes the knife on a handkerchief before passing it to me, jaw clenched. I draw the same blade across my own palm, trying not to wince at the sudden flash of pain. Cillian scowls as a rivulet of blood escapes my trembling hand, blooming on the periwinkle tablecloth below.

I clasp his hand before he can change his mind, sealing the pact. He grips my hand so tight my finger bones crack, but the deal is done. I will be heir to his magic.

If he doesn't kill me first.

CHAPTER
9

I come back the next day to find the "Closed" sign in the window and the bookshop dark. Even with my face pressed against the glass, I can't make out any movement beyond a few dust motes floating in the sunlight that the window lets in.

I pound on the door until my knuckles are scraped and raw, but no one answers. A jiggle of the door handle reveals a very locked door. Only one thing left to do.

Reaching into my pocket, I remove a packet of matches, striking one on the brick facade. The match flares to life instantly, insignificant in the glare of the sun. I wave it across the bottom of the door, the flames licking at the wood eagerly. The wood is old, and the fire devours it quickly, belching smoke as it goes.

"What in the blazes are you doing?" The window jerks open revealing a livid Cillian. I give him my best smile.

"I so hate being late to my engagements."

Cursing, Cillian disappears into the smoke again, reappearing with a kettle full of water which he attempts to douse the fire with. Although the fire hisses in response, it still takes three more kettles to kill it completely. Cillian stands, staring at his blackened and smoking door before turning to me with a sour look.

"Do come in."

Ducking past the remains of the door, I take a seat in the rose chair and wait expectantly.

Cillian takes one look at my folded hands and scowls. "You really mean to take my magic, don't you?"

I smile sweetly. "It's a better alternative than the gallows, isn't it?"

It's clear he never intended to teach me magic at all, of course, but the sooner he understands what will happen if he doesn't teach me, the better.

Jaw grinding, he scans the bookshelves with a finger as though he can read the books there by touch. His finger stops on a heavy navy tome that reads *Magic: Basics and Theory* on the spine in thick, serious letters. Tugging it out, he thumbs to the first chapter and skims it. My heart thrums; I've wanted this since I was a child and now I'm finally going to learn how magic, real magic, works.

The book lands with a thump in front of me.

"Start with the first five chapters and we'll go from there."

I look up at Cillian in disbelief.

"You want me to read? I thought I'd be learning magic!"

It's hard to keep the betrayal out of my voice. I'd expected spells and potions, not dusty old books.

Cillian casts me an offended look.

"Magic? Look around you, child."

I ignore the "child," even though it's rich coming from him. He's easily only seven years older than myself, at most. About the same age as my brother Edward would've been.

I look around, humoring him.

"Books," I say, flatly.

"Yes, books," he agrees, impatient. He pulls an ancient text, heavy and worn from the shelf. It's nothing much to look at, but he touches it with something close to reverence, running a finger along its fading print.

"This book," he says, jabbing it in my direction, "both started and ended a war."

He replaces it, removing one adjacent. It is slightly less homely, but not much. The spine is cracked from use.

"This one stayed the hand of a king from executing his unfaithful wife."

There's a clunk as he replaces it.

"And this one," he says, handing me a smaller book, practically a pamphlet, leafed in gold, "seduced a god."

I run my fingers along the gilt. It's a beautiful little book, but I find it hard to believe there's any actual power inside.

Cillian holds my gaze, emerald eyes stormy. His voice is little more than a whisper.

"There is magic in words. Power in persuasion. The subtle difference between the words *melancholy* and *sad* can unravel a kingdom. Learn to use words with the precision of a sword, and you will have more magic at your disposal than Gantric the Great."

I consider the unassuming little book in my hand, still not entirely convinced. Cillian blows out a huff of exasperation.

"And of course, there's the fancy, pointless stuff as well."

Snapping his fingers, he lights my entire dress on fire. The flame burns so bright, it sears my vision, but doesn't so much as singe. I marvel at the flames, watching them shift and grow without even charring the fabric beneath.

Cillian watches me, distinctly annoyed. With another snap of his fingers, the flames disappear, leaving spots in front of my eyes.

"That was amazing! When can I do that?" I ask, checking my dress for even a hint of a burn. Cillian's expression is murderous.

"You have much to learn," is all he says, shoving his precious book back at me. "Read this and we'll meet again in a week."

Opportunity comes in the form of an invitation slipped under my door while I bathe. It's a pretentious thing, full of curlicues and gilt, and smells faintly of rose petals.

An invitation to dine with the queen.

Heart pounding, I finger the elegant script bearing my name. The last time the king chose a new Jester, he invited all his favorite acts to a feast. It would seem the queen is following in her husband's footsteps.

But what to wear to such an event? Recalling the queen's stuffy attire, I dress in the most formal dress I have, another borrowed gown from backstage at the Bleached Skull. The entire thing is adorned in peacock feathers that shimmer and catch the light. Twisting my hair with a number of pearl pins, I survey my reflection and pray I'm suitable enough to impress a queen.

The dinner is held in the Beehive, the Crown's formal conference room, available by reservation only. Upon entering, it's all I can do not to gape. A magnificent gold chandelier, easily the size of the table beneath, takes up half the ceiling. The rest is frescoed with watercolor flowers, and lazy bees buzz across the arched ceiling. The floor is inlaid with the same marble tiles as the rest of the hotel, hexagonal bordered with gleaming gold grout. Delicate tables, draped in lace and only large enough to seat four comfortably, dot the room. Lush floral centerpieces, sprays of color against the white of the tablecloths, adorn the tiny tables. And in the center of it all, practically groaning under the weight, is a table laden with food. My mouth waters at the abundance.

I don't even realize I've stopped walking until I'm elbowed from behind.

"Excuse *you*."

I swallow my apologies as a couple, much more ornately dressed than myself, pushes past.

"I see you got my invitation."

I turn, arms crossed to face Luc, who looks devastatingly handsome. He's foregone his usual gaudy blood-red costume for a sleek charcoal suit with gold thread. It's obvious he's shaved too, his jawline sharp. Without the usual kohl lining them, I can finally make out the thick lashes that line his amber eyes.

"*Your* invitation?"

But it suddenly makes perfect, painful sense. Why would the queen summon a mediocre performer like me when she has the entire Noose to choose her Jester from? Luc smiles, pleased that I've caught on so quickly.

"Forgive me. I do so love to watch you make a fool of yourself though."

I grind my teeth, wishing I had something to stab him with. "Go to hell."

His eyes glitter. "Isn't it interesting how the prickliest cacti have the most beautiful blooms?"

"What's really interesting is how poison can taste just like honey," I respond. Instead of provoking him as I'd intended, however, my words seem only to amuse him. To my surprise, he takes my arm, guiding me toward the tables.

"You know what they say about rattlesnakes, right? If you waste all your time trying to kill the snake that bit you, you'll die from the venom."

I tighten my grip on his arm, nails biting into the thick fabric of his suit.

"The only question is, which of us is the rattlesnake?" I ask, as we make our way to one of the tables farthest from the queen's, on the outskirts of the room. Luc leans in, adjusting my cheap necklace, lips brushing my ears.

"Isn't it obvious?"

I shrug him away, ignoring the way my ear still burns.

"Oh dear, no room for you," Luc says, flicking one of the table cards. "Perhaps you can have the leftovers once we're finished."

He's gone before I can respond, lean figure cutting back toward the center of the room. I bite my tongue so hard I taste blood, as he takes a seat at the queen's table, where there is only room for three besides the queen herself.

The realization hits me with the force of a train. The queen doesn't even know I exist. Without Luc's invitation, I wouldn't even be here. His supposed chivalry was just an excuse for him to grind me under his snakeskin boots. I clench my teeth, hugging the wall as the true guests take their seats.

The competition has yet to begin, and I'm already losing.

I should leave, but I'm frozen, watching as the guests taste the first course, slices of raw salmon, so thin they're transparent, laid gracefully over a mouthful of rice, sprinkled with roe and garnished with a bite of ginger. As we are so far inland, seafood is the height of luxury. My mouth waters, watching.

It's been more years than I can count since I last had fish, and the sight of Luc savoring his own food as he chats with the queen rankles me.

"Peacock feathers are bad luck, you know."

I look up to see a dour-looking girl staring at me from across the table with what is apparently deep disapproval. I'd been so caught up in watching the queen, I hadn't even noticed the nearby table watching me. Limp curls frame the girl's scowling face, and her fur dress is so tight that it squeezes her visible flesh like a sausage casing. She's dotted in a number of large moles, like constellations.

"I don't believe in luck," I say, throwing her a glittering smile. Her lips purse.

"The nerve of these servers," she mutters to the woman next to her. "See if I tip *her,* how's that for luck?"

They both break into amused titters. Because of course, even here, she thinks I'm nothing more than a serving girl. I clench my fists, hating Luc with every fiber of my being.

"There's a seat here."

A young woman, electric purple hair sliced in a bob seated at an empty table nearby, gestures to the seat next to her. It's obvious why it's empty; a giant black panther is sprawled on the floor next to it. I hesitate as the panther eyes me, but the girl's brown eyes sparkle.

"He won't hurt you," she says, rubbing the panther's silky ears. "Not unless I tell him to, of course."

She winks. The words are anything but reassuring, but the smile beneath them does the trick. I slide into the empty seat.

"Thank you," I say, face still burning from my interaction with Luc. "Someone else must've stolen my seat . . ."

"Happens all the time," the girl says, mouth twitching into a smile. "Don't let it get you down. I'm Yasmin, big-cat trainer at the Panther."

She extends a hand, which I seize gratefully. I've heard of Yasmin; she was a big deal on the Noose a few years ago, a long-time headliner.

"I'm Mirage."

A laugh from the queen's table catches my attention. I'm just working out an excuse to drop by and introduce myself, make her notice me, when the queen stands up.

The room instantly quiets, the clinking of silverware and side conversations evaporating into expectant silence.

"Thank you all for joining me."

Her voice is so quiet I have to strain to hear her. She's exchanged her heavy garb for the summer clothing of the North—lighter but no less formal.

"As you all know, I will be taking my husband's place as judge for the position of Jester. This competition was very important to my husband. He loved a good show more than anything."

From the little I've gathered about her, the queen does not share this particular passion with her late husband. She looks down at the tablecloth as though steadying herself. I expect tears, but none come, and when she looks up again, her face is as unreadable as stone.

"I look forward to the performances."

Several of the male guests, and even one female, leap up to assist the queen as she sits again, but it's Luc's hand she takes with a grateful smile. My stomach clenches.

I study the queen from my place in the corner. Every other bite is interrupted by yet another performer, eager to introduce themselves. I wonder how many of these introductions she's been forced to sit through already. Her eyes are glazed, her gestures the result of years of etiquette training, automatic. In a room full of the elite of Oasis, she looks . . . bored.

Death before boredom.

It's the motto of the Jester. Anyone can be Jester, magic or no. All the late king really cared about was who could entertain him best. The last Jester wasn't even a performer; she was a chef. Flavia hailed from the East Isles, and word on the Noose was that her iced-coconut cakes were so good, a fight once broke out at the king's dessert table over the last one, ending in the death of a courtier.

This is the first time a Jester is to be chosen since the king's death. It's been seven years since the king's selection, and three years since the queen retired the chef, shortly after her husband's death. Whatever the king felt about entertainment, it's obvious his wife does not feel the same.

I'm on my feet, across the room before I have time to plan, before I have time to remember I don't belong here. Luc catches sight of my approach and nudges his neighbor. I ignore the satisfied smirk that sweeps across his face and drop a heavy knife next to the queen's dish with a thunk.

Startled, she looks up.

"Your Majesty, have you ever played 'hilt or blade'?"

The guard across the room straightens, hand drifting to the revolver tucked neatly in his waistband.

The queen stares at the knife, then me. "I beg your pardon?"

"It's a game. You pick one person at the table and ask them to choose, hilt or blade."

"I don't believe I've played—"

"Is there a problem, Your Highness?" The guard materializes next to my shoulder, grabbing me not so gently. I jerk away, but his grip is iron.

"It's only a game, relax. Can't you see how bored she is?"

The queen considers me. For one terrifying moment, I'm sure she'll arrest me. Instead, her face smooths, and she waves away the guard.

"It's been a long time since I've experienced the many amusements and pleasures Oasis has to offer. Let her continue."

The guard lets go reluctantly but does not resume his position at the door, choosing instead to station himself directly behind the queen. Picking up the dagger, I point it directly at Luc, who chokes on a mouthful of shark-fin soup and scrambles to regain his composure.

"Hilt or blade?"

Luc's eyes, which are watering from coughing, dart to the queen, and I know I have him. There's no way he'll refuse to play now. He straightens, clearing his throat.

"Hilt. Obviously."

"Very well, give me your hand." Luc cautiously stretches his hand across the table. It's warm, and I can make out the steady pulse beneath.

Quickly, I prick his fingertip, just enough to draw blood, and let it drip onto the hilt before he can pull his hand away.

"Now you must reveal a secret to the entire table."

The queen's eyes jump from me to Luc and back again.

Luc considers me, eyes narrowed. "And if I lie?"

"This is a truth blade." I set the dagger on the table, so he can make out the ruby eye on the hilt. "If you lie, we'll all know, and you'll be forced to play blade instead."

"Something tells me I won't like blade much more," Luc says, giving me a lazy smile. "Although I do wonder if that cheap trinket can truly detect a lie with nothing more than a shiny glass 'ruby.'"

I should have known that with his expensive taste, he'd be the first to pick out the faux gemstone. Scowling, I rub at the chipped stone as if I can make it real by wishing hard enough.

"Just spill your secret already."

Luc's mouth twitches in amusement.

"Hmm, let's see . . . I don't know if I even have any secrets. I'm quite an open book, you know."

Chuckles erupt from the tables around us. At this point, most everyone nearby has started to watch the proceedings with great interest.

"Oh! There is one thing."

He pauses for effect, and the room is so quiet, you could hear a snake slither, and I wonder when this became his show and not mine.

"I'm in love with you."

Even though I'm expecting something ridiculous, the words are still a punch to the gut.

There's not a hint of deception in those golden eyes. They burn as he watches me, as ravenous as a wolf. Catcalls and whistles fill the room as my face heats.

"Lie," I respond, showing him the hilt, where the false ruby glows as red as my face.

"Of course it is," Luc says, smile sharp enough to slice. "Just testing the veracity of your 'truth blade.'"

"Since you lied, now you must play blade."

Luc's smile never wavers. "Pray, tell us how."

"You must throw the knife at a target of my choosing. If you miss, you'll be forced to remove an appendage of your choice."

I let the words sink in, enjoying the way his eyes tighten at the corners.

"It's a good thing I am an excellent marksman with a knife," Luc says, draining his glass. "Well, what bull's-eye would you like me to hit, then? A crystal from the chandelier, perhaps? The pearls on Madame Bouvier's necklace?"

More chuckles. I wait until he's finished peacocking.

"I want you to hit me. Right here."

I tug at my bodice, revealing the tender skin below my collarbone. Enough to tease, but not enough to start a scandal. The shock on his face is delicious. He doesn't even protest when I hand him the knife, hilt first. He just stares at my collarbone, as if befuddled.

"You can't possibly be serious," he says finally, looking up, all traces of bravado gone.

"Of course I am," I say, affecting an innocent look. "After all, who better than a master marksman?"

Luc scowls and twirls the knife. "Fine. Stand where you will, then."

I take my place several tables down, where even if he misses dreadfully, no one else will be in range.

"Ready when you are."

First, he weighs the knife in his left hand; then, as if unsatisfied, he switches it to the right. He aims, then lowers the knife again, and cracks his neck.

"Before we're all dead, if you please," I say dryly, and the knife comes at me so fast, I hardly have time to prepare.

True to his bragging, he hits the intended target dead-on, and I drop like a sack of rocks on impact.

There's a flurry of chairs scraping, gasps, and one shattered glass, and then Luc is by my side, carefully lifting me to a sitting position.

"Is she dead?"

The queen. I'd be touched at her concern, if I didn't currently have a knife lodged in my chest.

"I can heal her."

Luc. He's pale but confident, as he pulls at the hilt. His face is dismayed as it slides out, revealing not a gaping wound beneath, but unblemished skin.

"What in the—"

"Trick knife," I smirk, standing up easily. For the group, I demonstrate the retractable blade. The magnetic strip concealed beneath the bodice of my dress ensured the knife would stick once thrown. It's a cheap trick indeed, but judging by Luc's bloodless face, it had its intended effect. Applause rings out, and I don't miss the queen, joining in the clapping. Nor do I miss the murderous expression on Luc's face as he tosses the fake dagger onto a table and stalks back to his seat. I cast him out of my mind, dropping into a dramatic bow.

"Thank you for playing! My name is Mirage, and I'll be performing at the Saguaro tomorrow night. Remember who entertained you during this *fascinating* dinner when you consider your choice for Jester."

The applause is deafening. I want to enjoy the moment, but I can't seem to erase the image of Luc's frightened face as he pulled out the dagger. I thought for sure he'd see the dagger for what it was, a clever fake. Just like me. It's not even a real truth blade, its ruby eye controlled by a carefully concealed button. Luc's confession could have been the absolute truth and that cheap blade would never have been able to tell the difference.

Just like me.

CHAPTER
10

The next morning, I'm early again for my lesson with Cillian, but this time he is prepared. He answers the door before I can even raise a hand to knock, gesturing wordlessly for me to follow him down the street. Intrigued, I follow him all the way to the outskirts of Oasis, where there are more tumbleweeds than tourists.

"Here." Satisfied, Cillian cracks his knuckles. "Out here, there is nothing to distract you. I have eliminated every external force."

I see nothing that would make this a good spot to learn magic. The land around us is barren for miles, nothing but red rock and scrubby bushes. Flies buzz around my head; the sun beats down on us. I'm fairly certain Cillian insisted on having our lesson outside in the middle of summer, not to "eliminate external influences" as he claimed, but to convince me to give up on our lessons.

But I would spend a week in the desert if it meant I'd have my own magic.

"I want you to close your eyes and picture your reason for summoning the magic. Why do you need it?"

I do as he says, shutting my eyes. There are many reasons for wanting the magic, but one in particular surfaces from the murk of my mind, floating to the top like a dead log.

"I want to be liked." It's the most honest answer I know how to give.

"That's a *terrible* reason."

My eyes fly open.

Cillian looks offended. "Magic is not about being *liked*. It's to be used for noble purposes, like getting rid of disease or furthering mankind's progress."

"Oh, like you're furthering mankind by setting buildings ablaze," I snap, my face red. Cillian pours iced tea from a thermos, his face a mask.

"I'm afraid I don't know what you're talking about." He doesn't offer me any of the tea, even though he must know how thirsty I am. Sweat trickles down the back of my neck, and my mouth is gritty from lack of moisture. Taking a long draw, he smirks as I swallow reflexively at the sight of the amber liquid.

"Concentrate," Cillian scolds, clearly enjoying himself. "Clear your mind. Feel the magic—"

"I don't have any magic!"

It takes every ounce of willpower I have not to strangle him. It's clear he's not taking any of this seriously.

"I could report you at any time," I remind him as he snaps open a massive umbrella and takes a seat in the shade beneath it.

"Sure, sure," he says, taking another pull from his thermos and removing a dainty cookie from his shirt pocket. He takes a delicate bite and looks at me, eyebrow raised. "Well? Are you concentrating?"

"What's the point of all this? You're just mocking me." I jab a finger at his cookie. "And if I can't pass the Apprentice's Exam, I'm going to shout from the top of the Crown what you did—"

"Oh, relax," Cillian says, dusting cookie crumbs from his trousers. "Just having a bit of fun. You can hardly deny me that luxury."

Sweat trickles down one temple as I glower at him. Pushing up his glasses, which have slid down his nose, he leaves the umbrella in the sand and turns to me.

"All right. I actually did prepare a real lesson, and it would be a shame to let all that preparation go to waste."

I roll my eyes, but relief courses through me. I can threaten all I want, but if he doesn't care if I reveal his secret, I lose any hold I have over him.

"Magic is power. Power over your fellow men, power over the elements. That power should never be used without accountability."

I relax, nodding. This, I understand. My father's entire job was built on holding people accountable for their misuse of magic.

"Which is why you need a good reason to use your power, or at the very least not a harmful reason," Cillian continues, oblivious to the heat. His messy black curls gleam in the sunlight as he paces in the sand.

"Being liked isn't harmful," I counter, wishing he'd let me have some of his tea. I lick my lips, which are salty from sweat.

"Not inherently, no," Cillian says. I can sense a "but." "But the need to be liked is like a disease. To what lengths will you go to impress others? What lines will you cross, what parts of yourself will you shed, just for a taste of approval?"

I study my feet, pretending his question doesn't make me uncomfortable. I'd never considered how far I'd go to impress. There was never a set limit, just a goal, the goal of being acknowledged by the Crown. And I'd do anything for that.

"I'm sure you can see why there's a problem," Cillian says almost gently. "With true power there are few, if any, limits. Which is why you must set the bar yourself, hold yourself accountable. Because if you don't, who will?"

Not the high judge, I think. The only man with more power than a king, sentenced to execution for his own loss of control.

"I want you to think about your reason for using magic. Come back with a good one next week, something better than 'being liked.'" Cillian thrusts a mountain of books at me and I curse, struggling under the sudden weight. "Oh, and read these."

Cillian's words follow me all the way back to the Saguaro. What are my limits? Deep down, I know there is no cost too high, nothing I wouldn't sacrifice.

The bruising on my chest from Luc's knife throw is spectacular, a colorful reminder of the cost I paid to get the queen's attention. And now that I have it, I need to make sure my first show is worth the sacrifice. I need something new. Something I haven't used on the streets, that people haven't seen before. Nothing impresses crowds more than novelty.

Which is how I find myself with a sword three inches down my throat. I know sword swallowing is possible—I'm not completely insane. There was a street performer several years ago, with a similar act on the Noose, who'd styled himself as the "Bottomless Pit." The Pit was exactly what you'd expect from a man who claimed to swallow anything: massive, built like the bajhu wrestlers of the South, and completely covered in tattoos. According to local legend (which I suspect was fueled by the Pit himself), each tattoo was something he had once swallowed, the most impressive being the twenty-inch flaming sword that bisected his entire back. When I'd asked him how he did it, he'd told me the trick was to go slowly. Even the slightest movement could rip apart the esophagus, he'd warned, jowls quivering, so it was very important to relax. And never, *ever* really swallow.

How he could relax with a live porcupine wriggling in his esophagus was beyond me. Of course, he'd probably used magic too. Nothing I can do about that part though. Thankfully, I don't have to worry about being accused of stealing his act, because the Pit died mid-show a little over two years ago. Ironically, it wasn't the lit torch halfway down his gullet that did him in but heart failure.

The sword I'm using is thin, barely an inch across, dulled at the edges but still sharp at the tip. It doesn't hurt exactly, but it is terribly uncomfortable. The only problem is, I'm not sure if I'm doing it right. I have my head tipped all the way back to make my esophagus as open as possible. The sword tickles my gag reflex, which threatens to reject it, as well as my lunch, at any moment. It occurs to me then, mouth flooded with saliva, that I should have started with something easier. A butter knife, maybe, or my finger.

Eyes watering, I carefully pull the tip of the sword from my throat, gagging as it slides up over my tongue. I mark the measurement on the sword, pleased when I realize it's a centimeter and a half farther than the last time I tried it. I pull out a notebook and jot down my observations.

Find something smaller to train the muscles of the throat. Try lubrication?

I have what seems like thousands of notebooks just like this one, full of these kinds of notes, everything I've learned as a performer. Some are falling apart, I've used them so extensively, with loose pages that flutter out when opened and script that's faded from years of desert heat and obsession.

In any case, how can I expect to be the best if I don't learn everything there is to know? I tap the pen on my teeth, wondering what I can use for lubrication but overall pleased with my progress. Stretching, I eye the tourists that wind through the streets from my grimy window. It's been a while since I've been to the Panther, I realize. It's time I paid the devil a visit.

My water sits untouched in front of me, the ice long ago melted. I haven't come to the Panther to drink or dance, as most people do. Instead I'd hoped that being in Luc's territory—the den of the lion, so to speak—might help me come up with a way to beat him. But I have nothing more than a headache from the strobing lights and pounding music of the club.

I'm about to leave, when a flash of electric purple hair catches my eye. Seated alone is Yasmin, the girl from the queen's party. It's hard to miss that razor-sharp bob—and the panther lounging at her feet.

I approach her, glad to see a familiar face. She doesn't bother to look up, just continues reading a book, long brown legs crossed on the table in front of her.

"I sign autographs every night at six in the lounge," she says automatically.

"I'm not here for an autograph," I say, flustered. She looks up, blinking, as though just remembering where she is.

"Mirage!"

The panther lets out a velvet growl. "Sit," she instructs the big cat. He does so balefully, yawning, the lights from the strobes catching on one gleaming fang. A thick tail flicks my ankle, and it's all I can do to remain nonchalant.

"Hilt or blade," she muses, snapping the book shut. "That was a riot."

"Thanks."

She's not rude or condescending like some of the other big shot performers are.

"Anything to make the devil squirm," I say.

"Personally, I'd prefer him writhing to squirming."

The book lies forgotten next to an empty glass, her spot marked with a napkin. Yasmin's smile is sharp, slicing. The panther licks at one enormous paw, his golden eyes fixed on me. I'm not surprised she and Luc don't get along, even though they share a stage. "Sibling rivalries," as they're known in the business, tend to crop up when two acts compete for ticket sales. And I know of more than a few theater managers who play off these natural rivalries to drive up sales.

Her fingers tighten on the edge of the table before she remembers herself. She flags down a serving girl and grabs a bright blue drink, then gestures to me.

"Thirsty?"

I shake my head, but she grabs one anyway, pushing it toward me. The liquid inside is tropical and smells like the ocean, if the ocean were made of fruit.

"Word on the Noose is you're Luc's biggest competition for Jester." Her dark eyes survey me over her drink. I take a sip of my own, hoping to downplay the thrill her words send through me.

Her fingers tap her glass absently to the heavy beat of the music as she considers me.

"I'm having a party on the rooftop tonight," she says finally. "You should come."

I catch the stupid smile that threatens to cover my face just in time and settle instead for a casual nod. I've waited my whole life to be acknowledged by someone like Yasmin, an actual headliner.

"I'll see if I can make it." There's no way I'm missing it.

Yasmin smiles, pleased, and leans back to sip her drink. "Can you imagine a street performer actually winning Jester?" She shakes her head at the thought, scratching under the panther's bristly chin.

"That's the plan," I say.

"Oh, it's not that I don't think you can," she says, placatingly. "I just don't know if Luc's ego could handle it."

I laugh. In the spirit of friendship, I take a sip of the blue drink. It feels like a thousand tiny bubbles fizz in my bloodstream.

"So, what's your plan?" she asks, leaning in conspiratorially. I mimic her without meaning to.

"What plan?"

She lets out an exasperated laugh. "For beating Luc, of course."

"Well, I've got a fantastic show lined up . . ."

Yasmin's already shaking her head. "That's not enough. You've got to find out his weakness and exploit it."

"You mean, like cheating?" I'm not above it, but a weird part of me wants to win without cheating. Prove that I'm good enough.

"Oh, you have got a long way to go." She sighs. "You're not on the streets anymore. Listen, you want to beat Luc? Check the storage closet backstage at six fifteen."

She winks at me surreptitiously and nudges the big black cat with a toe. "Come on, Iko. We've got a show to get ready for."

Six twenty-three. Crouched in the dust backstage at the Panther near a box of masks, I'm beginning to feel a fool. The glow from Yasmin's unexpected attention fades more and more with each passing minute, leaving me with something like a hangover. I wouldn't be surprised if Luc himself were somehow behind the whole thing, Yasmin just another of his plants.

I'm about to leave, when a loud retching sound comes from inside the storage closet. I tap lightly on the door.

"All right in there?"

The voice that answers is hoarse. "Go away."

"Nerves?" I ask sympathetically, leaning against the door.

More retching. Poor sop. Twisting the handle, I tug open the door. And there, hunched over a mop bucket, pale and shaking, is Luc. My hand flies to my mouth.

"Devils!"

Luc looks up, wan, dragging a hand across his mouth.

"Of course it's you," he says, resigned.

"Are you okay?" I ask, even though it's obvious he's not. He'd better pull himself together. I glance at the clock. His show is in less than thirty minutes, and I can't help the eagerness that rises inside of me. If Luc is too sick to perform . . .

"Ate some bad quail or something," he mutters, pushing the bucket away. I furrow my brow.

"You have stage fright." It dawns on me with certainty. This was what Yasmin wanted me to see. Luc doesn't bother to contradict me, just holds his head in his hands as though he can stop the shaking that way. It's almost too much: the great Luc, performer of death-defying feats, afraid of the stage.

"Go on then," Luc says, waving me away, still pale. "You know you're dying to tell everyone. You finally have an advantage over me, may as well use it."

I pause. He's right, but it feels so cheap. I lean against the door, taking in the sight of my enemy brought to his knees from fear. It should be delicious, but it's more pathetic than anything.

"Why do you do it?"

Luc looks up, as though surprised to see me there still.

"What? Vomit up a perfectly good meal before every performance?" I swallow back a smile. "Yes and no."

Luc studies me for a moment. "Do you take me for a fool?"

Now, I don't bother fighting the grin that slides across my face. "You are competing for the spot of queen's fool."

"Jester," he corrects.

"Same thing."

A small smile curves Luc's lips, although it's a touch bitter. "True enough."

He's silent for so long, I assume my question will remain unanswered, until he blows out a sigh.

"I hate performing."

The admission is a shock. I think of his face, the light that seems to suffuse him when he performs. I'd always assumed we were the same, he and I. Two ends of the same spectrum. He may hate performing, but he's a born actor.

He goes on. "Every single act, I wonder if it will be my last. The one where I slip up and get myself killed for real."

"Can't you just heal yourself?" I ask, brow crinkled.

Luc's laugh is hollow. "All magic has limits. If I overstrain my magic one day, or don't give myself adequate time to heal from a previous act, or even just let my heart go too long in between beats . . ."

He shrugs, letting the rest of the thought dangle like the feet of a hanged man. Reeling, I try to process what he's telling me. I'd always assumed Luc was invincible.

"Even I don't know all my limits," he admits, playing with one of the many silver rings that adorn his slender fingers. He falls quiet for a moment, as if sobered by the thought. "But this job . . . the position of Jester . . . I need it more than anything. And I'll do anything to get it."

His eyes bore into me. Perhaps we don't have the same motives, but the fire that burns within us is the same.

"Why?"

The question rouses him, and he seems to recall who he's talking to. I can see the mask slip back on, in the guise of an easy smile. "Same as you."

But it's not. I don't push him further though. One of the stagehands scurries toward us, startling when he sees me there.

"Master Luc, you said to let you know if anyone came backstage—"

"I'd noticed," Luc says, dryly. "A little late, but I appreciate the warning nevertheless."

The stagehand has the decency to look chastised. "Shall I escort her out?"

"You'll do nothing of the sort." I cross my arms over my chest, glowering at the little man.

Luc slips his own arm around me, guiding me away before I can so much as protest. "I'll handle this, Johan."

Johan gives him a short bow before backing away cautiously, throwing me nervous looks as he does so.

"You stink," I say, shoving Luc away. Reaching into my bag, I pull out a tin of ginger candies. "Take one of these, it'll help with the nausea. And your *breath*."

Luc smiles at my wrinkled nose, as he pops in the candy. "Are you always this charming?"

"Just be glad I don't poison you."

He doesn't try to put his arm around me again. Sneaking a glance at him from the corner of my eye, I absorb the fact that Luc is not who I thought he was. How much of Luc is the mask, how much is really him? Although I hate to admit it, I'm fascinated with this new side of him. I tell myself it's simply knowing he has a weak point, but there's something more. Something I can't name.

Something I'm terrified to name.

CHAPTER
11

*S*uccess.

It suffuses Edward with warmth, despite the ice-cold drink his father presses into his hands. His brain feels like a wrung sponge, his eyes are grainy from exhaustion, but elation buoys him.

A perfect score.

Sure, he'd hoped and studied and prayed for as much. But even he would have been a fool to believe he could actually achieve it. Only two perfect scores existed in the history of the Apprentice's Exam. Not even his father could claim such an honor.

"Come, have another drink, boy!" Joy, uncharacteristic in his father's voice, seems to fill the whole room. Guests, colleagues of his father's, well-known aristocrats as well as several high-level court officials, circle him like planets, offering hearty congratulations and drinking to him. Edward feels as if he will drown in all the praise.

It would not be an unpleasant way to go.

He does not say no when the daughter of the lord general asks him for a dance. Tonight is his night, and he will dance with every girl here.

They swirl, the moonlight above the courtyard sparkles in the auburn of his partner's hair, and his heart squeezes at the absolute perfectness of the moment.

A flash of burgundy catches his eyes near the tables. Excusing himself, Edward crouches near one of the refreshment tables, lifting the hem of the exquisite lace cloth that covers it.

Lisette, tucked neatly under the table and away from their father's line of sight, startles when she sees him. She recovers quickly, donning a scowl.

"Go away."

Edward smothers the smile that rises unbidden to his lips at the sight of her. She has avoided him for weeks now. "I had planned to offer you some of this lovely éclair, but if you're certain—"

He lets the gauzy fabric fall, nodding as Madam Oakley strides by, giving him a curious look.

"Wait!"

Schooling his expression, Edward lifts the tablecloth once more. "Yes?"

"You can come in." It is grudging, but it is an invitation, at least. Forcing his long limbs to obey, he crams himself under the table with his sister. She extends an impatient hand, into which he deposits half the promised pastry.

"I'm still mad at you," Lisette says around a gooey mouthful. "And you didn't even invite me to your party."

Edward smiles at the chocolate smear on her nose. "You're right, that was very rude of me."

Sucking the frosting from her fingers, Lisette nods, solemn. "I shall never forgive you."

"Never?" Edward leans against the wooden pedestal of the table, trying his best to keep his cramping legs hidden.

"Never," Lisette affirms, fixing him with narrowed eyes. Her curled hair is messy, and she wears only a nightshift. Even in the dark, he can make out the pinpricks on her fingers—souvenirs from her new apprenticeship with Madam Luelle.

Inspired, Edward leans in, conspiratorial. "What if I made you my heir?"

Her brow furrows almost comically. "What?"

"I have to retire sometime, right?" He shrugs, as though this is a completely normal conversation they're having and not a complete upheaval of decades of inheritance tradition. "When I do, I'll pass my magic on to you."

"You—you can't," Lisette stammers, eyes wide. "You're supposed to pass it on to your children—"

"I don't have to," Edward says, tugging one of her curls. "Captain Flint didn't."

"He didn't have any kids," Lisette argues, but he can see the way the idea has caught hold in her mind, ensnared her.

"How about this, then," Edward says, thinking fast. "If I have any children one day—your future nieces or nephews—when you're ready to retire, you pick your favorite and make them your heir."

He sits back, pleased. Sure, his future wife might hate him one day for this little agreement, but Edward can't think of anyone he'd rather choose for his heir. Lisette scrutinizes him, face screwed up, as if waiting for him to yell "gotcha!"

"I mean it, little Lis," Edward says gently, grasping one of her warm hands in his. "If you want it, it's yours."

Her mouth opens and closes, as though the night breeze has stolen the words from her. "Yes, please."

Edward laughs as she wraps him in a stranglehold, his head knocking into the underside of the table. "Easy, easy! I've got a party to get back to."

Lisette releases him, unable to hide the smile that has overtaken her face.

"And you should get back to bed before Papa sees," Edward adds, doing his best to look stern.

"He's probably droning on about international law to Lord Dannily," Lisette says, rolling her eyes. "He'll never even know I'm here."

Edward stifles a smile. "Very well. But if you get caught, don't you dare drag me into it."

"I won't," Lisette promises. Smiling, Edward discreetly lifts the table-cloth, looking for any courtiers in the nearby vicinity before sliding awkward-ly out from underneath.

"Oh, good evening again, Madam Oakley," he says, brushing the dust from his suit as the old dowager stares at him from a nearby table. A hand tugs at one trouser leg, and Edward looks down.

"Edward," Lisette's stage whisper is loud enough to attract the atten-tion of several courtiers milling by, who as a courtesy, pretend not to see the daughter of the high judge hiding under a refreshment table.

"Yes?"

Her gaze is earnest. "I was never really mad at you, you know."

He leans down and chucks her chin. "I know."

CHAPTER 12

I can't remember the last time I experienced the Oasis nightlife as a reveler rather than a performer. The city, so hot and sleepy in the day, comes alive at night, in flashing billboards, lights so bright I have to squint, and the bells of the games. On corners, men in masks stealthily hand out flyers to illegal shows, animal fights, and peep shows. The casinos beckon like palaces, each promising a different pleasure: exotic girls, lethal animals, death-defying acts. I drink it in, savoring the taste of the city for once extending its thrills to me.

Yasmin's party is on the rooftop of the Panther, an exclusive VIP club. Clad in yet another borrowed gown from the Bleached Skull,—this one made of slinky black silk that whispers like air against my skin—I feel like a fraud.

A slick bouncer blocks the entrance, and out of habit, I fall into step with the group in front of me, trying to blend in.

"You."

I look up, heart sinking, at the bouncer's finger pointed directly at me. Whispers and mutters surround me as the group I've hidden in scatters, afraid my status as outsider is contagious.

"Yes?"

My haughty tone doesn't fool him one bit. "Name?"

My heart sinks still further. I never gave Yasmin my real name. "Mirage?"

He scans his list half-heartedly. "Don't see you on here."

"Yasmin invited me." Even as I say it, I know it's a lost cause. It doesn't matter how fine my clothes are or how much money I make, I'll always be an outsider.

"Sure, I'll bet you're best friends, aren't you?" The bouncer's tone turns gruff. "If you aren't on the list, beat it."

Someone jostles me from behind. "Try Club Flamingo, they'll let anyone in."

A gorgeous blonde in a short-furred dress pushes past, smirking, the bouncer too busy checking out her backside to worry about whether or not her name is on his precious list. Cheeks aflame, I turn to leave. It's obvious Yasmin was only being friendly in the club; I never should have taken her at her word.

"Mirage!"

I turn to see Yasmin, a crowd of partygoers parting at her passing as naturally as water flowing around a stone.

"Aren't you coming?" she asks. She looks fantastic, a clinging leopard-skin dress covering her petite frame and a slash of gold eyeliner offsetting her heavy purple bangs.

"I was just—" I have no answer that won't humiliate me, so I just nod instead. "Yes, I'm coming."

The bouncer says nothing as we pass, Yasmin's arm slung through mine. I gloat internally at his sullen expression and throw him a wide smile that darkens his scowl.

The rooftop is as lush as a jungle; thick palms with heavy fronds drape over an infinity pool. Even though it's nearly midnight, the pool is full, moonlight gleaming off exposed flesh and blue water. A rippling growl comes from a lion sprawled on a lounge chair, startling me as we pass. Wild animals roam the rooftop, mingling with the guests.

Yasmin's friends are an eclectic group. I see one girl whose nails have been sharpened into gilded claws. She throws me a smile when she catches me staring, baring matching gold fangs. A man dressed in a glittering mermaid tail splashes in the pool. They are the elite of Oasis's performers, made rich on tourist gold. Amid so much exposed wealth, it's not hard to see why the bouncer picked me out so quickly. Yasmin's guests do not miss the fact that there is an outsider in their midst either.

"What do we have here?" A snub-nosed boy with a pixie cut grabs my arm in a not-so-friendly way. I respond instantly, the dagger I'd concealed on my thigh at his throat.

"Be nice, Clement," Yasmin drawls from behind me. "Mirage is my dear new friend."

Clement chuckles, low in his throat. "It wouldn't be one of your parties without a little blood, would it, Yas?"

Yasmin laughs. "Do us all a favor, Mirage, and just kill him already."

I relax at her teasing tone, letting the knife drop. It's obvious she and Clement are close. He scowls at me, dusting off his clothing.

"Where'd you get this one anyway?" Clement jerks his head at me, clearly still offended.

"It just so happens that Mirage has big plans of unseating the devil from his throne."

Clement lets out a scathing laugh. "No one can beat Luc."

"I can."

The conviction in my own voice surprises me but does little to convince Clement, who drops a mock curtsy.

"Of course you can," he says, jeering. "After all, what is the Jester but the queen's royal fool? By the way, have you met Clarice yet?"

He waves over a stunning redhead with long waves tossed artfully down her exposed back. Although I've never met her, I know exactly who she is. Clarice has an escape act at the Gilded Hilt that is spectacular. The girl has broken out of everything from a cage to a coffin nailed shut and tossed into the ocean. Rumor has it, she can survive without oxygen, but no one's ever been able to prove it. Yasmin's smile becomes tight.

Clement's smile is mocking. "No doubt you've already met, seeing as you're both competing for Jester."

I decide to swallow my pride and smile at Clarice. I am here to meet other performers, after all. "I'm Mirage. I suppose we are competitors."

Clarice throws me a bland smile in response, no recognition in her pale blue eyes. "Where did you say you perform?"

"The Saguaro," I mumble, suddenly unable to meet those icy eyes. Clement snorts.

"That dive in the Sagebrush district?"

"Shut up, Clement." Yasmin's tone brooks no argument, but Clement ignores the warning just the same.

"Clarice, weren't you just telling me the queen sat in the front row for your last show?" he asks, innocent. "Quite an accomplishment this early in the competition."

His eyes are narrowed despite his mirth. Clarice feigns indifference, brushing the feathers that adorn her over-the-top gown.

"No doubt one of many shows the queen attended that evening. My seeker was very pleased," she says, eyes flitting to me. I intend to ignore the unspoken question there, but Clement, sensing my weak point, digs in.

"No doubt." He smirks, and it feels like my facial muscles have frozen into a forced smile. "What about you, Mirage? Who is lucky enough to be *your* seeker?"

They all stare at me, even Yasmin. Clement's smile grows wicked. Devils hang him, he has me, and he knows it.

"I don't have a seeker yet."

Clement looks as if I've just handed him the crown off the queen's head.

"It's very difficult to find a seeker, of course," Clarice begins in a tone so patronizing, I want to pluck the feathers from her ridiculous gown and throw them at her.

"I just got hired on as headliner," I rush on, hating the excuse, and wishing I had stabbed Clement when I had the chance. "I haven't even had my first show yet."

"Of course," Clement demurs, ducking his head, although I can see the laughs that wrack his body. Clarice, having lost interest, is gazing out at the pool. True to character, she slips away into the crowd, pretending to see someone she knows.

"Go bother someone else," Yasmin says to Clement, eyes darting to me.

Still laughing, he sways into the crowd, grabbing several drinks as he does so.

"Don't mind him," Yasmin says. "He's just jealous. Half the people here would kill to be Jester."

"I don't mind," I respond automatically, although his obvious disdain pricks at me. Even here as Yasmin's guest, I'm nothing more than a trained poodle, jumping through hoops. But better to be the dog they clap for than nothing at all. I grab a drink and down it without even looking at the contents. It burns my throat like acid. "Why would I mind? I'm here to have fun. This is a party, isn't it?"

My voice is too loud. Several partygoers turn to stare, but I can't seem to stop myself. Grabbing a torch, I wave it at the nearest group and clamber onto one of the tables. Yasmin doesn't try to stop me, only claps her hands in glee.

"Surely you've all seen someone swallow a sword," I say, twirling the torch at the growing crowd. Suddenly, it doesn't matter who I am and whether I belong here. No one, especially not these fools, can resist the lure of potential death or dismemberment. What is socializing but a small-scale performance anyway? "But have you ever seen someone swallow a torch?"

"Do it!" Yasmin pumps her fist, and several other guests join her. Emboldened by their enthusiasm, I tilt the fire toward my mouth. I've never swallowed fire before, but I'm not too worried. Fire eating is an illusion like everything else; put the torch in your mouth and there's no more oxygen to feed the flames. However, it doesn't feel like an illusion when the fire hits my tongue. I can actually smell my nose hairs sizzling. Eyes watering, tongue burning, I suffocate the flame, shoving the torch in until the fire is finally out. Cheers erupt and I snatch another drink, hissing as the concoction burns my injured tongue. Yasmin joins me on the table, lifting an arm in the air as I cough.

"You're insane!" she cries over the applause. She grabs me, wrapping an arm around me like a vice, as we jump off the table and wind our way through the party. The rest of the night, no one questions my right to be there.

Now, they recognize me as Yasmin's honored guest. Partygoers flock to introduce themselves, to praise my daring. I float on their approval, ignoring the searing pain whenever I speak, knowing deep down that I'll always pay the price for their acknowledgment, no matter how high it is.

After a while, Yasmin tires of the constant attention. She leads me to a private cabana, drawing the silk curtains tight around us, shutting out the noise of the party, and flops down on one of the chaises.

"Finally," she murmurs, reaching for a drink. I sit awkwardly on the seat next to her, trying not to lick my blistered lips. As silent as the desert night, Yasmin's lanky panther, Iko, slips in through one of the openings and nudges her hand. She caresses the big cat, who lets out a throaty rumble. I startle, then realize he's purring.

"Hiding at my own party." Yasmin chuckles wryly, rubbing the panther's ears. "I must be crazy."

"I totally understand," I respond automatically, even though I yearn to be back at the party, rubbing shoulders with the elite of Oasis's performers.

"No, you don't," Yasmin says, a faint smile on her lips. "You love the spotlight. You're one of those performers who never turns it off, aren't you?"

"No," I protest, even though she's right.

"I love performing," Yasmin says. "Being onstage is my life. But it's exhausting. Sometimes I just want to be me without the pressure to constantly dazzle and delight."

I can understand that, even if I don't relate.

"It's never enough for me," I admit quietly. "No matter how much they applaud, no matter how much they praise me, when the spotlight dims and I'm left alone on the stage after a show, all I want is more."

I've never admitted that out loud to anyone. I should be ashamed, but being in Yasmin's confidence, seeing her true self has made me bold.

"I wish I were more like that," she says simply, and the acceptance washes over me. "In our world, there are so many fakes. But you're genuine, and I like that."

I shift on the chaise, which is suddenly uncomfortable, too hard. If only Yasmin knew what a fraud I truly was, how much I had to lie and fake it to get here, we'd never be having this conversation.

"That's why I like animals," she goes on, tapping Iko's nose. The panther opens one golden eye and yawns. "They are never ashamed to be themselves, no matter how we perceive them."

I eye the big cat, curled at her feet as docile as a tabby. "Can I pet him?"

Yasmin's answering smile is wide. "He loves to be scratched behind the ears."

I allow the big cat to sniff my extended fingers before reaching to stroke his ears. The short fur behind his ears is velvety and his eyes close to slits. I let my hand roam down his thick, muscled neck, pondering Yasmin's words. All I've ever wanted is to be loved for who I am. But it wasn't until I started pretending to have magic that anyone paid any attention. Even Yasmin, who claims to love authenticity, wouldn't have given me the time of day if it weren't for my mediocre success at illusion. No one at this party cared who I was until I shoved a burning torch down my throat. My whole life has become an illusion, I realize. But at least they always applaud at the end.

The curtain whispers open, revealing a girl with a buzzcut and piercings that look like snake bites.

"Yasmin! We've been looking for you!"

Yasmin throws me a wan smile, a smile that only someone who knows her secret would understand. A friend. Turning back to the girl, the smile turns into something false and shiny.

"Coming!"

Then, in an undertone, she adds low enough that only Iko and I can hear, "The show must go on."

CHAPTER 13

I awaken the next day feeling as though I've swallowed a train. Blistered and swollen, my tongue sits like a fat snake in my mouth. Yasmin's words ring in my throbbing head: *The show must go on.*

My *show.* I groan as the realization that I'll be sticking a sword down my throat in just six short hours hits me.

No backing out though, not now.

Not when the queen herself could be in the audience. Mixing myself a chalky remedy my father used to take for heartburn, I pray it'll ease the burns in my mouth enough to perform. It's thick and sweet in my mouth and makes me gag, but it does take the edge off the pain enough that I can wiggle my tongue carefully.

"Ladies and Gentlemen!"

The words come out like I have a slug in my mouth, but it's understandable anyway. I take another sip of the frothy white liquid, wincing, when a knock on the door startles me.

Apprehensively, I open it, only for Rose to bustle in uninvited. Her wiry hair is especially frizzy today, as if statically charged by her energy.

"Tonight's your first show! I brought breakfast."

She sets a plate of watery eggs down on the bedside table and eyes me. "You look awful."

"Long night," I croak, and her gaze turns stern.

"You haven't been out partying, have you?"

"Networking." It's my best attempt at a joke, but Rose is anything but amused.

"You're still able to perform?"

"Of course." I'm insulted. I'd perform dead if my rotting bones would let me.

"Good. Had to fire our last headliner for partying too much. Well, gambling anyway," she amends. "Terrible habit."

That's odd to hear from someone who owns a casino. I give her my most professional smile, hoping my teeth aren't blackened from my fire eating. She grimaces but drops the subject.

"What do you need for your show tonight? Anything I can help with?"

She's like an over-eager stage mother.

"An extra ticket seller, maybe? For all the sales I'll rake in?" I deadpan. She swats at me, chortling gleefully, my late night transgressions all but forgotten.

"Dinner's on you!" she says, and finally, finally, she leaves. It's not that I don't appreciate the offer, but performing is something I'm used to doing on my own. Not only that, but most performers are very superstitious before a show, and I'm no exception.

I choke down the eggs, although they're bland and runny. No point in turning down free food, especially food I can tolerate with my scalded mouth. After a quick rinse with some cool water, I make my way down to the Saguaro stage. I never rehearse my show the day of, out of superstition, but I do go over the script and my blocking on stage. This usually takes a few hours and then I begin mixing powders. This part of my pre-show ritual really has nothing to do with my show and everything to do with my vanity. It's the one indulgence I allow myself. Pouring a handful of crushed diabantha seeds from a packet into my palm, I admire the rose-gold hue of the powder. Mixed with cactus water, the seeds make a hair dye that will last until my roots grow out.

There's nothing wrong with my natural hair color, of course. It's a mousey shade of blonde, right in between blonde and brunette. Dish-water blonde, my father called it. A perfectly respectable shade of hair for the daughter of the high judge. A girl I haven't been for a long time and refuse to ever be again. Although hair color on the Noose ranges anywhere from plain old brown to vibrant turquoise, this shade of rose gold is rare. Made from actual flecks of gold so fine they sparkle like tiny stars, one packet of powder cost me an entire month's salary at the Bird of Paradise. I went without dinner for two months to be able to afford the one I hold now. And I have just enough to cover my roots.

Only my elbow slips on the edge of the wet sink. I watch, in horror, as my precious powder goes down the drain. I tap desperately on the end of the little paper packet, hoping to knock loose just a little more. At five ounces of gold dust for one packet, I can't afford to run out, not to-day. Scraping the powder from the sides of the sink, fingernails turning pink, I scramble to save what's left of the precious mixture. Mixed with the sink water, the remnants of powder form a thick unusable paste that dyes my fingertips red. It's gone.

Breathing hard, I rinse the red goop from my fingers, aching at all that money literally down the drain. *Bad luck*, intones a voice in my head. *Or perhaps kismet*, I think ruefully. I'd purchased these seeds from Stefan, right before I'd tricked him into humiliating himself on stage for my benefit.

It's no big deal, I tell myself firmly, even though my hands shake. In-stead, I focus on relaxing, paying attention to the muscles of my throat.

I don't think about the fact that my throat is so swollen, I'm not sure I could swallow a biscuit, let alone a sword. I don't think about the fact that if I blow this, I'll lose my shot to be Jester. And I definitely don't think about the fact that the queen herself might be in the audience.

There's no way I can leave my hair as is, so I wrap it in a haircloth I used to use for my fortune-telling act. My costume is nothing special, the same old black leather pants and corset I always wear for shows. We all have our signature looks on the Noose; Luc favors snakeskin and red leather; Aria, the contortionist at the Palm, wears only sheer leotards. This is not the look I'd choose for myself if I had any real money, but it'll do for now.

I finish the look with a slash of black on my eyes, intended to look like a mask. There's no real point in concealing my identity, but it adds to the general mystique of the act. I check myself from every angle, and then curse when I catch sight of the clock on the bedside table. If I don't leave now, I'll be late for my first show at the Saguaro.

Ready or not, it's showtime.

I take the stage with my normal bravado, even though today my teeth are locked so tight, my jaw aches. Today, like all days, I have something to prove. But this time, I actually have a shot to do so. I'm hungry, I realize in that moment. Hungry from never having enough to eat, ravenous to prove myself.

I scan the audience, which is sparse enough to reveal that the queen is not in attendance.

Disappointment feels like a trapdoor opening underneath me. I swallow hard, burned mouth aching. I hadn't really expected she'd come, not to a first show, and certainly not without a seeker's recommendation. It's a huge letdown, to be sure, but not an unexpected one.

I'll just have to make sure this show is good enough that there's no way she would miss the next one.

"Can I have a volunteer, please? Someone with a hat, if they'd be so kind?"

I've gone without a plant today as a matter of pride. To show myself I'm good enough to be here without the cheap tricks that other magicians resort to. Several hands wave from the audience; I select a self-important man in a cowboy hat. The hat is nothing special, a common tourist purchase in Oasis, which is why I pick him. His boots clank as he takes the stage with me. He has a thick moustache and a leer.

"Well, aren't you a pretty thing?" he croons. The smile dies on his mustachioed lips when I draw the sword. It slides out soundlessly, thanks to the many layers of oil I coated it in before the show.

"Easy, love."

Both hands are up, as if I'm nothing more than a stubborn cow, rather than a girl with a steel blade. I lunge. It's greatly satisfying to watch his eyes bug as the sword slices neatly through his ridiculous hat, just brushing the thinning hair beneath. The two halves of the hat fall to the ground with a comical flop.

"You owe me a new hat!"

Mustache twisted in a scowl, my volunteer brandishes the remains of his hat at me. It's all I can do not to roll my eyes. With a flick of the sword, I swipe his belt and his trousers fall to the stage to uproarious laughter.

"You little—" he splutters, face red.

"Apologies," I say, winking. "If you'll give me your hat, I'm sure I can fix it up for you."

Clutching his pants, he staggers toward me and passes me the hat. The cut is clean, both halves even, but even I'm not skilled enough to actually fix it. Luckily, there are ten thousand other hats just like it.

"Rest both hands on the sword, if you please."

The volunteer does so, which causes his trousers to drop again, and I thank every star in the heavens I didn't go with a shill. You don't get comedy like this with a plant.

"One hand then," I say, biting my lip to keep from laughing. The volunteer does so, glowering all the while. While he's distracted, I toss the old hat offstage.

"Now, first, you must say the magic words—'Terrificus majesticus.'"

The words are part ancient Romo-latus, part gibberish. Most magic doesn't require an incantation to invoke, but it's a fun bit of theater. Not only that, but it distracts the audience from the switch, which is the most important thing.

"Terrificus majesticus," the man intones, face solemn, both eyes on the sword. With a flourish, I produce a brand new hat, an exact replica of the original. The man's eyes go wide, anger replaced with awe as he takes the replacement.

"Let's have a round of applause for our volunteer!"

His eyes never leave the hat, even as he stumbles offstage, one hand still holding onto his trousers for dear life. Now for the real magic.

"As you have all just witnessed, the sword I have here is very real, and very sharp."

The audience is fully invested now. I can feel it in the held breaths, the rapt expressions. And I've done nothing more than slice a man's hat in half and replace it with a new one when he wasn't looking. Sometimes it's depressing how easily fooled people are.

Sometimes, like now, it's the greatest feeling in the world.

"I have no more tricks up my sleeve, only a very sharp sword that I will now swallow whole. The only other magician to ever attempt this ruptured his own diaphragm and bled out onstage."

Gasps. Even a muffled shriek that sets my heart thrilling in my chest. I have them now. All I have to do is get through the rest of the act without severing my esophagus or vomiting all over the stage.

Throwing my head back, I do my best to relax. It's impossible. Adrenaline fires through my system, setting every nerve ablaze. I swallow once, concentrating on my breathing, but it's no use. Every muscle in my body is taut, tight as wire. I should have practiced in front of someone, I think distantly, but it's too late to second-guess myself. I'm going to swallow this sword even if I shred myself from the inside out.

I open my jaw so wide it cracks in protest. I picture my throat as a sheath, and the first inch goes down easily. There's a horrified choking noise from someone in the audience.

Centimeter by centimeter, the sword ekes past my gag reflex. My mouth is flooded with saliva and the urge to cough is like an itch. Blinking back tears, I will my throat to soften, to open up. Four inches are in now, and the tip of the sword is dangerously near my solar plexus. One wrong move and I'll tear it open.

My neck aches, but the sword is moving easily now, hours of practice coming back to me. It's now halfway down, ten inches deep. Vital organs cushion the blade, only a cough away from being eviscerated. Fifteen inches. I've never gone farther than this, fear of puncturing my own stomach keeping me from attempting anything deeper, but the last quarter of the sword still hangs out of my mouth.

I hesitate, the sword plunged down my throat. It's still an impressive trick, I think. No need to go all the way to the hilt, just to make a point. But isn't that why I'm here? To prove I'm just as good as the rest of the competitors? That I'll do anything to be Jester?

The last five inches are excruciating, but I manage to get it all the way in. I throw out my arms and the audience roars its approval. Pain blooms in my stomach but it's nothing compared to the deafening sounds of applause. Pulling the sword back out is like trying to breathe fire, the metal burning the entire way back up, but out it comes, covered in my own stomach acid and blood. Suppressing dry heaves, I hold the sword up and take a bow. They're standing now, wild at the sight of the sword.

My chest is going up in flames and the world is hazy, but it's worth it. I cling to the sounds of clapping as though approval alone can save me from bleeding internally.

Even if I die right here onstage, it's worth it, I think viciously. It's the last thing I think before I stagger backstage, to the sound of riotous applause.

⁓⁓⁓※⁓⁓⁓

Rose is there to greet me backstage, applauding, a single pink rose pinned to the lapel of her suit. She tucks it into my costume, but I barely notice. It feels like I've swallowed a bucket of nails. I cough several times, wincing as my stomach spasms in response.

"Well, you certainly didn't disappoint!" Rose says, with a clap to the back that almost causes me to black out. I choose that moment to collapse onto her.

"Holy cats! We need to get you to a healer!"

"No money," I choke out. With my face buried in her cheap suit, I can smell the chuck steak she ate for dinner and the whiskey she drank. Rose helps me to a chair, looking relieved once I'm off her.

"Well, we can expedite your first pay, if you need it—"

"I'm fine."

It's not a total lie. Seated, I feel the pain lessen to a dull throb. My father battled ulcers most of his life, and although I've never had one, I can imagine for a moment that this was what he felt. What's the difference really? He had a hole in his stomach from a lifetime of stress, I have one from the wrong end of a sword.

Rose watches me, her thick brows scrunched. "You should rest, kid. Let me get one of the bellhops to help you to your room."

I lean back into the seat, closing my eyes. Rose is right. I should see a healer, but I have neither time nor gold dust for that. *You can sleep for a month once you're Jester*, I tell myself. I've lied to myself so often, sometimes I forget not to believe.

"Do you think it was good enough for the queen?"

Rose leans in, a furtive look on her face. "Didn't want to spoil the surprise, but I suppose since you've asked . . ."

I sit up, ignoring the stabbing pain in my abdomen.

"One of the queen's maidservants was here for your show. Word is, the queen was quite taken by your little dinner theater the other night."

Warmth suffuses me, almost enough to make me forget the ripping pain inside. It's not what I'd hoped exactly, but if I impressed the maidservant, there's a chance, however small, that the queen will grace the Saguaro for my next performance. And maybe that will finally snag me a seeker.

I stand up slowly, holding the chair for support, and take a few experimental steps. Rose leaps to my side, arms out as though to shield herself from me falling on her again.

"Come on, kid," she pleads. "You did good, okay? Now go lie down for a bit, huh?"

The pain is a knife in my side with every step, but if I go slowly, it's tolerable. I straighten as best I can, sweat beading on my brow, and throw her what I hope is a smile. Rose winces in response.

"I can sleep when I'm dead. Tonight we celebrate."

CHAPTER
14

Rose insists I take the next day off, but I refuse. Now is not the time to cut shows, not right as I'm starting to get a following at the Saguaro. If I go to the Panther early enough, I can catch Luc's show before my own. I don't bother to disguise myself this time. Let him see me. Shaking out a measure of gold dust—the first money I've had to myself in years—I purchase a ticket from the Panther ticket seller. The letters are blood red, Luc's signature color, and embossed. I can feel the edges of his name as I run my fingers over the thick, black paper in my pocket. Taking a seat near the front, I settle into the plush chair. I can't remember the last time I sat in a theater, waiting to enjoy someone else's show. It feels all wrong. I yearn to be up onstage, rather than confined to the audience.

The chairs around me fill quickly. The Panther theater has a capacity of five hundred and historically has been filled to capacity only a few times. Luc doesn't sell out, not tonight, but the empty seats are almost nonexistent.

Not that it matters. I almost feel bad for him. No doubt news of my own spectacular first night has reached him. Poor fool must be scrambling to find something to match my act. What a shame it will be when he disappoints everyone in this vast audience.

The lights dim, the audience chatter dying to whispers. The curtains, thick, heavy velvet, slide open with a gentle murmur. Onstage, Luc sits tied to a chair, eyes closed. Thick chains bind his wrists, a cloth gag binds his wicked tongue. An escape act. I stifle a yawn, annoyed to have wasted so much gold on this.

A rustling from the opposite end of the stage catches my attention. An assistant fiddles with the lock on an enormous steel cage. Air holes dot the top of the cage, which is so high it almost brushes the stage lights, but whatever waits inside is concealed by the thick metal of the cage. It takes a while; the assistant's hands are trembling so badly, he can hardly get the key inside the lock. As usual, Luc's team is melodramatic beyond belief. It's a cheap way to heighten tension, but Luc needs all the help he can get.

The lock slides open with a click that rings out like a shot in the hush of the theater. With a squeak, the assistant darts to the safety of backstage. I roll my eyes. The door of the cage swings open slowly. Only a few feet away, Luc's eyes fly open. Sweat collects on his brow, beading and rolling down one temple. Grudgingly, I'm about to admit that although a mediocre magician, Luc is at least a phenomenal actor, when the first enormous hairy leg extends from the cage.

As though feeling for inconsistencies in the stage surface, the jointed leg probes before settling so softly it's hardly more than a tap on the stage. The rest of the beast emerges in stages: another leg, then another, then another, a mess of legs and eyes, clicking mandibles and fur. A gargantuan elephant spider. I hardly register the pain from gripping my armrests too tight, although my knuckles scream in protest. Luc pants, straining against his bindings. It's all for show, I remind myself, sucking in deep breaths that do nothing to calm the rapid staccato of my heart. Likely, there's an assistant with a tranquilizer offstage, waiting for Luc's signal. A slip in his bindings, tied just a little bit loose on purpose. But even though the spider is now right next to Luc, so close you can see Luc's terrified reflection in its many glittering eyes, no assistant comes to his aid. Although he thrashes, the bindings hold, the gag muffles his screams. Venom—heavy, clinging drops of the stuff—wells up on the surface of the spider's fangs, which jut like giant fishhooks from both shifting mandibles.

No tricks, I think, and before I can so much as register the thought, the spider attacks, those long fangs sinking into Luc's flesh. A startled scream escapes my own lips, as Luc goes limp in the chair. Like a dagger from its hilt, the fangs slide out again, leaving behind two vast puncture marks, bloody and oozing.

With neat motions, the spider wraps Luc in thick ropes of silk. *Where are the assistants?* I think numbly. There is no way even Luc can get out of this one. I remember his confession backstage, the catch in his breath as he admitted he was afraid of dying.

Satisfied with its prize, the spider leaves Luc immobile behind it. It takes in the rows of fat flesh filling the seats of the theater as if noticing this for the first time. It's then I realize there is nothing separating us from the spider. In a matter of seconds, the giant spider could devour half the audience. I'm not the only one with this realization; audience members stumble up the aisles, shoving and clawing their way out of the theater, too frightened to even scream.

But despite the danger, I can't bring myself to leave. Luc's prone, wrapped figure still slumps behind the giant arachnid, motionless. The poison has been working its way through his system for several minutes now, in an amount that would've killed a normal human in less than a minute. His words float through my numb mind, haunting: *If I let my heart go too long in between beats . . .*

And although it's obvious he's dead, obvious no trick in the world can save him now, I have to see how it ends.

The spider scuttles to the edge of the stage, long legs testing the walls, before scurrying up into the rafters. Widespread panic breaks out as more audience members flee. The spider wraps itself around the heavy swinging chandelier, which groans under the weight of the beast. Tiny cracks in the ceiling spread from the chandelier like spider webs. But it's not the spider that has my attention any longer; onstage, the white bundle housing Luc's body twitches. It's a subtle movement, hardly anything at all, and I squint, certain I'm imagining things.

Until it happens again. Another jerk, more obvious this time. Then another. The bundle rocks, as though it's an egg about to hatch. It trembles and rocks and falls still again.

And then, with a ripping sound that tears through the theater, Luc's arm emerges from the cocoon bearing a dagger. I can't breathe. Slashing and hacking, the rest of the silk falls away in strands as he struggles to free himself.

A cracking sound drags my attention away from Luc back to the ceiling, where the chandelier suddenly drops several feet, the wiring ripping under the weight of the spider. Bits of ceiling plaster hit the ground in explosive bursts. The chandelier swings, hanging by only a few fraying pieces of wiring. The lights of the chandelier flicker, then abruptly go out, the theater lit only by the glow of the stage lights.

"Come and get me."

Onstage Luc stands, dagger pointed at the spider, thick strands of sticky spider silk still clinging to his arms and back. His face is pale, his dagger hand shaking, but the torn holes in his shirt reveal smooth skin beneath, no sign of the puncture marks that ravaged his stomach only a few minutes before. The dagger Luc wields looks tiny in comparison to the great hulking creature. The spider tenses at his voice, which rings out over the hysterics of the audience. The shift in its weight sets the chandelier swinging again. With a snap, the wiring finally gives, the chandelier hurtling to the theater below with the spider on top. I'm already out of my seat, tripping up the aisles, even though I know I'll never get away in time. With a crash that jolts the entire theater, the chandelier hits the seats below, glass and crystal exploding on impact. Bits of glass spray the audience. I can feel a trickle of something warm on my cheek, a shard embedded there, but otherwise I am fine. The spider is thrown off, hitting the wall with a hiss. Before I even have time to hope that it's dead, it rolls to its feet, sharp mandibles bared. I duck under a seat, knowing all I can hope for now is that it doesn't see me.

"Now look what you've done."

Luc's voice is almost bored, although the dagger never wavers. The spider clicks in response, chairs cracking and splintering under its many legs as it advances to where Luc waits onstage.

Only he doesn't wait. With a leap, Luc spans the distance between them, landing squarely on the spider's swiveling head. It bucks, almost throwing Luc, who manages to grab onto the spiny hairs that cover it.

Grimly, Luc drives the dagger into one of the thousands of eyes dotting its head. Ichor splatters him as the spider thrashes, but it does little to stop the beast, infuriating it instead. Wild, the spider rams its body into the walls, sending more plaster crashing to the floor. Luc slips, hands scrabbling for purchase as he falls under the spider's rampaging legs.

I shut my eyes, afraid to see him crushed under all those legs like a bug. There's a shout, and then a wet, tearing sound. Saliva floods my mouth, and I'm certain I'm going to be sick, until a thud shakes the theater.

I open my eyes cautiously. The spider lies prone, a viscous yellow fluid oozing from a six-foot-long gash down its abdomen. And standing beside the felled beast, covered in spider ichor and silk, eyes wild but triumphant, is Luc. Alive.

He eyes the damage carelessly—the ruined theater chairs, stuffing bursting from yawning holes, the shattered chandelier, the shards of glass littering the aisles, the yellow blood coating the walls, the few remaining audience members staring up at him with bloodless faces—and sighs.

"I suppose I'll have to pay for all this."

A lone figure emerges from underneath a chair, a man covered in plaster dust and spattered with spider gore, hands hitting each other almost solemnly. The sound of clapping startles Luc, who stares at the man, uncomprehending. Across the room, a woman rises from the debris, applauding with the first man, albeit somewhat shakily. More and more audience members join in the applause, until the sound rings through the ruined theater, until it's deafening, until all I can hear is applause. I swallow plaster dust and bitterness so great it threatens to consume me. Even though only a handful of his audience remains, even though he's destroyed one of the grandest theaters on the Noose and almost killed his own audience, it's undeniably the best show I have ever seen. Perhaps even the best show of all time.

My hands clench, refusing to applaud, refusing to acknowledge what Luc has always known—that I'll always be second-best.

CHAPTER
15

I'm early for my next lesson with Cillian. I've read every single book he's given me, and if he won't teach me how to use magic, I'll teach myself.

I rap on the door impatiently, scraping my knuckles on the rough wood. I think of Luc stabbing the giant spider and my knocking becomes desperate.

The door opens with a jerk. Cillian's scowling face peers out.

"You're early."

I shove past him. "Ambition is always punctual."

Cillian makes a face. "That's the worst made-up platitude I've ever heard."

I ignore him, sitting without invitation in the rose chair. I arrange the books neatly in my lap, flipping open the notebook I've written my questions in.

"In chapter thirteen of *Possessing the Magic*, it says you must center your mind on the magic. What does that mean? Is it like meditation?"

Surprised into compliance, Cillian takes the seat across from me, setting down a still-steaming teacup.

"You read all of these in three days?"

"Of course, that was the homework, wasn't it? Also, on page forty-seven of *The Anatomy of Magic*, it says something about blood flow that I didn't quite understand—"

Cillian removes his spectacles, emerald eyes serious. "Why do you want magic so badly? I saw your show. What you're doing *is* magic."

I snort. "Swallowing knives is not magic. It's stupidity combined with ambition."

Cillian considers this, swirling his teacup. "I highly doubt those pompous fools at the Crown can tell the difference."

"It doesn't matter." My own voice, sharp as fangs, surprises me. "I know. Every show I work ten times harder than everyone else, only to have a show that's ten times less impressive."

"Learning to work harder is not a bad thing," Cillian puts in mildly. "More often than not, it's not talent that grows success—it's work."

Sure. And wishes are borne on dandelion seeds. I blow out a huff of air. "What do you know, anyway? Your idea of magic is a fine cup of tea and a thick book."

"Underrated magic, to be sure." His thick eyebrows dance. George twines around my ankles, mewling, until I oblige him with a pet. His spine arches under my fingers, soft fur coating my trousers in a fine gray layer.

"Perhaps you should stick to lavender buds," I respond, as scathingly as I can manage. Cillian sets his tea down, unbothered by the attempted insult.

"I'd prefer to. Unfortunately, I'm being blackmailed by an annoying, overly-ambitious street performer." He smiles, teeth glinting.

I scowl. "Let's just get back to the lesson already, shall we?"

"As you wish."

I push Cillian as hard as he'll tolerate the rest of the lesson, but it's not enough. There's no way I'll be ready to pass the Apprentice's Exam anytime soon. There's still too much I don't understand. Still too much to learn. Drowning in desperation, I take as many books as Cillian will allow, knowing even as I stagger back under the weight of all that knowledge, it's still not enough.

The three properties of magick include inheritance, blood type, and . . .

The words blur in front of my exhausted eyes. I rub at them furiously, willing them to clear. Just one more book, and then I can sleep . . .

A knock on the door wakes me from a half doze. I don't know anyone who would visit at this hour, except for Rose. Reluctantly, I steel myself for the dull conversation that awaits, but it's Yasmin in the dim hallway, out of place in a gorgeous feathered gown with a train so long it drags on the dingy Saguaro carpets.

"Sorry it's so late," she says, flat. "Can I come in?"

I'm too surprised to say no. She's missing her trademark purple hair today, forgoing the gaudy wig for her natural hair, which is wild, dark, and curly. Perched on the edge of my bed, the feathers from her dress spilling onto the ground while she picks forlornly at a loose thread on the coverlet, she looks like a depressed tropical bird.

"He killed my spider."

For a moment I don't have the slightest clue what she's talking about, can't fathom the lone tear that rolls down one round cheek. Then I recall Luc's show, the monster arachnid he slew. Without meaning to, I blanch.

"That was *yours*? I mean, I'm so sorry."

Yasmin doesn't seem to hear the disgust in my tone, she just keeps picking at the bedspread.

"She was going to lay eggs in a week," she muses, as I struggle to keep the horror off my face at the thought of thousands of cat-sized spider babies terrorizing the Noose. I'd never say it out loud, but I'm grateful Luc stabbed that horrible spider when he had the chance.

"How awful," I manage to say weakly. Yasmin gives me a watery smile. With her eyeliner smudged down her cheeks and quivering mouth, she looks nothing like the girl who sticks her head in the jaws of tigers. I drop onto the bed next to her and pat her hand. I may not understand her specific pain, but I do understand what it's like to have Luc ruin everything.

"Thank you," she says, exhaling loudly and swiping at the black trails running down her face. "Devils, this is embarrassing. Sorry."

Wordlessly, I hand her a tissue to blot the makeup. She takes it gratefully, rubbing until her eyes are bare, swollen, and red from crying. That's twice now she's let me see her without the mask. The fact warms me, even through my exhaustion, and the ache I feel for her.

"You have to beat him. Luc."

As if she could possibly be referring to anyone else.

I clench the bedspread, recalling his last show. "I don't know if I can."

Yasmin shakes her head as though I'm daft, the last of her tears drying.

"You're spades more talented than he is and far more original too. Luc is lazy, he doesn't have to try. But you . . ."

Her confidence is contagious. And it doesn't hurt that I'm starved for praise.

"I'll beat him," I vow, catching her fervor like a plague. "I'll make him pay."

Her brown eyes shine as a sinking feeling threatens to envelop me. It's one thing to try to beat Luc on my own, but another to get Yasmin's hopes up like this. What if I can't deliver on my promise?

⌒⌒⌒✳⌒⌒⌒

I'm late to my next show. Not that it matters anyway. I swallow the sword, not even bothering to get it down all the way. The audience doesn't care, they go wild just the same. Only this time, the applause means nothing. I bow, unseeing, hands slapping and unslapping before me like a wave. How could I have ever expected a Saguaro audience to get me to the Crown?

I pull out all the stops in my next rehearsal—a stage assistant locks me in a coffin, saws the box in twain, and I emerge, whole and unscathed. There's even a bladder of pig's blood that spurts everywhere dramatically at the first cut. It's my best trick, and judging by Rose's enthusiastic clapping, it's effective.

Just not effective enough.

Escaping from a fake wooden coffin feels as dull as the edge of my sword after watching Luc escape true death. Without magic, my acts are as fake as I am. I pace the stage, ignoring the wooziness that washes over me like a wave. Ever since the sword swallow, I've had little appetite and I'm paying for it in alternating nausea and dizziness so great it threatens to overwhelm me. At night I scour the books I've borrowed from Cillian, trying to absorb everything in as short a time as possible. My eyes are gritty; I'm exhausted, sick, and no matter how hard I push myself, it's never enough.

"If that doesn't blow the queen's skirts up, I'll eat a scorpion."

Rose has joined me onstage, beaming. I've more than doubled her ticket sales over a single weekend, and she's happier than a pig in mud. I'm glad, but I know it's nowhere near the crowd Luc draws in every night. And there's still been no sign of the queen at any of my shows, in spite of my growing popularity.

"It's not good enough," I mutter, kicking the coffin. It's a fitting prop, since my entire career is dead if I can't get the queen to the Saguaro.

Rose sips her coffee, oblivious, the acrid smell making my nose crinkle. "What are you on about?"

"I need a better trick," I repeat. As though trying to infuriate me, Rose just continues giving me the same baffled look.

"It's a great trick," she insists. "I loved the blood."

"It's fine, it's good," I say, wishing my head would stop pounding. "It's also completely mediocre and cliché."

Rose waves me away. "Bah. You're too hard on yourself. All the good shows are cliché."

"*Not my show.*"

The words rip out of me. I'm dangerously close to passing out, chest heaving. The world spins, and Rose's face, dismayed, spins with it.

"Good isn't good enough, do you hear me? I need something fit for a queen."

And then because I can't stand to faint on her again, can't stand to see her not understand what Jester means to me, I leave her onstage alone, squinting after me.

I can't focus on Cillian's lesson. I keep replaying Luc's show in my head, over and over. How does he do it? I wonder. How does he manage to beat me every time, without even trying? Not that it really matters if I pay attention, because today's lesson involves scrubbing out teacups.

My mind wanders as I work at a particularly stubborn stain. When it's good enough, I set the teacup on the counter, where Cillian lazily inspects it.

"You've missed a spot," he says, dropping it back in the soapy sink.

"How exactly is this supposed to help me learn magic?" I snap, slapping the sopping dishrag into the sink. Cillian's expression becomes furtive, evasive.

"The proper execution of magic involves minute hand-eye coordination, and if you don't have that—"

It dawns on me then, like a wave of dirty dishwater. "You never planned to give me your magic, did you?"

Cillian's emerald eyes are dark, unreadable, but it's all the answer I need.

I groan, and collapse onto the counter. "I *trusted* you."

"Whose fault is that?" Cillian says, but he has the decency to look at least slightly ashamed.

"You were going to make me do your housework for the next ten years!" I fling the wet dishrag at him, and he flinches away. "What about our deal? You swore an oath to me that your magic would be mine."

"And I never broke that oath," Cillian says, scowling, as he peels the dishrag from his now-soiled shirt. "I fully intend to pass my magic on to you one day."

"What, when you're dead?" I ask, breathing heavily.

He shrugs, and my fury mounts. It's too much.

"You'll give it to me now, then," I say.

Cillian's eyes darken. "Excuse me?"

"You've broken your end of the agreement, forfeiting our oath, which means I am entitled to collect on the debt."

"Terribly sorry," Cillian says, not looking sorry at all, as he toes George away from the bookshelf he's sharpening his claws on. "But I never agreed to give it to you on your timeframe."

"I'll report you to the authorities."

Shoving me aside, Cillian slams the door shut and locks it.

"I've done nothing but honor our agreement," he says, voice even despite the sparks of outrage burning in his eyes.

"You lied to me!" I cry, furious at the way my voice breaks, at the fact that I'm actually surprised.

"You blackmailed me," Cillian returns, voice cool.

We face each other, chests heaving.

"If you won't give it to me, I'll take it," I say, even though it's useless to threaten. If there were a way to take magic, I'd have taken my father's a long time ago.

At this, Cillian scoffs. "As if you'd know the proper spell to use. And not only that, but stolen magic corrupts your soul. So I suggest you wait—"

"You mean, it's possible?"

Cillian stops, looking as if he'd like to bite his own tongue off.

"No," he answers, but it's too late. "And if you try to take mine, I'll roast you alive, murder charges be damned."

Flames burst from his hands, barely contained.

"I'm not going to take yours," I assure him quickly, and it's the truth. I don't stand a chance against Cillian's fire magic, armed or no. Cillian doesn't relax, shoulders practically to his ears.

"How do I know you're not lying and won't report me as soon as you leave here?" he returns, twin flames still crackling merrily in both palms.

"Because I still need you." It's as honest an answer as I know how to give. "But you're going to give me that spell. The one for stealing magic."

Another idea has taken root, something dark and blighted. I can't steal Cillian's magic. That much is obvious. But perhaps there is magic I can claim. Magic that should have been mine all along.

"Not a chance." Cillian shakes out the flames in his hands, which extinguish in a puff of gray smoke. I cough, eyes watering, and pop open one of his tiny windows, fanning the rest of the smoke out.

"Please," I say, even though I already know it's useless. Cillian doesn't even spare me another look as he rinses the sooty smudges from his hands in the kitchen sink.

"Get out of my house."

"What about our lesson?"

Cillian wrings the towel as though he wishes it were my neck. "I need a cup of something strong."

As he digs around in his cupboards, I discreetly edge toward the bookshelves. There are so many books, I'm not even sure where to begin. Cillian mutters to himself about lavender as I scan the spines lining the shelves. How do you find something when you don't even know what you're looking for?

As silently as I can, I slide anything that looks even remotely helpful into my bag while Cillian sets the tea on to boil, still grumbling. Even laden with only a few books, my bag is nearly impossible to pick up. I leave before the kettle can shriek, before he notices the gaps on his shelves.

CHAPTER
16

"If you do not fail in your duty, one day this and everything I have will be yours. My magic, greatest of my gifts, will pass on to you." The high judge extends a hand to his son. His son accepts the heavy signet ring the high judge drops into his palm, admiring the gleam of the garnet stone inside, a red so deep it's almost black.

"Today you will pass judgment for me, as one of the final steps of your apprenticeship. It is a great honor to serve the king, and we must always live worthy of that position."

His son nods solemnly. The ring rests like lead in his palm, as if weighted with the responsibility of his future position. He has worked tirelessly under his father, sacrificing sleep, friendships, and even a beloved girl for this. Truth, his father's voice, always in the back of his mind, echoes. It is he who will be the deliverer of justice after his father's magic is finally passed on to him, and he wants nothing more than to rise to the privilege.

His robes, brand new, fit him well.

It almost feels as if he's donning the role of High Judge as easily as a costume. Although he's observed his father for months now in court as his apprentice, this will be the first time he'll pass judgment in his father's place. In the name of the king himself. But the boy is not nervous. How can he be, when he has worked so hard, prepared until his brain has room for little else?

He is ready.

CHAPTER
17

Whatever Cillian may believe about the magic of books, these ones are useless. Three tomes of self-important jabbering, as dry as the dust that coats their spines. The last one was a mistake, an illustrated book of fairy tales. Head pounding, I rub the ache from my eyes and flip idly through it, even though I know it's pointless.

The illustrations are gruesome; a maiden skewered for speaking idolatrous words to a god, the remains of two children devoured by crows. I wince; apparently its only purpose was to terrify its readers into good behavior.

I stop on the next page, an illustration of a coiled snake wrapped around a beautiful young woman. Her head lolls as the snake squeezes the life from her lungs. The serpent's golden eyes remind me of Luc. I remember this story, I realize; it is the tale of Elotia. It was said that after her husband left her for a kitchen maid and gave his magic to his bastard instead of their daughter, she sought to kill him. Without magic herself, in desperation she tried to convince the Snake King, one of the lesser gods, to kill her husband in exchange for her hand in marriage. Instead the Snake King ate her. I don't know what happened to the husband; likely he and his mistress lived happily ever after, never even knowing what became of his vengeful wife.

The story only stood out to me as a child because I too was a magic-less girl. Now, I relate for a different reason; her hunger is my hunger. Her desperation, my desperation. Both of us willing to do anything for what we cannot have.

There is only one option left for me. My stomach churns at the thought of what I must do. Surely there is another solution, something I'm missing? No doubt I'll be damned in all nine hells for stealing magic, but I know what I've always known. That I'll pay any price.

I close the book with a snap. Maybe there is no way to steal magic. Or maybe it's been right under my nose the entire time.

I know even before I enter the cemetery, I'm making a mistake. The rusted iron gate is still warm in my hand, even though the sun set an hour ago. I clutch a bouquet of wilting flowers, their scent cloying, and a shovel. A great horned owl, perched on the fence, watches, its head swiveling. I'm not here to mourn though. I'm here to take back what is mine.

There are no lights, and I almost trip over a headstone. I scowl at the crumbling rock memorializing someone so long gone that even the stone has forgotten their name. Headstones litter the space without rhyme or reason. It's clear no one has bothered to maintain the graves. Weeds spring up between the dusty stones.

What memorials there are, are small, faded, and impersonal.

Here lies Cade, murderer and thief. Locke, fornicator. Delgado, traitor and pirate.

Normally, the deceased are given a formal funeral by fire, their bodies turned to ash, free like their spirit. The only exceptions are the criminals. Those unworthy of freedom, doomed to imprisonment in the earth for eternity. Criminals, like my father.

This is the first time I've visited his grave. I'm not even sure if it's here. I pick my way through the stones, looking for his name. He's only been gone a few years, although it feels like a lifetime. For all I know, they might have just dumped his body out with the royal sewage. And if that's the case, I'm out of options.

I notice a lone heap of earth toward the back and make my way to the grave, marked only with a hastily-placed chunk of rotting driftwood. A widow spider spins in one corner of the wood, oblivious to the trapped soul beneath. I know what the name is, even before I get close enough to make out the scratchings knifed into the wood. A name that as soon as the wood rots will be lost to time forever.

Roland Schopfer. Kingkiller. May his soul find no mercy in the Beyond.

I shiver at the inscription, hardly noticing when the flowers slide from my grasp. My breaths come in shallow gasps. I can't do this. Throwing the remaining stems at the grave, I turn to leave.

The graves surround me, only now instead of the names of strangers, my mind sees names I know. Edward, pale hand reaching from the executioner's block. My mother, straining in childbirth, the last of her strength bleeding out on the carpet below her. Myself, gasping my final breath alone and insignificant, just like my father. I drop to my knees on the soft earth, gasping. My father was a sniveling coward who hid in the shadows. Who wasted his magic. I will never be like my father.

I refuse.

Pulling myself up, I return to his grave, no longer afraid. Not when I slam the spade into the ground, loosening the packed earth, pulling up shovelful after shovelful. Not when the spade hits soft, rotting wood. Not even when I uncover the shoddy coffin that holds my father's remains.

The coffin is nailed shut, and it takes some work to jiggle the rusting nails out. I lean back, breathing hard, wiping sweat with the back of one filthy and shaking hand. No amount of preparation can steel me for what comes next. Using both hands, I drag the lid off of the coffin. It hits the ground in a puff of red dust.

The sight hits me before the horror does. My father stares up at me, unseeing. Beetles scurry over his face, running in and out of his slack mouth. Wriggling masses of worms thrash where his eyes once were. No flesh remains, his bones are as dry as the desert around us. Even without eyes, his blind stare is as judgmental as I remember, eternally accusing. I empty my stomach into the earth until there's nothing left, and dry heaves wrack my body.

Scooting backward on my hands and knees, I scuttle away from the coffin, pulling in deep breaths. *Focus*, I scold myself, wiping my mouth with a shaking hand.

I don't want to go back, but I do, looking anywhere but at his face. Opening my pack, I pull out one of the textbooks Cillian gave me and turn to the page with the spell for passing magic on to an heir. According to *Possessing the Magic*, I need something of his to contain the magic once I've released it from him. Stolen it. A glint of black catches my eye, glittering on one of the bony hands folded across my father's cavernous chest.

The ring of the high judge.

Careful not to touch anything else, I grasp the heavy gold ring, tugging it up. It catches on his knuckle, refusing to budge. I swallow down the nausea, pulling still harder. There's a snap as the entire finger bone disconnects, and I promptly drop it in horror. I spend a good minute digging around the bottom of the coffin, grimacing as a beetle, fat from the flesh of my father, scurries over my hand. Shaking out the decaying digit, I wipe down the ring until it gleams. Setting it down next to me, I pull out another worn book of Cillian's, flipping to the page with the spell for choosing an heir. Normally, the spell would be read by the possessor of the magic, but in certain cases, the heir can read the spell.

There's a very good chance it won't work. For starters, the magic must be given willingly. What I'm doing here is nothing short of grave robbery. If my father still lived, he would simply deny me the magic. However, with the final breath expelled from his lungs forever, there's no one to stop me from taking it. Even that may not be enough, but it's my last and only shot. I've creased the corner to mark the page, and a hysterical laugh shudders through me as I realize Cillian would likely be more disturbed about that single folded corner than the unspeakable act I'm about to commit.

The first words of the spell I speak are weak, little more than a whisper. I shake myself, mentally.

Who am I afraid of disturbing?

I read the next stanza louder, the unfamiliar words harsh on my tongue. There's a taste to the words, bitter and acidic, and I spit each one out, eager to be rid of it. I'm halfway through the spell when I realize my father is glowing, a sickly greenish cast that frightens me so much, I stop mid-line and have to repeat it from the beginning.

At the final line, I pull out the ring, which is the color of rotted blood. The words pour out of me now, a forceful roar that feels like vomiting. The ring burns in my hand, so hot I struggle to hold on to it. With everything I have left, I shove the ring to where his heart once was, ignoring the way his crumbling chest caves in at my touch.

Blood of my blood. Bone of my bone. To dust I return, to blood let my magic return.

The magic resists my touch at first, sluggish in my father's bones. I will it to me, letting the fire of my own blood warm it, coax it. The first trickles of magic tingle, slow at first, and I realize I am starved for it. I need it more than air. With a scream that shakes the dust from my father's headstone, I strangle the magic, dragging it into myself, my thirst for it unquenchable. My veins burn, alive with magic. I can actually feel it coursing through my heart, pumping through every part of my body, and it feels wonderful.

It feels terrible.

The last of my father's magic finally mine, I collapse onto the coffin, chest heaving. The newly awakened magic is ravenous, eager to be used. It bursts out of me and I marvel at the rush of pure power flowing from me. Finally, I'll be able to see what my father's ability was.

Wind picks up the dirt and leaves, scattering them until they take the form of a man. It's hazy at first, so vague that I have to squint. Details paint themselves onto the man: thin gray curls, a dour downturned mouth, a forehead weighted by wrinkles. As disappointed in death as he was in life.

"Father."

The word gasps out of me. What is this apparition? Have I been cursed for stealing my father's magic?

The ghost takes no notice of me. Its black eyes stare far past me, at something I cannot see.

"Son?"

The voice is whispery, longing, infinite, but it is undoubtedly my father's voice.

"My son . . ." His voice breaks, and to my horror, great silvery tears roll down his cheeks.

"Father?"

My own voice is tremulous in response. My father's head jerks toward me.

"You must undo these wrongs," he intones, piercing me with those empty black eyes. I cower under his stare.

"I can't—I don't know how! Just take it back," I plead, holding out my hands.

"Justice must be delivered to the traitor."

His black eyes swallow me whole.

Wind gusts through the cemetery, dissolving the outline of my father until he's blurry again, indistinct, a part of the air.

"My son . . ."

The wind eats his last words, swirling them into the flat and starless night. I'm alone once more, left staring up at the sky, my father's words still ringing in my head. *Traitor.*

What have I done? I try to twist the ring off my finger, but it feels as though it's fused to my flesh. The metal is cold, burning, and blackness has seeped into the surrounding skin like a sickness.

What in the name of all that is unholy have I done?

I burst into Cillian's shop, surprising him while he files. Papers flutter like snow all over the tidy shop.

"I thought I got rid of you, for devils' sakes—" Cillian begins, exasperated, but I cut him off.

"What happens if you steal magic?"

Cillian blinks at me. "Beg your pardon?"

The ring burns on my finger, and I'm impatient. "What happens when you steal magic?"

Instead of answering, Cillian just gapes at me. Of course, the one time I need him to give me a quick answer, he's useless.

"You told me that stealing magic is possible," I say, pacing the tiny room. "But you didn't tell me what would happen if someone actually did it."

Cillian's eyes narrow. "What did you do?"

"That doesn't concern you—"

"Like nine hells it doesn't," he says, grabbing my wrist. "Whose magic have you stolen?"

My voice is a whisper. "My father's."

"Does he know?"

The memory of my father, rotted and cold, shudders through me. "He's dead."

Cillian's head jerks up. I hold out my hand to him. The black has spread. It covers almost my entire ring finger. Cillian stares at it, then at me, in disbelief.

"You mean to tell me," he says, voice low, "that you dug up your deceased father and stole his magic?"

I nod, helplessly. Cillian lets out a stream of cursing.

"And that's not even the worst part," I say, tugging futilely at the ring. "I saw him. My father. His ghost, anyway. I think I've been cursed."

I drop into the rose chair as Cillian attempts to process everything I've told him.

"You saw your father's ghost?" Cillian shakes his head, pacing the room. "I don't know much about stolen magic, and I've never heard of anything like that . . . But then, I've never heard of anyone stealing magic from their *dead father* either—"

He chokes on the last part of the sentence and struggles to compose himself. "I mean, you can't have been the first. Surely, there must have been grave robbers in the past, but I'll have to research it, of course . . ."

Cillian's fingers scan the bookshelves, nimbly picking out what I desperately hope are relevant books. Once he has a towering pile, he drops several on the little table next to me and settles in his own chair with the remainder.

"Start reading."

He doesn't have to tell me twice.

I flip through all the books he gives me, and when I exhaust those, I search through the shelves on my own, grabbing anything that seems even slightly helpful. *Beyond the Grave: Ghost Sightings of the Middle Century. Curses and Hexes for Beginners.* I even spend close to a quarter of an hour scanning a fictional tale of a cursed maiden who threw herself into the sea. I slam the last book shut, groaning. The only thing I have to show for my efforts are strained eyes and a neck ache.

"Hold on, this might be something—" Cillian's eyes rapidly scan the page he's on. "There's an account here of a man who stole his neighbor's magic. There was a court trial . . . one of the witnesses, the man's wife, said using the magic made him sick . . . but it doesn't say anything else."

Cillian closes the book with a sigh, stretching his neck. "Not much help. Have you used the magic yet?"

I close my eyes, remembering the rush of magic that threatened to consume me in the cemetery.

"I started to . . . but then the ghost appeared."

Cillian gives me a strange look. "Hang on—you tried using your magic, and that's when the spirit appeared?"

I'm not sure where he's going, but I don't think I like it. "Well, yes. Of course, I have no idea if I was even doing it right or not—"

His green eyes blaze. "Use your magic."

"What? Now?"

"Now." I shiver at the ferocity in his eyes. Reaching for the magic, I feel it lurking, malign and festering, in the darkest parts of me. Although the feeling is like wet seaweed wrapped around my ankles, I force the magic to obey me. Papers, forgotten in all the excitement, toss in an unnatural breeze. They dart and rush around the room, spinning and fusing into something human—

Cillian lets out a cry, backing into a bookshelf so hard, he knocks several books off.

In front of us, a young woman glimmers, head bowed.

"Who are you?"

The words scrape out of her, as if her throat is raw. Neither Cillian nor I can find the words to answer her. He's pushed up against a bookshelf, chest heaving, a fireball glowing in each hand. The woman's black eyes jerk toward me. Sweat prickles on my forehead, and it feels as if I'm being sucked into a whirlpool.

"You summoned me. What do you want?"

Every word that falls from her lips is the sound of something dead being dragged. I swallow down the oily nausea that threatens to choke me.

"What are you?" I finally manage.

The answer whooshes out of her in a sigh. "My name was Hannah. I am no one to anyone anymore."

Cillian's eyes bulge like a frightened stallion's. They dart from the ghost to me and back again.

"What do you want?" the ghost girl repeats. The hem of her dress, frayed and dirty, floats in an invisible breeze. Black stains cover the bodice.

I want her to leave. I twist the ring, trying in vain to pull it up over my knuckle. "I don't want anything."

The ghost girl stares at me, and chills ripple up my spine. What kind of curse is this? She doesn't seem malevolent, at least.

Finally, the girl that was Hannah nods her head.

"Very well."

The wind dissolves her into dust and a thousand fluttering pages. My legs give out and I slide to the floor, shaking all over.

"What in the blue demons was that?" Cillian gasps. His face looks as though all the blood has been leached out of him. A sickly sheen of sweat covers his forehead.

"The curse."

Cillian gives me a sharp look, wiping at his mouth with a hand that shakes so badly, it's a wonder he doesn't hurt himself. "That was no curse. That was stolen magic."

"What are you talking about?" I demand. Cillian doesn't answer me, just keeps staring at the spot where the dead girl was.

"Cillian."

He jumps at the sound of his name. I sigh and push him to his chair. Once he's settled, I put the kettle on to boil. His kitchen is small, and I find the cups and a canister of loose tea easily. I don't make tea often, so I err on the side of strong, and add a spoonful of honey to each. When I hand him the warm cup, his fingers wrap around it automatically, bringing it to his lips. He takes a long sip and then gags, spitting the contents back out.

"What is this?" he asks, shaking the cup at me.

"Tea." I take a sip of my own to demonstrate, and while it's definitely potent, it's not undrinkable, by any stretch.

"No, no, no." Cillian snatches the cup from me mid-sip, and dumps both into the sink, in spite of my protests.

"That took me a solid ten minutes to make!"

"I don't care if it took you a year," Cillian returns, rinsing out the cups. "That was utterly offensive."

Grumbling, I let him have this one. It's his money he just dumped down the drain, not mine. And anyway, at least he's acting more like himself.

"What did you mean about the stolen magic?" I venture. Cillian's face twists as he fills the cups again with steaming water, but at least he doesn't look like he's going to pass out anymore.

"What was your father's gift?"

The question stops me. My father never used his magic in front of us. When prodded, he would only answer, "I discern the truth."

"I don't know," I answer honestly. "He was the high judge for the Crown, and whatever his gift was, his skills were highly sought-after."

I still remember the day a neighboring king came to beg my father to work for him. He promised jewels, a sweeping estate, and all the wives my father could enjoy. But my father, although not a kind man, was loyal to the Crown his entire life.

Until he killed the King, that is.

Cillian slops some of the tea he's pouring onto his hand and lets out a hiss. "Your father was the high judge? Well, that solves it then."

"Solves what?" I ask, baffled.

Cillian sucks on the end of one burned finger, put out. "Honestly, Lisette, when are you going to put it together? Your father was an evoker."

I ignore the jibe. "A what?"

"Evoker. He could summon the dead."

The air rushes out of my lungs. Evoker. My dull, listless father, summoner of the dead. It makes no sense. It makes complete sense.

"It's a rare gift," Cillian goes on, oblivious to my turmoil. "Highly useful for ferreting out murderers. After all, who better to determine the guilty than the innocent they injured?"

I discern the truth. My voice is no more than a whisper. "Couldn't they lie?"

Cillian plops a mug of tea in my lap. He takes a long sip of his own before answering, breathing in the steam.

"Now, that's more like it. And the dead can't lie. Everyone knows that."

I stare blankly at the tiny pink buds floating in the cup Cillian handed me. Evoker. I can summon the dead. I can see how it's a useful gift—practical, just like my father himself. But what am I supposed to do with a gift like that? I wanted something simple and flashy: fire, ice, any of the elemental gifts. I picture my next show, the stage set up like a courtroom, lines of the dead waiting for me to pass judgment, as dull as all government work. I fight to stifle the scream that threatens to rip from me. This is what I corrupted my soul for? Unearthed my dead father for?

"I suppose we should work on teaching you to manage it then," Cillian says, looking ill at the very thought.

"What? No. I don't want it!"

Cillian gives me an odd look. "I'd have thought you'd be thrilled. I can't think of a better gift for the stage."

"Oh, right." I set the cup down harder than I mean to, as bitter as the herbs inside. "I'm sure crowds will line up for miles to watch me deliver justice to the dead."

"Not that I want to encourage this in any capacity," Cillian says slowly, "but just because your father used his gift to pass judgment doesn't mean you have to."

I stare at him. Because up until that moment, it hadn't occurred to me that the gift could be used for anything else. I can summon the dead. Like magic, the possibilities unravel in front of me, infinite and wonderful. I clap a hand to my mouth.

"Nine hells."

"There it is." Cillian swills the rest of his tea, looking as if he rather wished it were stronger. "I'll get my books."

CHAPTER
18

The first case is easy. Murder, over a quarrel regarding a stolen horse. The spirit is brought to justice, and the replacement of the horse ordered. Restitution, all in its rightful place, as it should be. There is a power to righting wrongs, the boy discovers. A satisfaction. The next several cases follow easily, and judgment is delivered through the information given by the dead. Although his father never once smiles or even looks at him, the boy can see the approval in the way he holds his shoulders and the set of his chin.

His father is proud, and this realization spurs him to impress him still further.

When the next spirit is summoned, the boy, filled to bursting with pride, assumes it will be just as easy as the first cases. The high judge summons the spirit to the stand and nods to his son, just once.

"I was murdered."

Aren't they all, *the boy thinks.*

"Who murdered you?"

The spirit, both victim and witness, a sallow man in his fifties, stares at the boy.

"The king."

Whispers erupt from the stands. The boy shoots them a look, although his own insides freeze at the accusation. The dead cannot lie, he knows, but no one accuses the king of murder. Not even the dead.

"What do you mean?" the boy asks, hoping to buy himself enough time to figure out what to do.

"The captain of the guard tried to enlist my boy, even though he's lame in one leg. I told him he was incapable of serving, under the king's own law, and the king had me killed for it."

The boy swallows hard. His father avoids his desperate attempts at eye contact, face hard and unreadable. Truth. Justice. All the principals he's had drilled into him make no sense now.

"So, you defied the king, then?" the boy probes, although even he knows it's a paper-thin defense, at best.

"I quoted his own law to him, statute fifty-two. 'No soul shall be recruited who is not capable in both body and spirit.' I did no more than that."

The boy needs more time. A better understanding of the law. But he knows only his father's magic keeps the spirit tethered in this plane, and as soon as he releases it, he will not be able to summon this spirit again. This is the only chance he has.

"Under the law, the king has the right to change whatsoever laws he will, without vote or precedence. Would you agree?"

"Yes," the spirit says, in a voice like dead leaves rattling. "But he did not try to change the law."

Another dead end. There is sweat gathering in the robes he had felt so capable wearing just this morning. There is only one answer, and the boy knows it. His father knows it too, the boy can tell by the way his shoulders, so proud before, hunch inward. An answer that will destroy his career before it has even begun.

But the boy is bound, as all the high judges before him, to deliver justice, no matter the price.

Even a king cannot escape the law when a high judge passes sentence.

"I find King Reginald the fourteenth guilty of murder."

CHAPTER
19

Cillian is relentless in his attempts to teach me how to master my father's gift. We summon ghost after ghost, Cillian's face growing paler with each apparition. Secretly, I wonder if he hopes that if he teaches me how to control my father's magic, I'll relieve him of our pact.

"Can you control whom you summon?" Cillian asks, after I evoke a particularly awful ghost, the spirit of a man who called himself Jean and threatened to hang Cillian by his own entrails. Up until that point, I hadn't even considered the idea that I might be able to choose who I evoke.

"I can try."

Taking a deep breath, I think of the only other person I've lost and reach for the magic. Pages flutter as the spirit forms, a young man, head bowed.

For a moment my heart leaps, but then the spirit looks up and his face is round, forlorn, nothing like my brother's.

Disappointed, I let the spirit fade. It tries to resist, calling to me, but the words sound distant. Cillian pulls off his glasses, wiping them wearily on his shirt.

"I take it that wasn't the spirit you meant to evoke?"

"No." I stare at the spot where the spirit disappeared, wishing more than anything that it had been my brother.

"Were you concentrating?" Cillian's voice cuts through my sorrow. "Remember, you can't just cast out a line of power and expect it to follow your will, you need to control it—"

"I *know*." I don't mean to snap at him, but exhaustion and disappointment have made me peevish.

"Well, then, try again."

I shove Cillian's book in my bag, ignoring the order. "Leave me alone."

"You're the worst student I've ever had," Cillian says, rubbing his temples in mock exasperation. "Of course, you're the only student I've had," he adds with a wry smile.

And although I know he's only kidding, the jibe feels like a cactus needle in my side, pricking.

"Who are you to judge me?" I ask, slamming my bag down, not caring if I damage one of his precious books in the process. "You're one of the most powerful magicians in Oasis, and yet, you hide in a bookshop all day."

Cillian sags. "You're right."

"What?" I ask, certain I've misheard.

Cillian sinks into the emerald armchair. He looks defeated, and for a moment I feel bad for my harsh words.

"You're right. I lecture you about using magic properly, and here I am, only using mine to heat my kettle."

Cautiously, I sit in the rose chair. "That's not true. You're teaching me."

"Only because you blackmailed me." Cillian lets out a mirthless laugh, letting his head fall into his hands. "My mother would be so disappointed."

"Is she . . .?" I don't finish the sentence. Cillian shakes his head emphatically.

"No, she's alive . . . doing well, last I heard. I haven't exactly been in contact." He looks ashamed.

Although I can sense we're treading on dangerous ground, curiosity gets the better of me.

"Why not?"

The sigh that gusts out of Cillian is loud enough to rouse the dead.

"My mother is one of the king's scholars," he begins, absently shredding a napkin. The fact doesn't surprise me, although I am surprised Cillian didn't follow in her footsteps. He would have made a wonderful scholar.

"My father was in the king's militia. General. He and my mother . . . didn't exactly get along, so I didn't know him well. I didn't even find out about his death until an entire year after the fact."

His deft fingers continue to pick and shred, a mountain of paper like snow in front of him.

"My mother raised my sisters and me on her own. Scholars aren't paid much, you know, just a modest stipend and whatever grants they can earn, so we lived simply, but we were happy together."

His face takes on a wistfulness. "She was so proud when I was chosen to attend the academy. Worked double shifts every day for a year so I'd have enough money to go."

I nod. The academy is where prospective scholars are apprenticed and trained. It's notoriously difficult to get into and entails a rigorous four-year program before scholars graduate.

"She passed her magic on to me the day I left for the academy. Told me I was going to be the best scholar the academy ever had."

All the paper now gone, Cillian stares at his empty hands.

"What happened?" I ask, because it's obvious his story doesn't have a happy ending.

"I flunked out." The admission is flat.

"*How?*"

Cillian's smile is brittle. "Nervous breakdown during exams. I got up halfway through the test and never went back. My mother still doesn't know I left."

I do my best not to gawp at him. Know-it-all Cillian, an academy dropout?

"Obviously, I couldn't go back after that, and I certainly couldn't run home crying to my mother, so I came here to Oasis, where no one cares about your past." His voice is harsh, mocking.

"Devils."

"And now, here I am, trying to prove I'm not the worthless, anxious wreck my professors thought I was." Cillian shakes his head, as if by doing so he can dispel the memories there. He leans back, rubbing at his jaw. "I haven't spoken to my mother or sisters in three years now."

I think of Edward, who I'd give anything to speak to again. "They must miss you."

"I can't go back." He's shamefaced, voice barely a whisper. "After everything my mother sacrificed—"

I sniff, still not convinced. "Surely they'd be more upset at you ignoring them all these years than the fact that you flunked out of school."

To this, Cillian has no response. He stares at the mound of shredded paper as though he can find the answers there.

"You remind me of my youngest sister," he says, finally.

I smile in spite of myself. "She's incredibly charming, I assume?"

"A spoiled brat," Cillian says, but there's a smile behind his lips that wasn't there a moment ago. He pauses, gaze far off. "I miss her terribly."

"I'm sorry," I say, and I find I mean it. I wish I hadn't asked. I don't want to feel bad for Cillian, and I definitely don't want to feel bad for blackmailing him.

My apology seems to rouse him.

"Don't feel sorry for me," he says, curt, sweeping the little pile of shredded paper neatly into his hand. "You're the one who can't control your magic."

And, after shoving another ridiculous stack of books at me, Cillian dismisses me for the day.

Although the Saguaro stage is mine to use whenever I like, I've been rehearsing alone in my rooms. I don't want anyone to see my act before the queen does, especially not Luc.

The spirit I'd managed to evoke, a bland young man about my own age, evaporates as something is shoved unceremoniously under my door. Frowning, I release my hold on the magic.

Tearing open the tiny black envelope, I find a single crimson ticket inside. A ticket to Luc's next show, tomorrow morning. Instead of advertising the Panther theater, the ticket only gives "The Crown Hotel" as the location for the show.

Likely another of Luc's tricks. Rolling my eyes, I toss the ticket on my desk and try to ignore it.

Although I do my best to focus on my own act, my attention keeps wandering back to Luc. Like an ember, the stupid ticket burns through my thoughts all day, rendering me useless. Devils knows I'm dying to see what Luc has planned for his next show.

Tossing aside my notes for my own act, I try to get some sleep. I'll decide in the morning if it's worth it or not to bother seeing Luc's performance.

A rumbling sound wakes me early. Wrapping a robe around myself, I stumble to the window, tugging open the privacy blinds, and gasp.

A crowd of tourists fills the streets. It's hard to see exactly where they're going, but it looks like the Crown. I squint at the mass of people streaming like water down the Noose. Why in the nine hells—

Out of the corner of my eye, I see Luc's ticket, still sitting where I left it, innocuous, on the desk. Scrambling, I tug on a pair of trousers, grab the ticket, and race down the stairs. The lobby is characteristically empty, but outside there are so many people, I almost can't push open the doors to leave. Following the crowds, I jostle and push my way to the Crown.

On the steps of the Crown, Luc awaits, clad only in a pair of worn blue jeans and his trademark boots. A simple brass buckle from the belt slung low on his hips winks, catching the sunlight. I try hard to drag my eyes away from the sharp bones of his hips. He catches my eye and winks. Flushing, I turn away, pretending to be interested in the sunlight glinting off the Crown.

It's obvious why we're here, why he chose this location instead of the Panther stage. What better way to get the attention of the queen? My gaze sweeps the crowd; the queen is nowhere in sight. A vicious satisfaction thrills me. Luc can't get the queen to come to his show, even right on her front steps.

Luc gives a short bow, neglecting his usual speech. He wipes at the sweat already beading his forehead, even though the morning sun is still cool. He's nervous, I realize, my own heart pounding in response. Stretching his neck, he shakes out his hands. Running them along the glass of the hotel, his fingers wrap into a nonexistent crevice, pulling first one leg up, then another. He's climbing, I realize, dumbfounded. Up the side of the largest hotel in the Oasis.

No wonder I could never find him rehearsing. Unlike the other hotels on the Noose, the Crown boasts floor-to-ceiling windows in every room, giving the illusion of a giant, many-faceted mirror, reflecting the Noose back on itself. I stare up the side of the building, which is so sheer, a single miscalculation on Luc's part could be fatal.

Squinting against the sunlight, we all watch as Luc carefully makes his way up the side of the building, which reflects the golden sun so that it's dazzlingly bright. How he can see anything that close to the glass is beyond me. His progress is surprisingly quick, and my eyes scan for the telltale sign of a rope or cable, but there is nothing. Nothing but the taut muscles in his back and the unrelenting strength of his arms.

About halfway up, he stops to rest on a windowsill. I calculate madly; the Crown Hotel boasts 118 floors. Which means he's fifty-six stories high right now. With the grace of an acrobat, he lets go with one hand to knock on the window. Even with my own feet planted firmly on the ground, a wave of dizziness forces me to look down for a moment, the palms of my hands tingling. I hate heights.

It takes a moment, but the window finally swings open, revealing a woman. Even from here, there's no mistaking the shock on her face. Her golden hair tosses in the wind as Luc gives an over-the-top bow from his perch on her windowsill, and suddenly I realize. Luc didn't pick just any random windowsill—he picked the queen's suites.

They speak for only a moment before the window glides shut again. Luc lingers in the windowsill, stretching the muscles in first one arm, then the other. He wipes the sweat on his jeans and stares up into the sun, seeming to steel himself. Then he starts again.

It's obvious the first half has drained him. His pace is slower now, and there's a noticeable shake as he reaches for the next handhold. I can't fathom what he has planned. Is this the whole show? Scaling the side of the queen's hotel?

It's a daring feat, but where is the magic?

A commotion at the front doors of the Crown steals my attention from Luc. The doors open, revealing the queen and her entire retinue. My heart sinks as she takes her place in the crowd, craning her long neck to watch Luc's ascent. That's one way to get a queen's attention, I admit grudgingly.

A collective gasp from the crowd returns my attention to Luc, who hangs, one-handed, from a window ledge. It's the final floor, 118 stories from the ground. Heart thrumming, I watch as he reaches for the sill, arm shaking, and misses. Someone near me screams. Perhaps it's the queen.

I can't even make out his features, he's so high up, a speck against the great hotel. Letting out a roar, he swings the other arm and makes contact. Even from here, I can see the way his muscles quake as he strains to pull himself up to the roof of the hotel. Once over the edge, he collapses in a heap. The audience around me erupts in cheers.

He savors it for only a moment, throwing his arms into the air in triumph. I clap with the rest of them, not sure if I'm applauding because I'm impressed or because I'm relieved he didn't kill himself. I don't know if even Luc could survive a fall from that height.

Luc leans his head back as the wind tousles his blond hair. So high up, he's a speck against the blue of the wide sky. And then, with his arms still spread wide, he falls, plummeting over the side of the hotel.

I scream. I can't help it, but I'm not the only one. Even some of the men let out shocked cries as Luc hurtles to the ground. It happens so slowly it feels surreal. Luc's face is serene as he tumbles to the earth. I scan the audience frantically for one of his plants, for a cushion of some kind, anything. But there is no one and nothing to greet him when he lands, nothing but the dusty street, and the eyes of the crowd. I close my own eyes just in time, but I don't miss the wet crack as he lands.

There is no way he could've survived that. My eyes fly open at the ensuing commotion. Luc's neck is bent at an odd angle, those golden eyes staring blankly at the sun. His entire body is shattered, seemingly beyond repair. The queen's servants flutter around her; she's fainted, and this time I don't judge her for it. I draw a shaky hand to my lips, wondering if I'll be sick.

A young man darts out of the crowd and kneels at Luc's side. Gently, he angles Luc's neck so that it's not bent at such a violent angle. With an expert hand, he unstoppers a tiny glass vial, dribbling its contents into Luc's mouth. Steam pours from Luc's lips. The boy stands, eyes scanning the crowd.

"My master requested a volunteer before he died."

No one responds, still too stunned at the sight of Luc's broken body lying mangled on the pavement. The boy points a finger at me.

"You. The girl with the rose hair."

I shake my head. I want no part in this. But the boy is not so easily deterred. The crowd parts as he makes his way toward me and grasps my hand. I have no choice but to follow him to where Luc lies.

"In order for my master to resurrect, he requires the kiss of a pure maiden."

Several of the audience members scoff at the boy's words, which are antiquated, but I'm still caught on the word "kiss." The boy gestures to Luc, pleading in his blue eyes.

"Please. Play along. If you don't, he'll die."

The words are soft, meant only for me and not the audience surrounding us. Biting my lip, I dare a glance at Luc. His chest is still, lips parted. A ghost of steam from whatever the boy poured into his mouth still wafts like his spirit has already left him. I've spent the last year hating Luc with every fiber of my being. I don't anymore, I realize.

Steeling myself, I lean over and let my lips brush his, so faint it could barely be considered a kiss. Nothing happens. My heart thuds dully inside of me. What if he dies because of me? I think again of the girl he couldn't resurrect, lips blue, blank eyes staring at the sky.

The same way Luc's eyes stare beyond me to the sky he fell from.

"Kiss him," the boy pleads, eyes desperate. "He's *dying*." And I oblige, crushing my lips to Luc's. Luc gasps, pulling me into him. His pupils constrict, the veins in his neck bulge. His grip is painful, as though he's using me to claw his way back from the Beyond. Maybe he is.

I wince as the shattered vertebrae in his neck realign with a series of pops. The broken bones reconnect, the open wounds zipper shut as Luc heals in front of my eyes. He pants, and from his tortured expression, I can tell he's in excruciating pain. His body spasms under me, my face buried in his chest, which smells like copper and tastes like salt.

Finally he releases me, blood rushing back to my arm in a river of tingles. The crowd erupts into cheers, but he ignores it. It's as if we're the only two people in the world. With a shaking hand, he reaches up to brush a lock of my hair away.

"Well done, my little plant."

I startle. "What?"

I steal a look at the boy, but he's gone. The realization hits me like a sinking stone. Of course. It was all planned, all a trick. Revenge for my own show, likely. As the knowledge hits me, Luc sweeps me in for another dramatic kiss. I slap him with all the force I can muster. Recently dead or no, he's made me furious. He's tricked me again. I stalk away, realizing there are actually tears in my eyes, and this makes me even more angry.

The clouds gather quickly, shrouding the sun in gray. Lightning cracks across the sky, lighting the valley below in flashes. Rain in the desert is never a peaceful thing. It comes in violent torrents, quick and deadly. The first fat drops hit my face like a warning, followed by a downpour. I slog through the floodwater back to the Saguaro, passing a man carrying a tiger cub on his shoulders and two girls in feather headdresses crying, feathers drooping.

My lips sting where Luc's lips met mine. How can I ever hope to beat him? Somehow, he always knows my weakness. Somehow he is always better. I promised Rose and Yasmin I would beat him, and yet, I have nothing. Nothing but a legion of ghosts awaiting justice. How am I supposed to impress a queen with that?

The rain rolls down my face like tears, soaking my clothing through.

In less than an hour, gallons of water have flooded the Noose. This is power, I think, as the water pulls at my legs. Not even magic can turn an entire desert into an ocean. The same rain drenches all of Oasis, soaking queen and commoner alike.

It hits me then, like a lightning strike.

I know what my next show is going to be.

CHAPTER
20

"What in the nine hells have you done, boy?" His father is not angry, and that is perhaps the most distressing thing to the boy. He is anguished.

"I did what you taught me—"

"I never taught you to go against the Crown! You absolute, mewling fool . . ."

Scraggly bushes and sun-beaten fences blur in front of the boy's unseeing eyes as the high judge's motorcar speeds them away from the debacle at court. After the boy's outrageous sentence, before his father could spirit him away, the court had quickly devolved into madness.

"Perhaps there's a way to still make this right. You are still only an apprentice, which means according to law seventeen, statute B . . ."

The boy listens to his father ramble in silence. In all his nineteen years, he has never seen his father frightened before. Angry, yes. Disgruntled, certainly. But never afraid. The high judge pours himself a drink with shaking hands but doesn't drink any of it.

"*After everything I've done for the Crown . . . there's no way . . . a silly, youthful mistake . . .*"

"*What else could I have done?*" the boy protests. "*The evidence was irrefutable, spoken from the mouth of one who cannot lie!*"

His father, the man with a resolve of stone, of unwavering morality, or so the boy thought, regards him with an ashen face.

"*The dead cannot lie. But you should have.*"

CHAPTER
21

Luc's kiss still burns. I don't think about how badly I wish to strangle him, wrap my hands around his neck and squeeze until my fingers ache, because I can't kill him. I'm not even sure I can beat him.

The ink on the invitation I've written smudges, leaving a black smear. Wordlessly, I throw it into the trash and begin anew. If the queen won't come to me of her own volition, I'll ask. I'll beg if need be. I hadn't bothered to invite the queen to any of my shows until now. Because this show will be different.

This time, I at least have a shot.

Of course, there's always the chance that this invitation won't even reach the queen in time. I waited too long, and without a seeker, well . . . I bury that thought down deep with all the others as I finish signing the invitation with a flourish.

I'm startled by a knock at the door, causing me to leave another trail of smudged ink on my invitation. I crumple it up and toss it in the direction of the trash, not caring if I miss. Expecting housekeeping, I fling open the door, surprised to instead see Yasmin, looking small and out of place. I usher her in, forgetting in my concern to be ashamed of my tiny quarters. Yasmin doesn't seem to notice; her eyes are glazed as she traces the pattern on my bedspread.

"Are you okay?" I ask when she doesn't say anything, just keeps staring at the bed.

"You're in love with Luc."

The accusation comes out dead, flattened. I flinch, as if burned. "Excuse me?"

"It's obvious, Lisette. Everyone on the Noose is talking about his show. The one where you *kissed* him."

She's never called me Lisette before. That's the only thing that registers in my numb mind. I let out a startled laugh.

"I don't love him. He tricked me."

"Yeah, sure he did." Yasmin rolls her eyes, but I don't miss the way she holds herself, arms crossed, as if afraid of my response.

"It's the truth." My hands grit into fists at the memory of the kiss, stolen from me like everything else. "He was mocking me."

Yasmin's eyes flicker up to mine, wary. "Really?"

"Really."

"Thank the devils," she says, gusting out a breath, collapsing at my desk. "I really didn't want to have to hate you too."

Her foot knocks one of the crumpled invitations on the floor. "What's this?"

I shake my head. "Just trying to get the queen to my show. I'm starting to think I'll never be able to get her attention."

Yasmin picks up the invitation, smoothing out the wrinkles. Her sharp eyes narrow as she reads.

"This will never reach the queen in time, if at all. Her mail is heavily filtered. You're better off asking her in person."

I can feel my face fall. My show is tonight, in a mere three hours. There's no way I can secure an audience with the queen in that short a time, and even if I could, what are the odds she'd listen to me anyway?

Yasmin seems to sense my despair. Folding up the invitation, she clicks her long nails on my desk as she ponders the dilemma.

"I know one of the maids at the Crown. There's a good chance even she can't get anywhere near the queen, but maybe . . ."

I hardly dare to breathe. "You would do that for me?"

"Of course," she says, pocketing the invitation, turning to leave. "Anything to make Luc suffer."

Her words burn for reasons I can't put my finger on. I want Luc to suffer more than anyone else. After what he did to me at the Crown, I don't care if his next act leaves him splattered all over the Noose. The thought of his golden eyes, the feel of his lips, full and lush against my own, the taste of his betrayal . . . of course I want him to suffer.

Don't I?

Five minutes until my show, and the Saguaro theater is only half-full. My numbers have flagged ever since Luc threw himself off the Crown. No sign of the queen, which is more than a problem, considering I've based the entire act around her. It occurs to me then that Luc has never bothered to come to one of my shows, even though I've seen all of his. My whole world revolves around beating Luc, and yet, he doesn't even consider me a worthy opponent.

I'm nothing more than a fly in his periphery, a minor annoyance to be waved away.

I can't stand to watch the empty seats, so I focus on my magic instead. Feel it rage inside of me, as angry as I am. As hungry. I shove away my anxiety, the screaming voice in my head reminding me that I still haven't figured out how to choose which spirit I evoke. I know only a few things about my father's magic, the most important being that it seems easier to evoke a spirit if they have a connection to someone nearby. Even so, I have just as much chance of evoking someone completely random as the spirit I hope to see tonight.

I dare another look at the audience, but it's just as sparse as before. The queen has not come. I bite back the humiliation that rises up, the urge to run from my own show. It's over. Luc has always had me beat.

Taking a deep breath, I cross the empty stage. I've left it barren on purpose. No props, no stagehands, nothing to distract from what I'm about to do. Nothing but a single beam of light, hitting exactly center stage, and a chair. I enter the stage from the right, relishing the sound of my footsteps echoing across the theater. The audience is silent, waiting, expectant.

My costume is simple. I've adorned the musty powdered wig my father used to wear. The rest of my ensemble is navy blue, the traditional robes of the high judge. There's a slight murmuring from the audience as I walk into the light and they take in my appearance. The feeling that, once again, I'm making a huge mistake threatens to overwhelm me. I shove it back down.

Leaving the chair empty, I face the audience. I'm about to ask for a volunteer, when the door to the theater opens, casting a harsh square of light. An usher hurries to stop the interloper.

"Please, the show is already in progress—"

"My apologies, we did not mean to be late."

My already rapid heart rate shoots up. The audience members rise in their seats at the sound of the voice. The queen and a handful of ladies-in-waiting fill in the remaining seats, while the queen's guards station themselves at the doors.

"Be seated," the queen orders, then beckons to me. "Madam, your show?"

Yasmin did it. I swallow the hope that rages like wildfire inside me and give the queen a gracious bow. I clasp my hands behind my back so that the audience can't see the way they tremble, evidence of my own nerves heightened to an almost painful extreme in the presence of the queen.

My shot is finally here.

"Thank you, Your Highness. I was just asking for a volunteer."

No preamble, no silly speeches tonight. Tonight, it's all about the magic. My magic.

A number of hands rise, although they are wary. Tension runs through the theater, and I tug at it, manipulate it like the strings of a puppet.

"Your Highness," I call out, even though her hand is not raised. "Would you be so kind as to assist your humble servant onstage?"

As one, the heads of the audience swivel toward their sovereign. Her face turns sallow. I groan inwardly. I hadn't counted on the queen having stage fright.

I keep my expression easy, but inside I'm dying. I think I can do the trick without her, but it'll be a lot more impressive if she cooperates. To my surprise, she finally rises, nodding her assent. Making her way to the stage, she allows me to take her hand when she gets close enough. Both hands are cool and dry. Her gray eyes lock on to mine as I pull her up, a warning in her expression. Before I can react, she pulls away, waving demurely to the crowd. I do my best to collect myself, although my heart is pounding and there's a dryness to my mouth that wasn't there a moment ago. Oh devils, let this work.

"Please, have a seat, Your Majesty."

The queen does as she's instructed, albeit hesitantly.

Closing my eyes, I summon the magic. It still feels wrong, like thorns choking my soul, but it's quicker to respond this time. I barely hear the gasps as the figure onstage forms.

The queen lets out a scream, a single, piercing note that shatters the silence of the theater.

I open my eyes. I did it. The dead king stands before us, as clear as the day he died. He has no eyes for the queen, however. His stare bores into me as though we're the only two people here.

"You must deliver justice."

His voice is like gravel tumbling in a stream bed. I sweep into a low bow.

"It has already been done, Your Majesty."

His black eyes blaze. The gold burial clothes rotting on his emaciated frame rattle.

"The traitor lives."

Understanding dawns on me. He's clearly mistaken me, in the robe and wig of the high judge, for my father. I dart a look at the queen. Her fair face is green. This isn't going at all how I'd planned. I'd only hoped to allow the queen another precious moment with her dear departed husband.

I pull off the wig, breaking character, holding up my hands in a placating gesture. "Your Highness, I'm not the high judge. I'm just a lowly magician. Your murderer was executed."

"*Kingkiller!*" It's only one word, but it rips out of him, blowing the crown clean off the queen. She doesn't bother to retrieve it, just clutches at the chair as though it can save her from her late husband's wrath.

Kingkiller. This is the only legacy I'll ever have.

I scramble to remember how I dismissed the other spirits. Summoning them is the easy part. It's getting them to leave that is a struggle.

The king turns to his queen, mouth agape. He's so far gone, I'm not even sure he recognizes her.

"Leave." My voice cracks as the King advances on the queen, burial clothes flapping. Heart beating so fast it hurts, I plant myself in between him and the queen.

"Begone, spirit!"

The king hisses at me and reaches for the queen. As soon as his decaying outstretched fingers make contact, he bursts into a cloud of dust. The queen swoons, hitting her head with a crack on the stage.

There's a moment of stunned silence, and then everything goes to hell.

CHAPTER
22

H er brother is dead. Her perfect, silly older brother, who made faces at her when Papa was in one of his moods. Who read her stories. Who kept the nightmares at bay. Dead.

And Papa. She'd thought Papa would save Edward. After all, Edward was so dear to Papa, dearer than Lisette would ever be. But Papa only stood there, mute, when the king's guard clapped heavy iron shackles on her brother and shuffled him away, as if he were nothing more than a petty thief. That's all he did, stand there. Long after trumped-up charges were read, accusing her brother of everything from conspiring against the Crown to treason. Even after her brother's head was separated from his body in the name of the king.

There was no one to keep the nightmares away now. Nightmares of her brother, headless, howling at Lisette for justice. She'd wake alone, screaming, but no one ever came. Because her father turned to stone after his son's death, and Lisette would never be good enough to break the spell.

CHAPTER
23

I don't bother to move as servants and guards alike swarm the stage, checking the queen's pulse. Not even when one of them catches sight of me, shrinking into the shadows, and shouts to his comrades. Or when one of them cuffs me in chains and drags me from the stage.

What have I done? The question follows me all the way to the makeshift holding room, the laundry room of the Saguaro. I'm dumped unceremoniously in a plastic chair and left with only the company of stained bedding, wet towels, and the smell of mildew.

All I wanted was to impress the queen. Instead, I've committed worse than treason, and onstage, no less. Will I suffer the same fate as my father? I sink my head into my hands, the chains dragging at my wrists. Cillian was wrong. This magic *is* a curse.

An hour passes. Perhaps this is my sentence, left to rot in a hotel laundry room. Two guards chat outside the door. I can hear them, babbling about which shows they plan to see this weekend. I don't bother summoning my magic. What good would the company of a spirit do here? The blackness from the ring has crept up my wrist, which I've hidden with gloves. I wonder what will happen when there's nowhere left for it to go. When the magic has consumed me entirely.

I'm watching the clock, which sticks every other second, turning one second into three, when the door opens. It's the queen. One of the guards accompanies her, holding her arm as if to keep her from blowing away. I stand, knocking over the chair in my haste.

"Your Majesty, I meant no harm. I only intended to give you a moment with your beloved. I had no idea—"

My mouth dries at the memory of the vengeful King.

"—you have to believe me." I finish. The queen studies me. And although I'm not on trial, not yet anyway, the look in her eyes makes me feel as though I am.

Finally, she nods. "An unfortunate lapse in judgment to be certain, but I don't believe you intended to be malicious."

I blow out a breath, avoiding looking at the gash on her forehead, which has been bandaged neatly.

"Thank you, Your Highness."

The queen watches me, light eyes unreadable.

"However, such behavior is not without consequence, of course. You're competing for Jester, are you not?"

Relief has made me near hysterical. I swallow the giggle that threatens to escape. For months I've tried to get the queen's attention, and now I finally have it. And all it took was to injure the queen.

"Yes, Your Highness."

She considers this. With her stiff, formal robes and gilded crown, she is at odds with everything in the laundry room. One long finger, dripping with rings, taps the edge of a washing machine. My heart drums with it. This is it. She's going to eject me from the competition.

"I'd like you to join me for tea tomorrow."

What? I stare at the queen, struggling to formulate a coherent thought. Perhaps she is going to wait to deliver my sentence in private? Like the shadow of an axe, the unknown swings over my head, which drops in submission.

"Of course, Your Majesty."

After our conversation, the guards return me to my room at the Saguaro, where I am still processing what just happened. Sinking onto the bed, suddenly exhausted, I stare up at the ceiling.

Why wasn't I tried? I set a vengeful ghost on the queen. Unintentional or no, I should be swinging from the gallows right now.

The coffin prop in the corner of the room catches my eye. There are only two weeks left to prepare my final act, if there was any way I was still in the competition.

There's no way. I've been spared from execution; I should be content with that.

I'm as punctual as Death himself for my meeting with the queen the next day. I enter the room indicated on the formal missive delivered by one of the queen's handmaidens early this morning, a small, sunlit parlor where the queen is tending to a strange, prickly plant. What look like tiny mouths hang off the plant in abundance, gaping blindly. I sweep into a curtsy, but the queen doesn't even look up. Awkward, I clasp my hands behind my back and clear my throat.

"Please, come in. Lisette, right?"

I nod, afraid of the wrong words tripping off my tongue in my nervousness. The queen plucks a live mouse by the tail from a silk drawstring bag at her waist. As she dangles the wriggling creature over the plant, the many green mouths come to life, snapping at the offering. She drops the mouse and I watch, horrified, as it's ripped to shreds, each tiny mouth snatching greedy bites until the mouse is completely devoured—not even the bones are left. While the many mouths are occupied, she takes a gleaming pair of clippers from the same pouch and neatly snips two white blossoms from the plant.

"I'm glad you could make it," the queen says, replacing the clippers in the silk bag, ignorant of the specks of mouse blood spattered on her hands. "Please be seated."

I drop like a rock onto the tiny pouf next to me, not realizing in my haste it's intended as a footstool. Thankfully, the queen doesn't point out my folly, only sits herself in the divan across from me, as though my behavior is completely natural and appropriate.

"Welcome to my greenhouse," she says, gesturing to the tangles of leaves, thorns, and blooms around us. I tug my foot away from a wandering root, hoping the queen doesn't notice. The sunlight catches her golden hair, making it sparkle, and she sighs as she leans into the warmth. "I find much peace here. My gift is with plants, you see."

"That was a plant?" I ask, and instantly regret the question. The last thing I need is to offend the queen. But to my surprise, she doesn't seem offended by my query. A smile creeps across her lips like a vine.

"A *fitica*. Mine is only a juvenile. Fully grown, they can consume an entire cow in one feeding. They're quite finicky though, and hard to care for."

I dart another look at the tiny plant, seemingly innocuous now that it's sated. It could be sleeping. I swallow back nausea, feigning a smile.

"How intriguing."

"Most people find it appalling," the queen says, that same smile still playing at her mouth.

"It's horrible," I finally say honestly.

The queen lets out a startled laugh and it's all I can do not to slap a hand over my mouth.

"I forget myself, Your Majesty. My apologies."

"No, no." She waves away my words, still chuckling. "I find it quite refreshing. The plant *is* awful. However, when pressed, the oil from the buds makes a rather potent remedy for the infant sleeping sickness."

"Oh."

"Sometimes even terrible things can yield beautiful results. There is often beauty in death, agony, and despair if one chooses to see it." The queen toys with one of the buds, spinning the tiny bloom. Although I'm not certain I agree, I dip my head in assent.

"Of course, only a teaspoon more and the oil becomes a vicious poison. Also useful." The queen tucks the innocuous little flowers into the bag and smiles warmly at me. "So. You also have an interesting gift. I've only seen such a gift once before in my life."

The words are innocent enough, but my stomach clenches.

"In fact, if I recall correctly, it was once possessed by the high judge himself."

Kingkiller. She knows. The room spins, suddenly too hot, and I choke against the humidity.

"Peace. We are not to blame for the sins of our parents," the queen says, noticing my discomfort. "I was unaware Roland had passed on his gift before . . . his death."

I nod, biting my lip, not trusting myself to speak. The ring burns on my finger as I discreetly tuck my blackened hand into the folds of my dress.

The queen doesn't seem to notice, her gaze distant.

"Your father was one of my most valued servants, until . . . well."

Her eyes sparkle with tears. Abruptly she jerks her head away, daubing at her eyes with a pristine lace handkerchief.

"Your Majesty, I'm so sorry for your loss . . ." I begin, the words awkward and heavy on my tongue. Because of my father, she lost the one person she loved more than anyone else. A need to atone, to right the wrongs of my father rises up within me.

"Thank you." The queen clears her throat, shaking away the emotion as if embarrassed. "My husband was very dear to me. His loss has left a wound that all the gold in the world cannot heal. But tears won't bring him back," she goes on, suddenly brusque. "You, however, can."

I freeze, uncertain where she's going with this. The queen leans in, conspiratorial, and I find myself mirroring the action, until our heads are nearly touching.

"Your Majesty, I can't bring the king back again," I begin, awkward, but she talks smoothly over me.

"I need a new high judge."

I jerk back as if stung. "Your Majesty, I have no desire to assume my father's former position at court."

Visions of myself, crowned in my father's dusty wig, banging a gavel as an endless line of spirits waits for me to pass judgment . . . the thought churns my stomach.

The queen studies me, head cocked. "The position of high judge is one of extreme wealth and power, as well as honor. You would turn it down?"

I've said the wrong thing again, but I can't make my lips form an acceptance. "I cannot take it."

Wrinkles crease her smooth brow. Once out, the words continue to tumble as if they have a will of their own.

"I would rather rot in a cell than stop performing . . ."

The queen arches an eyebrow.

". . . although I thank you for the honor," I finish lamely. I've no doubt just condemned myself but I can't find room for regret. I meant every word. Sentenced to the dungeons would be a kinder fate than a life without performing.

"Truly?" The queen looks baffled.

My lips are numb. "Yes, Your Majesty."

She sits back, considering.

I await her sentence with more than a little trepidation. Although I meant it, I've no desire to die prematurely in a sweltering prison. There's also the chance that she'll just force me to take the position, regardless of my own thoughts on the matter.

"Then I'd like it if you moved to the Crown," the queen finally says.

I stare at her, not registering the words.

"I beg your pardon?"

"You'll headline for the Crown from now on."

She sits, hands clasped daintily, completely unaware of the shockwaves her words have sent through me.

"I'm certain you already know that the Crown performers are given . . . special consideration when it comes to the position of Jester?" she continues, smoothing her skirts.

Devils. I knew my father's gift was sought-after, but this . . . I'm still incoherent, gaping at the queen like a stupid fish. She raises an eyebrow at me.

"I'm aware," I finally croak. The room spins as adrenaline pumps through me. For the first time, my dream hangs so low I can almost grasp it, if I lean just enough . . .

"Better to have you as my Jester than nothing at all." The queen sighs. "Although you will be required to assist in any court issues I have need for."

I can still perform. My head jerks up and down, as if on puppet strings. "Of course, anything."

"And if you do anything to upset me, you will be ejected from the Crown, as well as the competition, immediately."

I swallow hard, my dry throat clicking. "Yes, Your Highness."

She nods, settling back as if pleased. One of the blooms, a giant orange blossom, nudges her hand and she strokes the downy petals absently. I notice then that even the flowers seek her, as if she's the sun.

"I suppose that means you had better win."

The words aren't entirely encouraging; a vein of threat laced through them like poison. I nod furiously, wondering what will happen if I lose.

It doesn't take long to gather my things. Dazed, I stare around my room at the Saguaro one last time. Room 304. Although it's not much, it's been my home these last few weeks. In a strange way, I'll miss it.

Lugging my suitcase down the stairs, I run through the speech I've planned to break the news to Rose.

Thank you for everything you've done for my career, unfortunately, I will miss tonight's show, as well as the rest of my shows, for the foreseeable future . . .

The last hour has been a dream, but the thought of talking to Rose quickly brings me back to reality. Knocking on the scarred "Management" door, I shift from foot to foot. I've left my suitcase in the lobby. Better to ease into the bad news. Even though this was only ever supposed to be temporary, I still feel guilty leaving Rose, especially after everything she's done for me.

The door swings open, almost hitting me in the face.

"My star act! Come in, come in!"

Rose hurries to relinquish her own chair, a leather thing with holes that gape stuffing. I take the proffered chair before realizing there are no other seats in the cramped office. Rose leans against her desk, beaming at me as if I'm a winning racehorse.

"What can I do you for?" she asks. Devils, this is going to be harder than I thought.

"I was offered a job at the Crown. Effective immediately."

Rose pauses halfway through stuffing a giant wad of tacco seeds in her lip. Gripping the armrests, I steel myself for her disappointment, but it never comes.

"I'll double whatever they're offering."

I choke back my surprise as she grins at me, red from the tacco seeds staining her teeth. I don't think the Saguaro even makes enough in a month to cover a quarter of the Crown salary, but I don't say so. Instead I try a new tact. Unfolding the decree from the queen, I pass it to Rose.

"I don't have a choice," I say, trying to keep my tone light, although I can finally see it, the expected disappointment watering down the grin she keeps plastered on.

"'By order of Queen Sonora' . . . devils, kid, I knew you were good, but—" She spits a gooey wad of shells into a metal cup on her desk, shaking her head. "Guess I'll have to find another act, huh?"

"I'm sorry," I say, but she waves away my apology.

"Always knew you were too good for this place," she says a little wistfully. "All right, kid. Get out of here before we both lose our heads."

"Thanks for everything, Rose," I say, sticking out a gloved hand. She stares at it for a moment, before gripping it in her own callused one.

"Take care of yourself," she says sternly. "I'd better not hear about you choking on a sword or devils knows what else in pursuit of glory."

Smiling, I tug the glove up to hide the black of my poisoned veins, hoping she doesn't see how close she is to the truth.

The Crown Hotel, jewel of the Noose, looms in front of me. It's absolutely massive, panes of glass from the floor-to-ceiling windows reflecting the setting sun so the entire building glows gold. Squaring my shoulders, I march past the valet, certain he'll call me out any second. Deny me entrance. Have me arrested. Instead, he hurries to hold the door for me.

"Welcome to the Crown."

Doing my best to hide my surprise, I give him a curt nod in thanks and push through the open door. Although I've been in the Crown before, the entrance never fails to steal my breath. Marble tile, grouted in gold, forms a diamond pattern on the vast floors, a tiny golden honeybee in each corner. The queen's portrait, easily ten feet tall and painted in warm colors in spite of her austere expression, smiles coldly down on me. A stately golden chandelier, wrought with ornate flowers, suffuses the room with warmth and light.

Sucking in a breath, I make my way to the reception desk. I am out of place in this grand, beautiful place, and every echoing step across the immense lobby reminds me of that fact. The receptionist is an unsmiling man with hair as golden as the chandelier above us. His sneer deepens as I approach him.

"Can I help you?"

Shaking back my hair, I toss the decree at him. He allows me a sour look before smoothing the paper, scanning it with pursed lips. I wait, smile as cold as Sonora's, until I see the telltale widening of his eyes.

"Deepest apologies, Miss Schopfer. Let me see if your rooms are ready."

Rooms. I feign nonchalance, although adrenaline pumps through me. Suddenly all charm, he smiles apologetically as he checks the massive hotel ledger.

"Of course, here we are. You'll be staying in the Peony suites, room 5470. Please let me know if there is anything we can do for you."

His tone is now oily, ingratiating. I pocket the heavy gold key he passes me, my heart pounding. It's really happening. I am the headliner for the Crown.

"Enjoy your stay at the Crown."

I make my way to the elevator bank, surprised to find not one but four. A bellhop stands straight next to a pile of trunks, a pinched expression on his pimpled face.

"Going up?" he asks, without looking at me. I check my room number.

"Floor fifty-four."

The door shuts with a muted chime and the bellhop eyes me, taking in my ragged costume and single suitcase.

"Street performer, I take it. Must've made quite the handful of dust down at the slots to be staying here."

His tone is dismissive. Already his eyes have wandered away, searching for someone or something more worthy. Arrogant sop.

"Actually, I'm the newest headliner for the Crown." I should let it go, but I can't stand when people underestimate me.

The boy sneers. "And I'm the mob queen of Oasis."

I grip my suitcase, wondering what would happen if I launched it at his cratered face. Surely even the queen's favor couldn't save me from the consequences of that decision. I'm saved from the temptation when the elevator glides to a stop.

With a soft ding, the doors slide open, revealing my floor. The bellhop shoves past me with a clatter of luggage. Dumbfounded, I stare after him, until the doors almost shut on me again, and I have to jam an arm through to escape.

The elevator is set in a honeycomb of hallways, all branching off from its door. A sparkling chandelier shaped like a beehive spirals overhead. Every hallway is the exact same, each with only a simple gold plaque denoting which room numbers lie that way to differentiate them.

My room is in the opposite direction the bellhop went. I walk past door after door, the impossible hugeness of the hotel making me dizzy, until I reach my room, almost at the end of the hall. The large golden door is tucked neatly in the corner, next to a flight of stairs. The golden placard next to the door reads "Peony Suite." Setting down my trunk, I scan the hallway for other guests, but only a sea of doors greets me. I fumble for the key and have a brief moment of panic when it doesn't go in. With a little wiggling, I manage to open the door.

And gasp.

In keeping with the hotel's general bee theme, the lush carpet is the color of raw honey. The bed is airy and white, accented with gold. The wallpaper is old-fashioned but elegant: golden bees glittering against a background of white. There's also a curious buzzing sound that takes me a moment to place.

Everywhere, carefully-manicured plants breathe life into the golden room. Pink peonies the size of cabbages, tucked in a white vase, decorate the bedside table. A tiny cherry tree in full bloom is propped next to the doors to the bathroom. Lilacs perfume the air. A bundle of lavender is set against the enormous down bed pillows. And buzzing improbably throughout the entire room are live honeybees.

Setting down my trunk, I pick up a small glass jar set on the bed. It's filled with rich dark honey, and next to it lies a tiny golden card.

Please enjoy today's complimentary flavor: lavender

It's a good thing I'm not allergic to bees, I think, dipping a finger in the honey. Although odds are the expensive spellwork in the hotel prevents the bees from stinging guests. Eager to test the theory, I reach to brush one of the thickly-furred abdomens protruding from the mouth of a rosebud. Sure enough, the bee leaves me alone, after a perfunctory investigation of my hand.

It's an exquisite room, a living garden. Rumor has it the king built the Crown as a tribute to his queen. The magic used to sustain all the flowers alone must have been extraordinarily expensive, let alone all the fine finishes. Only the Panther rivals its magnificence on the Noose. It's terribly romantic, I think, sucking in a lungful of the scented air.

Something slides under the door, followed by a crisp knock. *There it is*, I think. Surely I must have misunderstood the queen, and the square of thick emerald paper on the floor is no doubt the bill for this exquisite room. A quick survey of the hall outside my room reveals nothing but the retreating backside of a servant.

Curious.

I close the door and lift the envelope by the corner as if it might suddenly grow teeth. My stage name, surrounded by enough curlicues to render it almost illegible, graces the front. I rip it open with my teeth, dread pooling in my stomach. What a way to start my stay at the Crown, owing somebody money—

Dear Ms. Mirage,

After your unforgettable performance at the Saguaro last week, I would love to offer my services as seeker. As you know, I have a prestigious history with the Jester competition, and my last two choices were selected by the king personally as winners.

I would love to meet and discuss your options for winning. Meet me at the Lone Agave tonight, at six sharp.

It's signed Raster MacMillan. I blink, the ridiculous penmanship blurring in front of my eyes. I read the entire thing again, then again, to be certain I haven't misread. Raster MacMillan wants to be *my* seeker?

It's a trick, I think with sudden clarity, another gaffe by Luc, but no, that's definitely Raster's crest—an erupting volcano—on the envelope. I scan the letter yet again, as if there's a clue I might have missed, but it's just as perfectly baffling as the first two times.

The only way to figure out what this is all about is to meet with Raster. According to the elegant gold timepiece on the bedside table, I have a little under an hour to ready myself. I dress in a gown I recently purchased with some of my earnings from the Saguaro. It's a bit over the top, even for Raster's taste, studded with pearls that catch the light from the setting sun.

I've heard plenty about the Lone Agave, the Crown's world-class restaurant, but I've never dined there myself. At a nugget a plate, it's never come close to being affordable for me. A quick calculation of my gold dust confirms what I already suspected—I'll barely be able to afford an appetizer. I tuck the gold dust back in my wristlet and pray Raster is paying.

At 5:55, I make my way to the entrance of the Lone Agave, the beginnings of anxiety setting my heart racing. Was I really fool enough to believe Raster, renowned seeker for the Crown, would want me?

Situated in the center of the extensive, manicured gardens, the restaurant is tucked away from the massive luxury shopping center and casino the Crown boasts. Lush palm trees frame the entrance like overgrown bouncers. I pause near the ornate iron doors, pretending to fix the heel of my shoe, the hostess watching me curiously. I don't belong here, that much is obvious. Even the hostess is better dressed than I am, from her glittering opal stud earrings to her sleek plum gown. Déjà vu needles me, the irritating realization that no matter how far I climb, I will always be an outsider.

At 6:01, I can't seem to make myself enter the restaurant. Fear roots me to the marble floors, fear that once again, my pride has gotten the better of me.

Luc knew. The thought is electric, jolting.

He was there when I was trying to impress Raster at the party. Of course it's another trick, another snare Luc has cleverly set. The realization makes me woozy, the strings of garden lights above my head suddenly too bright. I turn to leave, disappointment pooling like molten lead in my stomach.

"Mirage!"

I cringe, expecting to see a taunting Luc, but it's Raster himself at the entrance of the Lone Agave, dressed to the nines in a suit decked in what looks like crocodile scales. His crisp white boots snap on the stone floors. Could Luc have actually gotten Raster himself in on the ruse?

"You're late," he says, pointedly. "And I'm hungry. Shall we?"

I have no choice but to follow him into the Lone Agave. He leads me to an intimate table surrounded by softly flickering torches. When he pulls the chair out for me, the picture of gentility, it hits me—the realization that all of this is real.

Raster MacMillan wants to be my seeker.

It's a struggle to rein in my exhilaration, but I manage to whip out a performance even Luc would be impressed by. Sipping my ice water, I survey the restaurant as coolly as though I dine here every evening.

A server appears as if out of thin air, bearing two delicate plates, which she places, mute, in front of Raster and me. It occurs to me then that there are no menus on the table, and I'm not even certain I can afford the handful of greens tossed artfully and drizzled with a mouthwatering dressing on the plate in front of me.

"I didn't order—"

The server doesn't hear my plea; he's already melted into the verdant gardens. Raster watches me carefully, one thick eyebrow raised.

"Dinner's on me," he says, gesturing to my plate.

I duck my head, cheeks burning. "Thank you."

He doesn't say another word until after his plate is clear of even the dressing. The salad, though barely enough to sate a rabbit, is bright and citrusy, each mouthful like a bite of spring. As soon as my fork scrapes my empty plate, another server collects our used dishes. Behind him is the second course, a thick curried soup with a sprig of cilantro on top.

"So, what did you think of my letter?" Raster says, sipping the steaming soup delicately. In spite of his flashy suit, which borders on gaudiness, his manners are impeccable.

I burn my tongue on my own spoonful, wince. "To be honest, I thought it was a joke."

Raster lowers his spoon, brow furrowing. "Oh?"

Oh devils, I've offended him.

"It seemed too good to be true," I rush on, hastily trying to smooth the disapproval scrawled on his brow. "And I thought you had already chosen a competitor for Jester."

The flattery works. The storm clouds gathering in his countenance dispel, leaving his face neutral once more.

"It's true, I did have a competitor," he says, taking a long pull from his drink. "Cerulea, the mermaid."

I'd assumed as much. Next to Luc, only a few other performers had the clout to catch the eye of the queen. Cerulea, although one of the youngest performers in Oasis at only thirteen, shows more promise than most veteran performers. Her show, performed almost entirely underwater, includes a battle royale between pirate ships, a variety of trained sea life and an actual humpback whale in the finale.

My mind snags on the past tense. "What happened to her?"

"Nothing," Raster cocks his head, confused. "I fired her when I heard about you."

The soup sits heavy in my stomach, curdling.

As if he can sense my unease, Raster throws me a warm smile. "Not to worry, my dear. I'm certain you won't disappoint me the way Cerulea did. I have it on good authority that you've become quite close with the queen."

Disappointment mixes with guilt in my gut, thick and sludgy. Stupid of me to assume he's sought me out because he actually likes my performance; he probably didn't even see my last show—

"And of course, that last show was absolutely brilliant," he goes on, eyes sparkling at the memory. "I've never seen Sonora so taken by a performance before. Of course, I follow her to every show she attends. Good way to keep tabs on who is ahead in the game."

Sure. If you counted swooning on stage and almost cracking her head open being "taken" by a performance.

Still, the words soothe something deep and aching in my soul. "You really liked it?"

The words tumble out before I can stop them, reeking of desperation. I almost cover my mouth, horrified as I am that I actually said them aloud. Raster doesn't seem bothered, however. "I should have known you were one to watch after that stunt you pulled at my party."

I stare at the next course, pulled pork tacos garnished with a mango chutney, my eyes burning. I've waited longer than I would ever admit to hear someone like Raster say something like that.

"You know what I have to offer a prospective competitor," Raster says, smoothing his napkin, suddenly all business. "I don't gamble or waste my time on luck. I pick winners."

I balk under his unblinking gaze. I hear every word he doesn't say, how easily I could meet the same fate as Cerulea if I disappoint him.

"What do you think? Would you like to be my competitor for Jester?"

Even though our entire conversation has been leading up to it, the question still surprises me. I turn around, half expecting to see Luc swagger out of the shadows, laughing at my guile.

The answer is automatic, already on the tip of my tongue. I try not to think of Cerulea.

"Yes, I'd love to."

CHAPTER
24

I leave dinner feeling more alive than I've felt in months. Even my stomach seems improved, the constant searing dulled to an ache. Although it's nearly midnight, the light of the city is as bright as noonday. Neon lights advertising everything from hotels to cage dancers blink and flash, designed to ensnare wandering eyes.

The city calls. Back at the Crown, I dress in a new outfit, a short emerald dress decorated in shimmering palm leaves. Tonight, there will be no mistaking me for a mere street performer. I don't know where I'm going, but the pull of the city is incredible. The same bellhop from earlier awaits in the elevator and I cringe, but he doesn't recognize me. Gawking, he hurries to hold the door for me.

"Where to, madam?"

I manage to bite back the bitter words that hover on the tip of my tongue and give him the floor number instead. The door attendants scurry to open the giant gold doors as I leave. The night air hits me in the same breath as the Crown's doors shut, hot and dry. Exhilaration spurs me to do something rash and reckless. Something exciting. Street performers vie for my attention, promising to show me wonders I could never dream of. It feels strange to be on the other side. I pass a stately older woman bedecked in furs, giggling as her photo is taken with two enormous men in nothing but leather chaps, their gleaming abs and teeth on full display.

"Pick a card! Any card."

A deck of cards is fanned in front of me, held by a gangly street performer in an absurd top hat. Normally I'd tell him to shove off, but something about tonight, something in the air perhaps, has me feeling dangerous. I pluck a card, feigning ignorance, even though I've used the same trick on tourists millions of times.

"Now what?"

"Keep it close, don't show me," the performer warns. "Take a good look at it, remember it."

I take my time studying the card. It's the king of serpents, an ominous card if ever there was one. The fair-haired king's sneer reminds me of Luc. I show the card to the few tourists who have stopped to watch.

"Got it."

"Now, place it back in the deck, very good."

The magician shuffles the deck, making the cards arc and dance. He's really not bad, although his banter could improve. His fingers flash in front of me as he theatrically pulls a card from the deck using nothing but magic. Telekinesis, the ability to move objects without touching them.

A gift any magician would kill for, and this is how he uses it?

"Madam, is this your card?"

It's the three of doves. I hold back a smile. "No."

The magician's brow creases, and I know I've thrown him, but he doesn't miss a beat.

"Ah, couldn't make it too easy on you now, could we? Is . . . this your card?"

Rook of pearls. I shake my head innocently. The magician is panicking now, rifling through the cards. The small crowd gathered around us mutters.

"Only joking, of course. Here is your card!"

Panting, he holds up the seven of serpents.

"Close," I say, "but my card was a king."

With a flourish, I grab a card from the purse of a tourist standing just behind him and waggle it in front of the performer's dumbfounded face. The king of serpents. I tuck the card in the magician's ridiculous hat brim, smirking, and melt into the crowd. Above me looms a billboard advertising Luc leaping off the Crown. I scowl at it.

"You can never resist showing off, can you?" The real Luc falls into step beside me, as though I've conjured him with my thoughts.

"You're one to talk," I counter, pretending to be interested in a necklace that costs five times what I made at the Saguaro. Maybe if I bore him, he'll leave.

"That one does your lovely eyes no justice." Mute, I watch as he removes an elegant emerald necklace and clasps it around my neck. I study myself in the mirror the vendor eagerly supplies. He's right, devils hang him. The emeralds bring out the green gold of my eyes, making them sparkle. I stare transfixed, very aware of Luc's fingers on my neck, still holding the clasp.

He clears his throat, removing his hand. "Told you."

"Too bad it costs a prince's ransom in gold," I say, removing the necklace reluctantly.

"I heard you're making that and more now," Luc says, watching me carefully. I replace the necklace on its bed of crushed black velvet. How does he already know? I've been in the Crown for less than a day. I'd kill to have the same eyes on him that he has on me.

"What exactly have you heard?" I ask, but before he can answer, a young man in a suit grabs my arm.

"Are you Mirage?" he asks.

"I am," I say warily.

"I saw your show. With the queen. It was *spectacular*. Easily the best show in Oasis."

Behind him, Luc snorts.

"Was it really the king's ghost?" the tourist goes on, seemingly oblivious to Luc.

I nod. To my surprise, the boy takes my hand and fervently presses his lips to my fingers. His mouth is hot, and I almost pull away in surprise.

"You, madam, are an artist."

I gape at Luc, who is struggling not to laugh.

"Could you . . . could you do it again? Here?"

Other voices chime in, startling me. A crowd is gathering, to the jewelry vendor's delight.

"Bring back my uncle!"

"My grandmother!"

"Please bring my son back!"

I hold up my hands and the crowd silences. I could get used to this.

"Unfortunately, I am no longer a street performer."

The crowd mutters and grumbles its disappointment. In front of me, the young man's face drops.

"But I am headlining for the Crown now. Come and see me live—"

Tourists are dispersing, shaking their heads. *What's the harm?* I think. Devils knows I could use the publicity. Clenching my fists, I summon my father's magic. A spirit, a weary-looking elderly woman shimmers into being. The crowd gasps.

"Who are you?" I demand.

The spirit sighs, as though irritated with me for disturbing her. "I am Regina."

"That's my grandmother!" A little boy pushes through the crowd, face awed. "Grandmama?"

The spirit squints at him. ". . . Henry? Henry, my boy!"

"It's me!" the child cries. "I've missed you, Grandmama!"

His arms reach for her, but I can hold her no longer, try as I might, and she fades to night, the boy's arms still reaching for her.

Around me, tourists sniffle, reach for handkerchiefs, daub at moistened eyes.

"Thank you," the little boy says reverently, wrapping tiny arms around my waist. I freeze as the crowd erupts into applause. I almost forgot about the audience, caught in the moment as much as they were. I kneel to the boy's level. With his dark curls and flushed cheeks, he can't be more than five.

"You're welcome," I say, wiping a lone tear that tracks down his rosy cheek. Reaching in his trousers, he removes a tiny vial of gold dust, probably given to him for a pony ride at the carousel.

"This is for you."

Before I can refuse, he disappears into the crowd. I stand up holding the vial, still warm from the boy's hands.

"That was excellent, quite extraordinary!" The young man from before shakes my hand, pumping it up and down. "I'm telling everyone I know about your show."

And then he's gone too.

"Well, that was heartwarming," Luc says, sidling next to me. "Conning the children now, are we?"

"Shut up," I say, but I barely hear him. This—this is what Cillian meant. I could make a killing each night with a reaction like that.

I wonder if it was a coincidence that the spirit I evoked tonight had a connection to someone in the crowd. Maybe the spirits come easier if there is someone they had a relationship to . . . I tuck the thought away to turn over later.

"Perhaps you're less useless than I thought," Luc muses, studying me intently. He's dressed simply today, in jeans and a T-shirt. A gold scorpion winking from a chain around his neck is the only bit of glitz on him. It hovers near his exposed chest, just visible above the V of his neckline.

When he catches me staring, he grins. I bristle.

"Excuse me?"

"Always so easily ruffled." He chuckles. "My darling Lisette, we really should just throw away the whole charade and get together already."

"Burn in all nine hells," I spit, but his grin only widens.

"Save some of that venom, you might need it."

An explosion down the alley drags my attention from Luc, but it's only a street performer, coughing and waving away a cloud of black sulfuric smoke.

I turn back to Luc, but he's gone.

"Can't you ever just leave like a normal person?" I yell at the smoke, which is already clearing, and although it's faint, I swear I can hear laughter.

Devils, he's awful. I reach a hand to straighten my dress, but it catches on something. Baffled, I stare down at the emerald necklace Luc recommended, innocently sparkling around my neck. I curse his sleight of hand.

How did I not see him put it there, or purchase it, in the first place? Knowing Luc, he probably stole it.

My fingers twitch, wanting to both rip the necklace from my throat and admire the way it glitters. It's a fitting gift, considering I feel almost the same about the necklace as I do him—somewhere between loathing and lust.

Reluctantly, I leave the necklace where it is, hating myself for enjoying the way it reflects the lights of the city.

The next day burns so hot, even the desert is listless. Lizards and jack-rabbits alike take to their holes to escape the afternoon sun, which beats on us relentlessly. In the distance, the red rock canyon looms. I used to think the canyon was manufactured with magic, the alternating layers of red and white rock too beautiful to be natural. Green scrubby bushes dot the hills, and only a few puffy white clouds are scattered across a vast blue sky.

"I don't know how you stand it," Queen Sonora says. Her cheeks are flushed almost to the roots of her hair, and sweat beads on her brow like diamonds. Her entire retinue follows at a distance, carrying everything from voluminous tents to relax under, to glass jugs filled with water, balanced on the heads of servants. There's even a magician forming delicate veils of ice so thin it melts at a touch, to drape on the queen at a moment's notice. It's both ridiculous and expensive, and I savor every bit of the excess.

I stretch my legs; the heat seems to collect and prickle uncomfortably behind my knees. I've taken the queen out into the desert in the hopes that if she is able to acclimate, her suffering might decrease. My own blood has thinned to water after so many years in the desert, and the heat hardly bothers me anymore. Of course, there is also the fact that I'm still not sure where I stand with the queen. I know she needs my father's gift, which grants me some security, but I still remember well the threat, subtle as poison, that ended our last conversation. Being the best performer on the Noose is no longer enough. I must show the queen that I'm not just another entertainer; I'm indispensable. We've only gone a handful of steps into the desert and already she seems on the verge of wilting. I have my work cut out for me, it seems.

"It's not like Terraca, is it?" I ask. I've never been to the capitol, although my father and Edward often went there for business. I still remember Edward telling me about the towering evergreens and constant rain hazier than a cloud-covered sky.

The queen's face takes on a wistfulness.

"I miss the rain. And the greenery. Everything is dead or as desiccated as dried meat here." She laughs, a sound more bitter than amused. "I feel like a fish out of water."

"You get used to it," I offer. After living my whole life under an open sky, the thought of being surrounded by trees, trapped by the clouds, makes me feel claustrophobic.

"I hope I never do," she says, shuddering delicately. The queen turns her face toward the infinite blue above us, rubbing a wan hand across her brow.

"If only it would rain . . . the plants here could use a little mercy."

She eyes a cactus squatting next to her.

"The plants here thrive in the heat," I say, smiling. The cactus has put out blooms, bright floppy petals that are as soft as kitten ears.

"As hostile as the environment they are placed in," the queen murmurs, more to herself than me. "Does it affect people the same as plants, I wonder?"

For this, I have no answer.

My heart sinks. Perhaps this trip was a mistake. A Carcan vulture swoops lazy circles over our group, pronouncing my efforts to please the queen dead. Peering up at the intricate rock formations above us, squinting, the queen's face sours.

"All that red dust. My dress will be ruined."

I groan inwardly. I'd hoped the queen might finally see the beauty of the Red Canyon Desert. It's very different from the Adabi deserts of the east, with their mountains of white sand and little else. Although Oasis is the biggest attraction here, there are many people who come for the magnificent canyon vistas and stunning red rock landscapes.

"We can go back if you like—"

Without warning, the queen lets out a cry and bolts forward. Heart seizing, I search for the source of her alarm, praying we haven't stumbled upon a rock rattler taking an afternoon snooze.

Crouching next to a gnarled cactus, she fingers the thick pod that hangs from one of the branches. "Come, look!" she says, gesturing emphatically, and it's then I realize she isn't displeased.

She's excited.

More so than I've ever seen her. Suddenly unaware of the red dust that cakes the hem of her dress, she plucks the pod, handling it with something close to reverence.

"Get me a stone," she instructs, and half the servants drop their wares, scrambling in the dust for a rock. After choosing a suitable one, she strikes the pod with it until it cracks with a hollow thud, revealing a bright pink fruit inside.

"Kanab cactus fruit. Also known as dragon's belly fruit. Taste it."

I take the proffered fruit, sniffing before taking a tentative bite. It smells like the knifefruits of the tropics, bright, with a hint of tanginess. I suck at the juice, scraping the meat with my teeth.

"It's very good," I say, handing her the pod, and I mean it. The fruit is refreshing in the unrelenting heat. She barely seems to hear, focused on picking out the black seeds riddled along the inside.

"The kanab fruit can stave off dehydration," she explains, scraping remnants of fruit from the seeds. "You can survive on the fruit alone, if need be."

"Amazing," I murmur. The desert truly is a wonder.

"That's not the interesting part," she says, delicate brow wrinkling, clearly under the impression that I'm daft. "The seeds, when cracked, have an oil that can extend one's life by a year."

"Wow," I say, looking at the fruit with a renewed interest.

"They're very rare, and very valuable." Using a small bone knife to saw off several more pods, the queen wraps them in a soft cloth and pockets them. "Excellent. Tonight, we will enjoy the fruit at dinner, and you will be rewarded with one of the seeds, as a sign of my gratitude."

Surprised, I drop into a curtsy. "Your Majesty, there's no need—"

"I insist." Leaving no room for argument, the queen turns to snap at the servants, although it's clear her mood is much improved. Now eager to explore the desert's bounty, she leads the group, pointing out various wonders and sights, while I struggle to keep up.

"Are you coming or not?" she turns to ask, and I can only nod, still reeling from her unexpected approval, like the sun peeking out from behind a sky full of clouds.

With Iko curled at her feet, Yasmin lounges in the Crown lobby, ignorant of the receptionist scowling at the giant cat. Reclining in a plush armchair, she picks at fingernails as black as Iko's coat, seemingly oblivious to the queen's passing retinue. When she sees me, however, she leaps from the chair casually, tossing her violet hair. Iko remains in front of the fire, although his yellow eyes track Yasmin's every movement.

"Mirage! I thought you'd never get back. Where have you been?"

I struggle to contain the joy that has filled me all afternoon. "I was just showing the queen the beauties of the desert."

Yasmin cocks her head. "Is that supposed to be some kind of a weird metaphor?"

Laughing, I shove her. Allowing herself a wry smile, she taps my arm.

"I need your help."

Although I'm exhausted from chasing the queen from plant to plant, I'm intrigued. "With what?"

Yasmin snaps her fingers at Iko, who stretches out, shining claws extending briefly, but doesn't budge from his spot.

"Useless thing," she says fondly, shaking her head. "I need your help coming up with ideas for my next show."

"Excuse me, *madam*—" The surly receptionist makes his way toward us, shining shoes tapping against the tile. "There are no animals allowed at the Crown."

"They let you in though, didn't they?" Yasmin says sweetly, as the receptionist's face pinks.

"If you do not get that *thing* out of this lobby . . ." he splutters. Sensing the insult, or perhaps just the tension, Iko lets out a low growl in the receptionist's direction.

"Easy, baby," Yasmin croons to Iko, snapping her fingers at him again. "Come."

This time the big cat complies, brushing up against the receptionist as he passes, who visibly starts. The cat seats himself on muscled haunches at Yasmin's side, gleaming eyes never leaving the receptionist.

"I'll take you up to my room," I say, hiding a smile. The receptionist's eyes dart to me, then back to Iko.

"I'm afraid I cannot allow that—" the receptionist begins, swallowing hard as Iko bats at one of his overly polished shoes.

"Good thing I take orders from Queen Sonora, not you," I say, nodding at Yasmin. We leave the still-blustering receptionist in the lobby.

"Devils, what a prat!" Yasmin crows, throwing herself on my bed. Finding a thick rug, Iko drops to the floor and gets straight to work cleaning one massive paw. *The housekeepers are going to have a fit over all that black fur,* I think wryly. With an exhausted sigh, I collapse into the desk chair.

"You said you needed help?"

Suddenly serious, Yasmin pulls herself up. "I'm a has-been."

"What do you mean?" I ask, confused. Yasmin's show is anything but boring; her Night Tiger act was named one of the "Must-see Oasis Shows" last year.

"I'm sure you heard about the attack?" Yasmin's mouth is tight. Iko's tail flicks as he watches her closely. I nod. Everyone in Oasis knew about the mauling, even though the Panther did its best to cover it up after the fact.

"One of your tigers lost it mid-act, right?"

Yanking up her skirt, Yasmin reveals mutilated flesh, a crisscrossing of twisted scarring covering her thigh. I try my best not to wince, but the damage is obvious.

"That's what the Panther told everyone," she says, replacing her skirt. "Calliope was one of my most gentle tigers. I hand reared her as a cub. She *never* would have done this."

"Are you saying she was provoked?" I ask, not following. Yasmin shrugs, leaning back against my pillows.

"Hard to say. All I know is after the attack, Natalia suddenly had a very good excuse to retire me as headliner and hire Luc in my place."

Her eyes follow me, daring me to contradict her.

"I mean, wild animals are unpredictable . . ." I trail off.

"Not Calliope." Yasmin's eyes flash.

My head spins. Yasmin's attitude seems to border on paranoia, and yet her suggestion makes a degree of sense. Although Yasmin's act generates a fair amount of revenue for the Panther, the commission paid to the hotel responsible for finding the next Jester is more than her act could pull in in a year.

She's not completely insane. Especially considering the timing of Luc being hired . . . I file the information away, knowing it's valuable but not knowing how, exactly.

"That explains why you hate Luc so much," I finally manage. Yasmin grips the bedspread.

"'Hate' is such a shallow word for what I feel for Luc," she says, throwing me a bare smile, devoid of any real emotion. "If I could find a way to make sure he stayed dead during his next show, I would."

Taking a deep breath, she tosses my notebook at me. "That's why we have each other though, right? Together, maybe we can finally bring him down."

Without meaning to, my hand goes to the necklace at my throat, the necklace Luc gave me. The gems are cold under my fingers.

I laugh weakly. "What are friends for?"

CHAPTER
25

O*bsession. It dances in the high judge's bloodshot eyes, in the heavily marked* Book of Law *he flips through late into the evening. Night after night he works, long after everyone in his household has gone to bed. There has to be something, something he can use to convict a king.*

But there is nothing. The laws have not been made in favor of the people, after all. They have been made with monarchy in mind, shielding the king from even his own laws. It doesn't matter how many bylaws or loopholes the high judge finds. None of them apply to his sovereign. The king is, by all accounts, untouchable.

Removing his spectacles, rubbing eyes that stick from exhaustion and overuse, he sets down his books. They cannot save him or his son, not this time.

But the law is not his only option. If the king cannot be tried and convicted by the usual measures, the high judge will have to think outside the law.

After all, not even a king is invincible.

CHAPTER
26

I need to prove to the queen that my father's gift is not merely practical but entertaining too. And given the debacle that was my last show, I'm struggling to come up with a way to do just that. Which is how I find myself at Cillian's bookshop once again, hoping desperately that another lesson will jog the fog that has settled into my mind, a combination of both fear and exhaustion.

"Let's try something new, shall we?" Cillian paces the small room, absently kicking away the loose papers that evoking the last spirit unsettled.

After all our lessons, I'm not sure there is anything new left to try.

"Can you evoke two spirits at once?"

Closing my eyes, fighting against the exhaustion that threatens to consume me, I summon the magic. I'm getting quicker at it, although after the parade of spirits I've summoned in the last several days, it feels like tapping a drained resource.

I've pushed my magic and my energy to its limit the last week.

"Little Lis."

There are a multitude of memories contained in those two words. Hiding in the kitchens sharing cherry tartlets when Papa was in one of his stormier moods. Stealing Hattie's bonnets, stifling muffled laughter as we tied them on the ponies. Thousands of tears dried by his warm hand.

My eyes fly open.

Hovering before me, with a look of such longing my eyes water, is my brother.

"Edward."

Cillian watches, interested, as I reach for my brother's outstretched hand. It's like touching mist—cold and insubstantial.

"You're in trouble," Edward notes, the same sympathetic crease I remember from childhood furrowing his shimmering brow. I try hard not to look at the blackness that oozes from a line that looks like a smile across his neck.

"Edward, I've done something terrible—"

Edward's head jerks back and turns to look behind him, as though he can hear something we cannot. "My time here is limited, Lisette. I cannot help you. Justice must be delivered to the guilty."

His words, echoes of the same words my father said, chill me to my core. The pit of my stomach feels like lead.

"Me?" I say, in little more than a whisper, but Edward is already fading. "Don't go, please, I need you, Edward!"

Scrabbling at the air, I reach for him as his spirit returns to wherever I called him from.

Furious, I try to rouse the magic, but it's dormant inside of me, thick and slow, like molasses. I let out a frustrated scream and then Cillian is there, green eyes frightened.

"Lisette, you need to sit down."

I fight him, but he's stronger and manages to force me into a chair. I'm sweating all over and shaking, as if wracked with fever.

"I need to bring him back!"

"You can't. Lisette, listen to me. You've strained your magic. If you keep trying, you'll kill yourself."

The panic in Cillian's voice, uncustomary and raw, stops me. But I continue to stare at the spot where my brother was.

"Your arms . . ." Cillian takes one of my arms, where the blackness spirals up from my glove and disappears into my sleeves. Absently tugging up the sleeve, I follow the path of the blackened veins, where they form a spiderweb across my shoulder.

"Magic poisoning," Cillian breathes. "I've only read about it. If it reaches your heart, you'll die."

I hear his voice as if from a great distance. "How many more spirits can I summon before that happens?"

Cillian stares at me the same way he stared at the ghosts. "Lisette . . ."

"Don't tell me I shouldn't try, just give me the answer." I tug my glove up even though it barely conceals the evidence of my own madness, trying not to think of the magic poisoning, foul and sludgy in my veins and ever closer to my heart.

Cillian's face has a look of helplessness; he knows better than to argue with me. "I don't know," he admits quietly. "But listen to me, you can't bring your brother back anyway. A spirit can only be evoked once."

Edward's face, as gentle in death as in life, haunts my thoughts. I brush forgotten wetness from my eyes.

"Don't worry, I wasn't planning on it."

Cillian's relief is palpable. "Thank the devils. Go see a healer, there must be someone who can help you—"

"I'll deal with it after my next show."

I leave before he can unleash the arguments that hover on his tongue, leave before he can see me cry again.

Being the queen's favorite is exhausting. Although at least the social engagements are limited, what with the queen feeling too ill most days to tolerate anything other than a darkened room. Everything seems to sicken her, from the too-bright lights of the Crown to the desert heat. Although I'd never admit it out loud, her constant neediness is wearing on me. After an entire morning spent listening to the queen's numerous complaints, I finally manage to escape, claiming a migraine of my own. In spite of my pounding headache, my feet take me to the Crown stage. I've spent every moment away from the queen here, rehearsing my act. Raster doesn't seem to care if I die of exhaustion before I make it to the final show.

Closing my eyes, I reach for the magic, but it resists my touch.

"Come on . . ."

I strain for it, grasping. It feels thick in my blood, oily and foul, a canker to be rooted out. The outline of a spirit forms as I gasp, my vision going double, but I can barely make it out before my tenuous hold on the magic slips and it disappears.

"No!"

I collapse onstage, chest heaving. *It's killing me,* I think, stars popping in my vision. My father's magic is destroying me from the inside out. I can't seem to muster the energy to care.

"Devils, you look awful."

Luc's voice, taunting, floats down to me. *Somehow he always knows when I'm at my worst,* I think, the stage lights dancing in my fevered vision. I don't bother to watch his advance across the stage. His shiny shoes cross to where I lie, gasping like a caught fish.

"Better than you," I manage. Luc lifts up my chin so I'm forced to look him in the eyes.

"If that poor excuse for an insult isn't proof you're unwell, I don't know what is."

"I'm fine," I slur, jerking my hand away. The stage lights swirl above us, and I wonder what he'll do if I pass out. Probably leach the secrets from my own heart.

"What's wrong with your hand?"

Halfheartedly, I yank my hand away, tugging up the long lace glove, although it's too late. Luc peels the glove off, his eyebrows shooting up at the sight of my blackened arm. His fingers trace the paths of my veins.

"You're mixed up in some serious stuff, aren't you." It isn't a question. His eyes are golden, like melting honey.

"None of your business."

"What, I wonder, will happen when this—" he points to the thickest vein in my forearm. "—reaches your heart?"

I've been wondering that myself. Snatching my hand from his, I replace the glove and close my eyes. I could sleep right here, if I wasn't so worried about what Luc would try if I did. My eyes fly open as the bodice of my dress is ripped open, revealing my thin undergarments.

"Excuse you!" I cry indignantly, throwing my arms across my chest. Luc ignores me, following the blackness that covers both sets of ribs. He lets out a low whistle.

"How are you not dead?"

"Hating you keeps me alive," I say, the room swimming in front of me. Luc ignores me, probing the veins at my wrist, then fixes me with a serious look.

"You've had kanab seeds."

The queen's gift, I realize with a jolt. I'd eaten the seed without much thought, more thrilled with the queen's approval than the gift itself.

"Well, I hope you have more," Luc continues. "I've never seen magic poisoning this bad before."

His hands are warm and I'm so tired. Maybe death will be a relief.

"Just the one," I say, letting my eyes drift shut.

"I could heal you."

My eyes flutter open again at the suggestion.

"I'm not sure I could do anything about that—" he gestures to my veins "—but I could try. At the very least, I could heal your exhaustion."

"For a price, I'm sure."

"Of course," Luc says, a wry smile twisting his features. "But not what you think."

There are any number of tortures Luc could bargain for. I'd be better off pandering my soul to some actual devil. In the distance I can hear the stage manager bellowing at a stagehand somewhere backstage. I have a show in mere hours that I'm woefully underprepared for. And I'm on the verge of collapsing from exhaustion and magic poisoning. Although I don't trust Luc, at this point, I don't have a choice.

"Fine," I wheeze, trying to struggle to my feet. "But I need to tell Raster—"

Luc picks me up in a heap of skirts. "That pompous git will figure it out, I'm sure. You, on the other hand, are teetering on the edge of consciousness, and I'd prefer you awake for this."

I don't argue as he carries me away.

He takes me to my own room, carrying me up the seemingly endless flight of stairs. Crushed to his chest, I notice that even in my fog, I can smell him. Like smoke and citrus. He sets me gently on top of the covers, then sets about assembling a number of seemingly random objects: a delicate bone, a shard of sandstone, some pungent alcohol, and a blood-spattered handkerchief. I'm quiet while he organizes his tools, thinking back on his past shows.

"Are you going to kiss me?"

Luc looks up, surprised.

My face heats at his expression. "That's what you do to the girls in your show. I thought maybe that is how your healing works."

His face is serious, almost somber. "It is. Are you afraid to pay such a price?"

Afraid of kissing my mortal enemy? Afraid doesn't come close. "Of course not."

Before I can prepare myself, he's crossed to where I lie, completely defenseless, on the bed. Taking the sides of my face in his rough hands, he lifts me to him, pressing his lips to mine. At first, I can only manage a startled gasp in response. His lips are like fire, and devils, it's no wonder girls are willing to be stabbed for the opportunity to kiss him. My body reacts instinctually. My hands tangle in his long hair, pulling him toward me. The beginnings of a beard burn against my lips. Stars flash across my vision as I drown myself in his kiss.

He's the first to pull away, disoriented. "What the devil was that?"

We're both panting. I reach a trembling hand to my lips, swollen and raw. "What do you mean? Did it not work?"

"You idiot," he says scathingly. "I was joking."

It takes me a moment to register. "*What?*"

He smirks at my reddening cheeks. "I had no idea you were so gullible."

"But the girl in your show—the one with the necklace—I saw her, she almost died!" I protest, refusing to believe he's gotten the better of me once again. "But then you kissed her and—"

Luc waves me away. "That was just to add a bit of drama. The same old routine gets dull after a while."

I stare at him, lacking the energy to stab him but desperately wishing to.

"And, of course, she was quite lovely. Nothing like you though." His eyes dance as he douses the edge of the blood-stained handkerchief in the alcohol.

"I'm going to kill you—"

"You don't have the energy to kill me," he reminds me, and although I'll die before I admit it, he's right. The room spins and weakness drags me back onto the pillows with a groan.

"I'll kill you later," I vow. Luc rolls his eyes as he engulfs the handkerchief in flames.

"Sure, sure. Give me your hand."

I eye the flaming handkerchief, which crackles merrily in his outstretched hand.

"You're wise not to trust me, you know," he says. There is danger in his words, but somehow, the honesty in them gives me the confidence to extend my hand to him. I cry out as he smothers it in the handkerchief. There's a brief flare of pain and then only warmth, as the flames dance across my infected skin. My fingers burn more at his touch than that of the flames.

Luc watches the progress of the flames up my arm intently, working his index finger in circles across the veins. I flush at the memory of his lips on my skin, hating myself for wishing his kiss really was the cure.

"How does it work then? If not kissing, then how?"

I'm blushing again, but Luc doesn't seem to notice. He doesn't even look at me, as the flames on my arm purge the infection.

"A magician never reveals his secrets."

I roll my eyes, which breaks some of the tension. Taking the handkerchief, Luc catches the fire as though it were a butterfly in the cloth, the last of the flames tickling my arm. I feel warm all over, like I've just had a hot bath.

And clean.

To my surprise, my veins flow unimpeded, a healthy greenish-blue again.

"You healed it!"

Luc says nothing, only takes my hand again, inspecting the veins there. "It's only temporary."

His fingers catch on my father's ring, snag on the red-black stone.

"What a lovely ring," he says, and before I can stop him, he slips the ring from my finger easily, holding it up to the light.

"Give it back." I keep my voice even, terrified he'll realize how much that ring really means to me. My blood surges at the loss of magic, as though free.

"Garnet, isn't it? And what a setting! Gold, if I'm not mistaken, all the way through, no gilt here."

"It was my father's," I say, even though my fingers twitch, eager to strangle him. "And as it's a family heirloom, I'd like it back."

Luc ignores me, holding the garnet up to the light. "Three carats, at least. The mark of the high judge, just there. And could it be? The source of your magic poisoning too! Quite an heirloom."

He knows. Oh devils, he knows. I reach for the ring, but Luc easily snatches it away. When I pry open his fist, the ring is gone.

"That's a fun little trick," Luc says, waving both hands to show they're empty. "Now you see it, now you don't."

"Give me the ring!"

"I don't think I will," Luc says, tapping a finger against his teeth. "Not yet anyway. I have something I'd like you to do for me first. And if this ring is as crucial to your act as I think it is, you'll do anything I say. Right?"

I gape at him, speechless.

"Right?" he prompts, an infuriating grin on his lips. "And do say it nicely, little Lisette."

"I'm going to hang you up by your entrails," is the best I can give him.

Luc pouts. "I said, *nicely*. I'd hate for your pretty ring to disappear for good, or worse yet—break."

"You wouldn't dare!"

Luc's smile is as sharp as broken glass. "Oh, I would. So, I'd advise you not to be tiresome, dear Lisette, and do as I say."

I grind my teeth, but no solution is forthcoming. I can't believe just moments ago I wanted to kiss him. Now, I'd rather stab him. But I can't even murder him, as satisfying as that would be, because then I'll never find the ring.

"Fine." The word growls out of me.

"I'm sorry, I didn't quite hear you."

Luc's face is serene, the countenance of an angel. I want to scratch his eyes out.

"I'll do whatever you ask." I keep my voice pleasant, although Luc would be a fool to miss the undercurrent of rage.

"Excellent!" Luc claps his hands together. "Follow me."

I have never been so angry in my life.

"I had a suspicion that ring was special," Luc crows to himself as we walk along. "I just had to wait for you to do something stupid enough for me to get a good look."

I glower at the back of his head. I'm not bound, at least not in any physical sense, yet I follow as obediently as a pup. I can't even sink a knife into his back, and he knows it, not even bothering to keep an eye on me as he congratulates himself.

"Where are we going?" I grit out, trying to change the subject.

"You'll see," is his enigmatic reply. I gnash my teeth. The Noose is filled with tourists, and I have a strange moment of disorientation when I realize I might never have to entertain on these streets again. If I win this competition, I'll perform in the Crown for the rest of my career. The thought is enough to bolster me, keep me from punching Luc and making a break for it. I'll get the ring back, I tell myself, taking deep breaths. Once I've done whatever he has planned, I'll get the ring back, and then I'll destroy him in the competition.

This thought is enough to keep me from doing anything stupid, at least.

Stars dot the desert sky, although behind the glow of the city, it's hard to make them out.

"All the wonders of mankind will never outshine the stars," Luc murmurs, and it's then I realize he's stopped and is following my gaze.

"Haven't we already?" I ask, tone thick with sarcasm, gesturing to the fluorescent overload around us.

"Hardly," Luc says. "Oasis is the brightest place on this earth. And yet, in spite of the billions of light years the stars' light travels, we can still see them, in spite of Oasis's attempts to drown them out."

His voice is awed, almost reverent. It's an odd sentiment coming from someone who lets a snake bite him once a week for a few claps. I again get that odd, itchy feeling that maybe I don't know Luc as well as I thought I did.

We've stopped in front of the Panther. Shaped like a diamond, balanced on one wicked point, the Panther is a combination of engineering and magical ingenuity. It glitters malevolently, its shining black surface seeming to swallow the lights of the Noose. There are rumors that it's even grander than the Crown, although I suspect most of the rumors are fueled by the mob queen and owner of the Panther, Natalia herself.

While I stare up at the rows of windows, Luc saunters right up to the bouncer. The man nods deferentially to Luc and then me. Luc takes my arm as though I'm his date, rather than his prisoner, and the man scurries to hold the heavy glass doors for us.

The Panther is everything the Crown is not. Loud, dark, and gaudy. The Jungle Club takes up the entire first floor, which means guests are forced to pass through it to get inside the hotel. Two lithe women in furs and little more, long hair tossed down their backs, greet us at the doors.

"Luc is here!"

They twine around him like cats, purring.

"Have you come to play?" One of the women, the taller of the two, runs a hand down his chest. I clear my throat and Luc extricates himself regretfully.

"Afraid not today, loves. I'm here on business."

Their sharp green eyes turn on me, noticing for the first time that Luc didn't come alone.

"Business." The blonde chuckles. "Is that what you're calling it now?"

"Save me a dance." Luc winks at them and they finally let us pass. The floors mimic the exterior of the Panther, gleaming slabs of black marble cut in diamond shapes, the stone reflecting the lights of the club. With some horror, I realize I've left a trail of dusty red footprints, marring the exquisite black stone. Before I can so much as drag a toe across the mess, try to hide it somehow, the stone seems to absorb it, once more pristine. Luc follows my gaze and smirks.

"Don't be fooled, my darling Lisette. The stone may not remember your sins here, but I certainly will."

"When you said you needed my help, I thought you had something more serious in mind," I shout over the skull-vibrating sounds of the music. Luc just shakes his head, pulling me past the throngs of clubbers toward the VIP tables in back. The Jungle Club is aptly named, all heat and sweat, bodies gleaming in the low light. It occurs to me that I'm vastly overdressed in this place, where flesh is as much on display as entertainment.

This time I'm not surprised when Luc bypasses yet another armed bouncer through a set of gauzy curtains. However, I am surprised by the almost complete silence that envelops us when the curtains fall shut behind us, admitting only the faintest thumps from the club beyond. The man standing guard must be an audial manipulator. I've heard of their use in places like this, altering sound waves to ensure complete audial privacy, even when people are seated right next to each other.

"Luc! Don't tell me you brought a lover to my table."

I tense at the raspy voice of a smoker and turn to face the speaker. Watching us carefully from one of the intimate tables is an older woman with sleek black hair and heavily lined eyes. She's an interesting-looking woman, with sharp, intelligent eyes that seem to miss nothing, high cheekbones, and a nose that looks twice broken. She's not a handsome woman, but she is a striking one.

"Hello, Natalia." Luc is all charm. "You know I wouldn't dream of it."

Natalia. The woman seated across from us is none other than the mob queen of Oasis. There's a reason the queen's rule is limited here. Everyone knows Oasis was built from the gold of mobsters, but Natalia reigns over them all. She has a monopoly on the Noose luxury hotels, with the Panther being her crown jewel.

"I can't see what other purpose she might serve," Natalia bites out, casting me a disdainful look.

Even though I don't even know this woman, the judgment still stings.

Luc produces my ring as if from the air itself and tosses it to the mob queen, who catches it easily. I swallow my protest as Natalia inspects my father's ring with the practiced ease of a jeweler.

"This is the ring of the high judge," she says, looking up. "A valuable little bauble, to be sure, but hardly worth interrupting my dinner for."

"It holds the high judge's magic."

At this, Natalia's thin eyebrows disappear into her fringe. Pulling out a tiny silver loupe, she inspects the ring more carefully, running a finger over the deep engravings along the sides.

"Sit."

Luc takes the seat across from her and gestures for me to take the one next to him. The remains of a steak dinner litter the table, half devoured.

"Who is she?" Natalia pockets the loupe as well as the ring—to my dismay—her sharp gaze darting to me.

"Lisette Schopfer, daughter of the high judge."

"The queen's new favorite," Natalia muses, suddenly interested. "You stole your father's magic?"

I can't tell if she's impressed or appalled.

"Yes," I admit. I could lie, but something tells me the mob queen has a low tolerance for deception.

Natalia does not react, simply picks up her knife and fork and continues eating as though we're not there. The knife she uses to slice into her bleeding steak is almost comically disproportionate to her other silverware. The hilt is studded with jewels and a carved golden lion, frozen in a snarl, eyes two chips of emerald. Bloody juices run down the polished tang.

"That's the Royal Crest!" The realization bursts out of me before I can stop it. I wince as soon as the words are out, wishing I could stuff them back in.

Natalia finishes chewing before responding. "The king's personal knife, yeah."

She stabs another piece of meat viciously. It seems an insult to such a fine blade.

"I take it you don't like the king."

Natalia takes her time, washing down the heavy mouthful with a swallow of beer. "On the contrary, I adored him."

The knife scratches between her teeth, removing strings of fat and gristle.

"Respect, however . . ." She licks the knife clean and smiles. "The king never had that from me."

"Her magic poisoning was quite extensive by the time I realized," Luc cuts in. "I healed her, but . . ."

"But it's only temporary."

Luc nods. Natalia considers this, twirling the knife idly. "It could work."

Although I'm dying to ask what, I keep my jaw clamped shut. Natalia settles back in her chair, hands laced behind her head.

"How much access do you have to the queen?"

The question is directed at me, but it's Luc who answers.

"At least several hours a day, one on one."

"What exactly do you need from me?" I break in. "Because I won't hurt the queen, if that's what you're planning."

Natalia's eyes glitter. "Do I look like someone who wants the queen dead?"

Luc shoots me a look. "Nobody is suggesting that. What we need is information, someone close to the queen to confirm some suspicions . . ."

"Do you love our dear sovereign, Lisette?" Natalia cuts in. Her voice is as sharp as the king's knife. "Does her goodness, her *compassion* inspire you?"

"Natalia—" Luc tries to calm her, but she's only just beginning.

"Funny you should be so protective of the woman who framed your father for murder."

Her words have their intended effect, a knife to the gut.

"What are you talking about?"

"You're dismissed," Natalia says, snatching another bloody bite. The juices pearl in the corners of her lips. Luc looks ready to strangle me. I stand up, still reeling.

"What do you mean, the queen framed my father for murder?"

"Here, your ring."

Natalia tosses the heavy ring without looking at me. It lands between us with a thunk, the garnet glittering up at me like an eye. I stare at it, not understanding.

"You mean . . . I can just leave?"

"Are you kidding me?" Luc bursts out, standing up. "I finally bring you what you want and—"

"I am not interested in wasting my time," Natalia shoots back, eyes steely. Luc drops his head reluctantly under her glower. Her eagle eyes turn to me.

"If you truly believe your father murdered the king, then go your way and live the rest of your life as the queen's little pet. What concern is it to me?"

What concern, indeed.

I should leave now, before I get in any deeper. But Natalia's words snag as intended, catching me as cleverly as any snare. The weight of the ring, of a chance at my father's—and therefore *my*—redemption drags me back down in my seat.

"Tell me," I say, keeping my voice soft.

Plates of a rich chocolate cake are brought in by a bland-faced server, as the remnants of Natalia's dinner are cleared. I pick at mine, impatient to hear Natalia's theory. As though savoring my impatience as much as her dessert, she doesn't speak until the last thick bite is gone and the dishes are cleared. Then she settles back, picking at her teeth again with the knife.

"What do you know about the queen?" I venture. It's obvious she's punishing me still, and one wrong word could send her into another fit.

"The bloody queen," Natalia mutters, throwing down the knife with a clatter. "And how fares dear Sonora? As pale and vapid as always?"

"She does not like the heat," I say, still unwilling to betray my queen.

"Of course she doesn't," Natalia says. "I'll admit, even I don't know if I really believe that washed-up madwoman is truly capable of murder."

She twists at one of many rings weighing down her spindly fingers as I seize gratefully upon the subject.

"You really don't believe my father killed the king?"

Natalia's eyes flick to mine like a vulture appraising a bit of roadkill.

Luc answers for her. "The high judge was found near the king's bed-side the night he was murdered. For such a careful man, don't you find that a bit too convenient? Suspicious, even? And of course, there's always the question of motive. Why would the loyal high judge murder the king? It just doesn't make sense."

Luc crosses his arms as though that settles it, and my heart sinks.

"That's it? That's your evidence?"

Luc's eyebrow rises at the flatness in my tone.

"My father hated the king," I go on. "He would have murdered him in a heartbeat, if he could find a way."

I remember the sleepless nights he spent poring over his texts, obsessed to the brink of madness, trying to find a way to incriminate an infallible king.

To make him pay for the death of my brother.

I lean back in my seat, hating the old disappointment that washes over me.

"We have other . . . evidence," Luc says, glancing at Natalia. Her face remains indifferent as she inspects her teeth in the reflection of the blade. "Your father was not the only one who hated the king."

"But the *queen*?" I ask. I'm desperate for anything, any kind of hope I can cling to that might prove my father's innocence. But for the life of me, I cannot picture meek, sickly Sonora killing her husband.

"No one hated the king more than the queen," Luc says with conviction. "I'm sure even you've heard the rumors of his rampant unfaithfulness."

"What king is ever faithful to his wife?" I scoff. "If you cannot convince even me of my own father's innocence, I fear your task a greater one than you realize."

"It is not our job to convince you," Natalia finally answers. "If there is even a chance that your father is innocent—the slightest shred of hope—would you not do anything to redeem him? Redeem yourself?"

Even with my face held in a carefully composed mask, I can feel her reading me as easily as if my thoughts were written on my face. The hope that pounds through me with every beat of my heart.

"Your father is innocent. It is up to you to prove it," Natalia says, tossing the king's knife on the table with a clatter.

I pick up the ring, relaxing as I slide it back on my finger, knowing it's safe from Luc. It's still possible she's lying. Using me. But deep down, I have my own suspicions about the night the king died. About my cowardly father being capable of not only murder, but murder of the highest authority in the land. Something about it never added up.

"What do you need from me?"

Natalia clasps bony fingers in front of her stomach, leaning back in her seat. "It's quite simple. You get close to the queen, learn her secrets, find out what happened on the night of her husband's death."

"That's hardly simple!" I burst out. That's their grand plan?

Natalia's eyebrows, thin, black painted lines, rise at my insolence. "In exchange for any useful information you provide, Luc will heal your magic poisoning."

It's a fair deal, fairer than I had reason to expect, but I hesitate just the same. What they're asking is treason. And if the queen truly is a murderer, do I really want to know?

"Don't forget your precious ring," Luc says, sharply, sensing my hesitance. "I can make it disappear again easily."

"Peace, child." Natalia flashes a warning smile at Luc, lipstick stains on her upper teeth. "You forget, persuasion is always more effective than force."

"I'll do it," escapes my mouth.

The words surprise even me. If there's any chance my father was innocent, there's no way I won't take it.

Natalia's smile widens and it occurs to me then that perhaps I've made a terrible mistake. Before I can take back my words, however, I'm escorted from the table, Luc's smug grin burned into my vision.

CHAPTER
27

The urge to summon his dead son is like an itch, one he knows he cannot scratch. He will not waste his son's final words on sentiment. Instead, he will find a way to convict the king, letting his son's testimony be the noose that steals the king's final, lying breaths.

If only, devils be damned, he could find the law that would condemn the king.

The door to his study creaks open, forcing him to abandon the obscure text he's pored over for the last twelve hours straight.

Shrouded in moonlight, the girl stands in front of him, so solemnly that for a moment he wonders if, in his exhaustion, he has accidentally summoned a spirit. The clenching of the girl's hands on the Book of Laws, his Book of Laws, brings him to the present.

"Papa, I am ready for the Apprentice's Exam."

He stares at her, surprised when she meets his gaze, shoulders proud in contrast to the way she stands with the book in front of her, as if to shield

*herself from him. Her words have hooks, hooks that sink into his aching
bones, remind him of his loss.*

"You are only a child," he says, harsher than he intends.

*"I'm fourteen. Most apprentices begin at twelve," she responds, and he
knows in this moment that she has an argument prepared for every one of
his objections. Foolish girl, he thinks fondly, although his heart squeezes at
the sight of her, where his son should stand. Perhaps she would have made a
decent judge in another life, but it matters not.*

"No."

*He uses the same voice he uses to pass sentence, the tone that no one, not
even a king, dares argue with. Omniscient. Unyielding.*

"I can pass," she insists, stubborn. "I know I can, just give me a chance—"

"No!"

The word rips out of him, making her jump. Let that be the end of it,
he thinks.

*But the infernal girl won't quit. "Papa, I know I could be just as good as
Edward—"*

"Enough!"

*His hands tremble, as he longs to strike out at the girl, return by physical
blow the pain she's wrought upon him by saying that name. Sucking in great,
gulping breaths, the high judge searches wildly for the control he's lost.*

*"Why in the nine hells would I give my magic to you, an untrained, un-
restrained, impulsive child?" The words are cruel, but he can't seem to stop
himself. The two things he has always prided himself on—logic, along with
his strict control of his biases—have fled him, gone the moment his son's
name fell from his daughter's lips.*

*The girl flinches as if slapped, and the words come hard and heavy, pour-
ing out of him in a roar.*

*"You lack all of the qualities needed for a judge." He ticks them off on his
fingers, spittle flying from his mouth. "Discipline, focus, strength of mind—"*

"But—"

"*You will never be my apprentice.*"

Finally, finally, his words hit as intended. Face crumpling, the girl spins to leave, the Book of Laws dropping to the carpet with a hollow thud that rings in the high judge's ears, more final than any gavel.

CHAPTER
28

I don't have to wait long for the queen. As if she knows of the illicit bargain I've struck, I'm summoned to the Crown lobby only an hour after returning from my meeting with Luc and Natalia. I wear my flashiest dress, a gaudy mess of sequins and sparkles, hoping that if I can't hide the suspicion in my eyes, at least I can distract the queen from it.

I meet her by the expansive sandstone fireplace that always blazes, even in summer, where she's waiting, stiff in a lace dress that looks like a set of curtains. I curtsy, low. As a performer, I'm used to bowing, but it feels wrong somehow, in front of the queen. I'm alert; eager to find any sign of guilt on the queen's visage. But she only seems tired, dark smudges under both blue eyes.

"Thank you for joining me, Lisette. Today is a difficult day for me, and I could use the company."

"Where are we going?" I ask, intrigued in spite of my better judgment.

"We'll be attending a charity ball. My husband—" she pauses, takes a deep breath "—*late* husband made many sizable donations to the Panther Hotel in his life. He was always a patron of the arts."

The queen coughs on the word *arts*, although I can't tell if it's intentional or not. I assumed the ball would be held in the Crown, where all the queen's engagements are held, but instead the sleek black car takes us to the Panther. I stare up at the marquee, the two gold eyes of a jungle cat flashing. Just to the left of the building is an advertisement for Luc's show. I don't know which gaze is more predatory, Luc's or the panther's.

Inside, we're directed to the VIP club, which has been reallocated as a ballroom. Gone are the caged dancers and exotic birds. Instead, gleaming tables dot the lush midnight carpet, and gorgeous tropical floral arrangements, many laden with ripe fruit, bow over the plates. I'm staring at the ceiling, where men and women hang from lines of silk like elegant spiders, spinning and floating, when someone taps my shoulder.

"Yes?"

"Lisette! What an absolute pleasure!"

My insides shrivel. Resigned, I turn to greet Del. His ensemble is clearly expensive but so over the top as to render it gaudy. He adjusts his tie, a floral monstrosity, self-importantly.

"Hello, Del."

He frowns, looking over my shoulder. "I didn't realize Louie was catering the ball."

His comment catches me off guard. Drunk on my new status as the queen's favorite, I'd almost forgotten my former life as a serving girl.

"He's not." I push past Del, making my way through the sea of tables and finely dressed aristocrats, suddenly feeling foolish and out of place. To my dismay, Del follows eagerly.

"Who did you come with then?"

The question and the implied assumption, that I could never have come on my own, sets my teeth on edge.

I whirl, nearly knocking over a server, and throw Del a sharp smile. "I'm here with the queen."

I say the words viciously, gloating. It's a pleasure to leave him gawping after me, too stunned to follow.

I take my time sauntering to the queen's table, feeling Del's eyes on me the entire time, and select a seat at the end. It's not as near to the queen as I'd like, but anywhere at the queen's table is an honor. I'm pulling out the chair, when a hand stops me, holding my chair in place. A guard smiles at me, bland and nonthreatening in contrast to the grip he keeps on my chair.

"The queen requests you be seated next to her."

Speechless, I glance at the head of the table, where the queen gives me a short nod. I don't hesitate again, warmth suffusing my entire being, as I take the seat nearest the queen. Scanning the room, I see a number of eyes on me, hands muffling whispered gossip. The realization gives me a strange thrill. Even Del watches my every move with a newfound awe.

A gentle clinking of china, like a bell, rings out over the genteel chatter, and the rest of the guests take their seats. On the other side of a massive podium sits a table full of important-looking people. I only recognize a few, the most notable being Natalia, who sucks on the end of a chicken bone, glowering at the crowd. Beside her sits Luc. As though he feels my gaze, he looks up, sending a jolt through me.

The speaker, a polished woman, gray hair pulled into a sleek updo, the wide expanse of her décolletage framed by a heavy pearl-and-sapphire necklace, adjusts the microphone.

"Thank you all for being here.

"As you all know, thanks to the numerous donations from King Reginald during his lifetime, we have finally completed our new gaming room."

Polite applause fills the room. To my left, the queen's clapping is dry and unenthused. It seems as if the queen is not a fan of her late husband's generosity, and the fact strikes me as odd. I dismiss it; more likely the queen is simply suffering from a headache or dry eyes or devils knows what ailment.

"In honor of our late and magnanimous sovereign, we have decided to name the room after him. The room will hereafter be known as the Reginald DeLuca Room."

All eyes on her, the pompous woman unveils a tiny gold plaque bearing the name to more applause. Is it really an honor, I wonder as I clap with them, to have a gambling den named after you?

With a smile more like a grimace frozen on her face, the queen shakes the hand of the woman and then takes the podium. She's pale as she surveys the crowd, the hand holding the microphone trembling.

"Thank you all for the honor you bestow upon my husband."

All eyes are on the queen, except for two. Across the podium, Luc watches me intently. I pretend to be interested in my fingernails, pretend that I can't feel his eyes on me.

"Reginald loved this city, and this would have pleased him very much." The queen is blinking rapidly, and for a moment I think she might faint, until I notice the wetness at the corners of her eyes and realize she's crying.

Clearing her throat, overcome with emotion, the queen is unable to continue. She lets out a loud sniff that echoes across the room, then digs about for a handkerchief. It's painful to watch, her obvious vulnerability. Extricating the heavy gold silverware from my fine linen napkin, I pass the cloth up to her.

She takes it wordlessly and lets out a honking nose blow. For a royal, she's surprisingly inept with her public persona.

"Thank you," she says to me and then, as if unable to think of anything else, she repeats it to the crowd. "Thank you."

She sits down heavily, dabbing at her eyes. A few of the aristocrats clap hesitantly, but it quickly dies out.

"Are you all right?" I ask the queen, low. Her watery eyes meet mine and then dart away as if ashamed. She clears her throat yet again and pats my hand, almost absently.

"Yes, thank you."

I jump at the contact; it's the first time the queen has done that. And not only that, but in front of everyone too.

Scanning the crowd, I notice more than a few courtier's gazes snagging on me, including Del's. He gapes like a dead fish. No doubt he understands my position in the court now, I think, glowing.

Once the speech giving and self-congratulating is over, platters of food are served. I'm just digging into a steaming bowl of soup when a hand taps my shoulder. I look up to see Del, hovering over me.

"Yes?" I ask, not bothering to remove the spoon that's already in my mouth. It's marvelous having an appetite again. It appears that Luc's magic has healed not only my poisoning but the wound in my stomach as well.

"May I have this dance?"

I look around the room in bewilderment. Light music plays in the background, but no one is dancing.

"I'm busy," I say pointedly, inhaling another spoonful of soup. It's creamy and rich, and just the fact that I can swallow it without burning pain makes it all the more enjoyable.

"Nonsense," Del chuckles. "You owe me a dance, remember?"

His hand grips my shoulder possessively. I've never met a boy less unable to take a hint.

I look to the queen for help, but she stares morosely at the menu, oblivious to my plight. *What's the point of having a friend with the power to execute your enemies if they don't use it?* I think, grumbling to myself. Smiling like an idiot, Del ignores my attempts to continue eating—his hand never leaving my shoulder—to the point of ridiculousness. Finally, I regretfully allow him to pull me away from my dinner.

Since it's a charity dinner, there's no official dance floor, but Del escorts me to a spot cleared in front of the tables to separate the rabble from the presence of the queen. In front of everyone present, Del grasps my waist as though we're married, pulling me scandalously close. I try to pull away, but his grip is like iron, holding me in place as though he'll drown without me. He's so close I can smell the cigarette smoke from the gambling den he spent his morning in and the overpowering scent of his cologne. My eyes water, and I'm not sure if it's the smell or the humiliation.

"Darling Lisette," he murmurs into my forehead. "How far my little star has flown."

I almost gag at his awful analogy. *One dance*, I think. *I just have to get through one dance.*

"I always knew you'd make a name for yourself, you know. You've always been so proficient in . . . the, er, womanly arts."

"I'm a magician, not a prostitute."

Del's cheeks pink at my bluntness, but he's undeterred. "And now you've captured the attention of a queen."

The song ends, but Del does not release me, even though the next is a livelier tune not suitable for close dancing. Del jostles me to the beat, unaware of the spectacle we're causing. Somehow, knowing Luc is watching the entire thing causes my cheeks to flame.

"Thank you for the dance," I say pointedly, trying to extricate my limbs from his.

"Now, now, Lisette, I'm not through with you yet," he says as every nerve in my body yearns to stab him with a fork. I can make hats and coins disappear, but in that moment, I'd give anything just to make him disappear. The room is starting to sway, dizziness making my empty stomach lurch as Del spins me even faster.

"Actually, I was rather hoping you'd introduce me to Her Majesty—"

"Excuse me, may I cut in?"

My entire face heats as Luc places an arm on my own, stopping our frenetic circles. I sag, grateful I'm no longer spinning.

Del glowers at Luc. "Not you again. I'm quite certain I asked you to keep your distance from my lady."

My lady? Before I can choke on that one, Luc responds.

"The lady looks as if your very presence makes her ill," he says mildly. Del's face twists. "And anyway, I asked her, not you."

"Of course you can cut in," I jump in, taking his extended hand gratefully, and letting him pull me as far away from Del as possible.

"Don't worry, I promise not to spin you." Luc's voice is light, teasing.

"Thank you." It's not a phrase I'm accustomed to saying to him, but it falls out easily, naturally.

Luc shrugs, a tic in his jaw as he eyes Del. "You looked like you needed someone to save you."

Across the floor, Del is livid. He paces, eyes never leaving Luc.

"Looks like I'll be able to return the favor in a few moments," I say, nodding at Del, who is fingering his overpolished sword. Luc chuckles, a low sound in his throat, dangerous.

"There's only one person I need saving from, and it's not that imbecile."

"Oh?" I try not to sound intrigued. The room is spinning again, but this time it's an intoxicating feeling, like falling in a dream. The courtiers, the queen, even Del, disappear into background noise. It's just Luc and I, floating through the song.

"I wish," Luc says, leaning down so that his breath flutters the hair on my crown. "That I didn't have such a taste for things that will kill me."

I can hardly breathe.

"Good thing you can heal yourself," I murmur. The hand on my waist tightens, his fingers burning through the silk of my gown.

We've stopped dancing, the song long ago ended, but still he holds me there.

Tentatively, his fingers tug my face upward, where the hunger in his eyes smolders.

"I'm not so sure I can," he says, so quietly I have to strain to hear him. "Not from this, anyway."

His gaze fixes on my mouth, and for a moment I think he'll succumb to the hunger, that we'll both succumb, but he catches himself just in time. Clearing his throat, he pulls away, face shadowed.

"Thank you for the dance."

He offers a polite bow and then leaves me there, alone, still burning.

Around me, other couples have filled up the dance floor. I stare at them unseeing, imagining for a second the feel of Luc's beard scraping across my exposed neck.

Devils. I need to get ahold of myself.

I walk back to the queen in a fog, hardly noticing the look she gives me as I take my seat.

"Good, you're back." The queen's greeting is curt, annoyed. *How long was I gone?* I think, but before I can respond, she snaps her fingers at one of the guards. "I can stand this party no longer. Will you accompany me to my rooms?"

I cast a longing look at my soup—as well as the several other courses that were set down while I was dancing—now cold and congealed, and sigh inwardly. "Of course, Your Majesty."

She leans heavily on me, cold fingers gripping my arm as we shuffle out of the Panther. She bemoans everything from the lighting to the choice of food, which she claims "unsettled her stomach." I listen half-heartedly, more focused on not tripping than on the many complaints that spill from her lips.

". . . and that awful woman who runs the Panther . . . the rumors about her abound. If I could only find the evidence to execute her and be done with it."

I do stumble now, realizing it's Natalia she's speaking about.

"Careful, clumsy girl!" the queen scolds as we nearly fall down a flight of stairs.

"Sorry, Your Majesty." I struggle to right us both. "But what do you have against Natalia?"

The queen's nails, always carefully neat and trimmed, pinch the underside of my arm.

"You mean other than the fact that she's a leader of a group of criminals, runs an illegal market right under my nose, and operates outside of my jurisdiction?"

I blink. I hadn't realized Natalia's illegal misdeeds were common knowledge to the Crown.

"Why not arrest her then?"

The queen laughs, a bitter sound. "Thanks to several laws my own husband passed, Oasis functions differently than any other city in my kingdom. My powers here are . . . limited, to say the least."

I've always known Oasis was different. Legal gambling and prostitution, as well as a thriving black market, are proof that the law doesn't function quite the same here.

I'd always assumed it was because of the mob's power here, not because of the king.

"I've sought to overturn the laws my husband enacted, but it's proved more difficult than I realized. There has been opposition from many, and now is not the time to challenge my already fragile position as queen."

We've reached the queen's rooms. Her speech has invigorated her; she barely leans on me, and I listen, fascinated.

"I want nothing more than to do right by my subjects. Rid the kingdom of lawlessness and scum like Natalia. Unfortunately, I can't help my people if they won't let me help them."

"Your husband . . . the king. He sounds like he was a difficult man," I try, tentatively. Oh devils, I may lose my head for this, but something about the queen's speech, the way she speaks of her recently deceased husband feels off somehow. If there's even a chance Luc and Natalia are right . . .

The queen stops abruptly, eyes flashing.

"I loved my husband more than life itself."

"Of course, Your Majesty—" I stammer under her sharp gaze. She stares as if only just seeing me.

A flash of something dark burns on the queen's visage.

"Be careful of Luc. I saw you with him tonight."

I stiffen, the memory of Luc's hand on the small of my back betraying my forced calm.

"He's involved with Natalia somehow, likely her lover. I've heard she has a taste for younger prey. It would not do for a member of the queen's retinue to associate with lowlife such as him." The queen's face shudders into a snarl. Then, as suddenly as it began, the passion leaves the queen like the sun going behind a cloud, and she leans on me, nearly dragging me to the carpet.

"Enough talk of politics now. My head does ache so."

The summonses from both Raster and the queen fill my waste basket. The first ones, I saved. *You are hereby summoned by Her Royal Majesty . . .* It was a symbol, a sign that I was finally reaching my goals. Now, they're just pieces of paper cluttering my room, demanding my time. Rehearsals, dinners, meetings . . . I don't even look up when another one slides under the door. My father used to send summonses just like these, on fine, thick paper.

Only his summonses were sentences, notices of criminal behavior, and to ignore them invited execution. Lately, the summonses I'm getting don't feel much different.

I ignore the neatly folded invitation for as long as I can, perusing my notebook for ideas for my next show, but the square of buttery white screams for my attention.

Throwing down my pen with a sigh, I retrieve the obnoxious little note and unfold it.

You are hereby summoned...

I scan the note. *The queen requests the presence of Lisette Schopfer,* blah blah blah. Of course it's for right now, right during the time Raster blocked out to prepare for my final show. And I can't just plead illness, because I need every chance alone with the queen I can get, if I'm going to prove she's the one who killed the king.

A knock on the door sends my heart jumping into my throat, and for a single dimwitted moment, I actually think the queen somehow sensed my reticence and sent someone for me. Pulling open the door, heart still skipping like a jackrabbit, I gust out a sigh when I realize it's Yasmin, not the Royal Guard.

The note is a reminder that I'm needed elsewhere, and so I prop the door open rather than invite her in. Yasmin peers into the room as if looking for someone inside.

"Yes?" I ask, trying my hardest to sound polite.

"Why won't you let me in? Do you have a guy in there or something?"

I let out an exasperated laugh. Of all the times she could stop and visit, of course she chooses now.

"I'm actually on my way out," I say, hedging. "Don't you have a show in like, an hour anyway?"

It's obvious she's performing soon, clad in nothing but a spotted leotard.

"I came to invite you to my show," Yasmin says, her gaze still darting around the room as if I'm hiding something. "I've got a new act, inspired by you."

I hardly even hear what she's saying. It's already been at least fifteen minutes since I received the summons, and I can feel the seconds pound by with each throb of my heart.

"Listen, can I check it out tomorrow? The queen summoned me."

"The queen? Summoned *you*?"

I try not to be offended at the disbelief in her tone. "As a matter of fact, we've become quite close as of late."

Yasmin crosses her arms over her chest, eyebrow raised. "I'd hate to think you only used me to get to the queen."

The accusation stops me cold, enough to dampen the urgency that pulls me toward the queen.

"Of course not!"

"Because it seems to me," she says, getting louder with each word, "that now that you have the attention of Her Royal Majesty, you don't seem to care much about me anymore."

It's not true of course, but my stomach curdles in shame anyway. It's not my fault the queen has taken an interest in me. And it's not like I can turn her down.

"Well?" Her jaw clenches and unclenches as she watches me hesitate. All I can think is that I'm going to be late, and if I displease the queen, I'll lose it all. My chance to prove my father's innocence. My shot to win Jester.

Yasmin's eyes harden and she turns away before I can stop her. I watch helplessly as she stomps down the hallway, her heeled boots leaving scuff marks in the wood, leaving me to wonder if she's right.

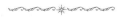

The queen is abed with a migraine and has asked me to keep her company, which mostly entails me running a toe through the thick plush carpet and watching the patterns change. I wonder how many hours I've wasted in this room, waiting on the queen, when I could be working on my final act. Of course, it's likely this was Luc's plan all along. Force me to play handmaid to the queen while he beats me in the final show. Even the queen's favor won't guarantee my spot as Jester if Luc or another performer proves themselves more worthy of the queen's attentions. I stare at my palm, where the faintest black webs have begun to bleed into the network of veins there.

"Your Majesty . . ." I begin, my voice too loud in the dark room.

The queen sits up with a groan, a hand over her eyes. "What?"

"What happened the night the king died?" The question falls from my lips before I can cram it back in. Hours of staring at the carpet must have made me insane. The glazed look leaves the queen's eyes in an instant. Sitting up against a wall of pillows, she clicks a tiny lamp next to her bed, shielding her eyes from the light.

"Why would you ask such a question?" Her voice is sharp, impatient. I cast about for a reason that won't leave me swinging from a rope by the neck.

"Please, I'd just like some . . . closure," I stammer. "He was my father, after all."

The queen's face softens some, although the hard line on her brow remains creased. Leaning back against the pillows, she closes her eyes, and for a moment I wonder if she's fallen back asleep.

"The night my husband died, our daughter was ill with a fever. I was up all night with her so she wouldn't bother my husband. He had a very important meeting with the council the next morning and I wanted him to get his rest."

She draws in a deep, shuddering breath.

"I wasn't there when he . . ."

Her hand flies to her mouth to muffle the choking sob that gasps from her.

Horrified, I realize she's crying.

"I'm so sorry," I respond, wishing the deep carpets would absorb me wholly. The queen waves away the apology, sniffing loudly.

"When I went in to check on him and bring him his nightly tonic, I found him already gone, and your father . . . standing at his bedside with a gun."

My heart sinks lower than my stomach. *Kingkiller.* Luc has played me for a fool yet again.

"How horrible," I murmur, cheeks burning. "Thank you for telling me."

The queen clears her throat, massaging her temples. "Will you do something for me?"

"Anything Her Majesty wishes," is the automatic response, although really, anything to get out of this dark, too-cool room where the only thing stronger than the smell of antiseptic is my own guilt.

"There is a plant in my greenhouse . . . *delantus mallowus.* Do you know it?"

"I'm afraid all plants look the same to me, Your Majesty, other than cacti," I say apologetically. "Green and of little interest."

"It's a cousin of the aloe plant," she says, as though this will help. "Tiny pink blossoms. Three leaves. I need you to get me a clipping for this infernal migraine."

I take the clippers she proffers with a grimace, and she sinks back onto the pillows with a moan. Like the plants she so loves, Queen Sonora is as dull and unremarkable as Natalia claimed. Of all the time we've spent together, she has done nothing even remotely suspicious or out of the ordinary, other than the time she bumped into a gambling machine and won the daily jackpot.

The greenhouse is humid, and my hair sticks to my neck in clumps. I'm unused to such large quantities of water in the air; it feels as if I'm drowning. I pass any number of small pink-blossomed, three-leafed plants, unsure which is the correct one. I'm forced to read the tiny handwritten labels on each plant—long, pretentious names that tell me little, if anything about the plant itself. Not only that, but I've already forgotten the name of the plant anyway.

Settling for the closest approximation of what the queen asked, I snip an entire branch and carry it back to her rooms.

"Steep it in some boiling water." The queen's eyes remain squeezed shut at my arrival.

I busy myself with boiling water and soon, a sweet, calming aroma wafts from the buds.

"I hope this pleases Her Majesty," I murmur, setting the cup on her bedside table. Her eyelids flutter open, and I help her sit up. Still squinting against the pain, she brings the cup to her lips—

—and spits.

I blink. "Did I do something wrong?"

The queen is suddenly completely alert, dumping the sweet-smelling mixture out. Ripping off a scrap of hotel stationery, she sketches a tiny flower in the corner.

"Since I assume it was not your intention to poison me, I need you to get me granda blooms as quickly as possible. The flowers are red, serrated leaves. Bring me six buds."

"Y-yes, Your Majesty," I stammer, taking the stationery and tripping over my curtsy. "I didn't mean—"

"Go now."

Heart pounding, I run back to the greenhouse, scolding myself every step of the way. First the stunt with the king's spirit, and now accidental poisoning. It's a wonder I still have my head attached. Why hadn't I been more careful?

With the queen's sketch, it's easy to find the right plant. I snip six of the delicate flowers as instructed, tucking them into my skirt pocket where they won't be crushed. Visions of the queen frothing on the floor alone spur me ever faster back down the hall to her suite. I almost crash into a maid dusting a bust of the late king in the hallway. She shoots me a foul look.

Expecting the worst, I burst through the door, but the queen is seated as I left her, face wan. Wordlessly, she takes the tiny flowers from me and crushes them in her palm, leaving a streak of pollen and crushed petals.

She swallows the mixture dry.

"Are you okay?" I dare to ask. My hands shake so badly, I'm surprised the queen hasn't noticed.

"I'll be fine," the queen murmurs, leaning back.

"Your Majesty, I'm so sorry. I promise it was an accident, all the flowers looked the same—"

Queen Sonora's eyes flutter open and she regards me. "This is the second time you've almost killed me."

I drop to the floor, head kissing the soft carpet. "Your Majesty, it was ignorance, nothing more—"

"Of course, it takes years of study to tell the difference between devil's tongue and poseygloves."

I sink into the plush carpet, relief washing over me in waves.

"I'm afraid my headache made me too lazy to attempt it myself," she continues, rubbing her temples.

"Was it—was it very dangerous?" I ask, in hardly more than a whisper. "The plant I gave you instead?"

"Not the worst, by a long shot," the queen says. "Death by devil's tongue is a quick, painless death. The poison targets the nervous system and blocks the effects of magic. Easy to recognize by its sweet smell when brewed, if you know what to look for."

I can still smell it, the ghost of the poison. It no longer smells sweet, but cloying, the scent of death and rot, of moldering flowers.

"Thankfully, it must hit the bloodstream to take effect." The queen leans back onto her mountain of pillows with a sigh.

"You mean those little red flowers weren't the antidote?" I ask, remembering her wide-eyed panic upon tasting the brew.

"Sleeping draught," the queen murmurs. "If I can't get rid of this headache by force, I shall sleep it off instead . . ."

Her breathing is steady and regular, and I assume she's asleep. Deciding to leave before I accidentally set the room on fire, I tiptoe across the room and slide open the door latch.

"Antidote," the queen chuckles to herself, eyes still closed. "There is no antidote."

Back in my own rooms, I chide myself for my stupidity. The scent of the poison still coats my throat, so sweet it makes me gag. Retching into the sink, I clasp the countertop.

Was there ever a greater fool?

The brisk whisking of something being slid under the door makes me cringe.

What in all nine hells could the queen possibly want now? Perhaps she's finally decided to have me good and properly executed.

With shaking hands I pick up the note, but even as I do, it's obvious it's not from the queen, the paper too thin, the ink smudged and hurried.

Meet me at the Panther. Room 667.
—L

I trace the *L* wondering if I wouldn't prefer an execution instead. I have nothing for Natalia and Luc, nothing except more evidence of my own ineptitude.

Sighing, I let the paper float to the ground, not even considering that a note like that is incriminating in more ways than one.

❦

"What have you learned?"

"Nothing."

My voice is flat, dull.

I've gone over every little moment I've shared with the queen with Luc and Natalia to no avail. I'm almost certain the queen did not kill her husband. As much as I hate to admit it, my own father still seems the most likely suspect.

And with the final competition only days away, I'm starting to feel as if the entire operation is a sham.

Luc shoots Natalia a meaningful look, which I pretend not to see. His hair has been hastily shorn since I saw him last, all those long, sleek locks trimmed close to his skull. I kind of miss the long hair, not that I'd ever tell him.

"What happened to your hair?" I ask, trying desperately to change the subject. Luc's mouth tightens and it's Natalia who answers.

"His hair got caught during his last escape act. The stupid boy had to saw it off in order to escape in time."

A giggle chokes out of me.

"No information, no healing," Luc says, pretending not to hear, although he rubs the back of his neck with more force than necessary.

"Why do you care so much anyway?" I ask, impatient, tired of being interrogated and manipulated over every meaningless exchange.

"I'm afraid that's none of your concern," Luc says, haughty.

"Isn't it, though? If I'm to be your mole, I'd like a good reason for doing so. And don't say proving my father's innocence, because quite frankly, I'm starting to believe you're just wasting my time to keep me from winning the position of Jester."

Luc's eyes widen at the accusation, but he doesn't dispute it. I've had enough; I stand up, daring them to stop me.

"You believe the queen." He never misses a beat, but I can feel the way he tenses, the frustration barely bridled under his cool demeanor. "You believe her, even though it's obvious she's lying."

"Why are you so sure she's lying?"

I know I'm supposed to be on my father's side, supposed to prove the queen's guilt.

But the memory of her tears, the defeat in her posture . . . there's no way she could've faked that.

"Do not forget that this is a woman who fooled an entire kingdom into thinking your father, a loyal subject of the Crown, was guilty of her crime."

The words hiss out of him.

"You of all people should see through a fraud, Lisette."

I jerk away, stung.

"Get the confession out of her," he says, not bothering to soften his tone or apologize. "She's starting to trust you. Don't waste that."

"I'm leaving."

Neither follows. I make it all the way to the elevator and hit the Lobby button as quickly as I can.

There's a moment of relief, of thinking I actually got away with it, when a hand stops the doors right before they glide shut. A sigh gusts out of me. So close. Luc squeezes into the elevator beside me.

"Mind if I take you somewhere?" His finger hovers over one of the floor buttons.

"I suspect you'll do it no matter what I say," I respond, sour. Luc takes this as a yes and hits the button. Neither of us speaks as the elevator glides down, down into the bowels of the hotel. The doors slide open on an unfamiliar floor. Luc steps out and waits for me, eyebrow raised. Huffing out a sigh, I follow. It's a gaming floor, although most of the machines have long since fallen into disrepair, and there are no patrons. Dust coats the room, giving it a ghostly feel.

"My parents met here," Luc says, trailing a finger absently through a layer of dust. I give the room a half-hearted once-over. Although it's obvious it was probably nice when it first opened, it's not much to look at anymore.

"How romantic," I say dryly.

"This was not the first casino my mother opened, but it was always her favorite."

"Natalia is your mother." The realization is like being doused in cold water. Luc nods once. It makes sense: the devil, demon spawn of the mob queen.

I'm honestly surprised I didn't put it together sooner. I sit at one of the ancient machines, fiddling with the broken handle.

"My father was a frequent visitor to Oasis, even though his wife disapproved. He was an important man, but a voracious appetite for gambling left him nearly bankrupt. While playing thief's hand one night, in this very room, my father drew the queen of rooks."

Luc pulls a card from his pocket, the queen of rooks. Unlike the queen of pearls, the queen of rooks is a sharp-eyed crow of a woman whose merciless gaze, along with her ability to steal all a player's points in one fell swoop, has earned her the title of "gambler's bane."

I click my tongue sympathetically.

"In an instant, my father was a ruined man."

Luc stares at the card a moment longer, than pockets it again. He rakes a hand through his hair, tugging at the roots as though willing it to grow faster.

"He was approached by the casino madam, my mother. Although my mother earned a decent enough living on casino games and hotels alone, she really amassed her fortune extending a special line of credit to those who had lost their money gambling. Second chance loans, she called them. A way to prey on those addicted to gambling."

I wrinkle my nose.

Natalia is an even worse person than I'd assumed, but Oasis is full of unsavory types.

"My mother saw the opportunity to have such an important man in her debt and took advantage of it."

Luc's tone is a hair defensive. I don't respond, tapping a dusty button.

"Unfortunately, my father was neither a lucky man nor a skilled man at gambling, and ended up owing my mother quite a substantial sum of money. By this point of course, they'd fallen in love."

I can't help the noise of disgust that escapes this time. I'm used to the unconventional morals of Oasis, but a loan shark falling for her prey is too much even for me.

"Why are you telling me this?" I ask, but Luc shushes me.

"My father's young wife back in the capital became suspicious of all his time spent in Oasis. When she discovered the infidelity, she was livid. At this point, I was seven months old, living with Natalia. But my father's wife had only uncovered a fraction of the true story. As my father continued to spend increasingly more time with his mistress and bastard child, his gambling debts mounted. By the time he died, fifteen years later, my father owed my mother a truly outrageous sum. Which meant the debt passed on to his wife."

"A terrible misfortune, indeed," I say sarcastically.

Luc shoots me a look. And then he delivers the gut punch.

"My father was the king. The king of Terraca."

"You're lying."

Even as I say it, I'm struck by his resemblance to the late king. The flaxen hair, strong jaw, lithe build, even the slight bend of his nose. His golden eyes, however, belong to his mother.

Luc doesn't bother to contradict me. "I wish I was."

"So, what then?" I stammer, trying to process everything he's just told me. "You think the queen murdered her husband—your father— out of petty revenge?"

"The queen, and therefore the Kingdom of Terraca, is in debt to my mother. By all rights, my mother could seize the throne. A paltry affair matters little by comparison."

"Why doesn't she then?"

It seems like an obvious choice. If Natalia can prove the queen is guilty of regicide, not to mention in debt to her, the throne would be hers.

"My mother has no desire to be queen, and I have no desire to be crown prince. My mother thinks her power over the queen is best . . . asserted from afar."

Luc is the crown prince. The information leaves me reeling. I recall the tiny princess, not even the true heir to a bankrupt kingdom, and feel a sudden surge of pity.

"That's despicable. And you still don't have any proof it truly was the queen."

Luc's face twists at the judgment. "Which is exactly why I attempted to become Jester. The queen does not yet know of my existence. I had planned to get close and prove she murdered my father."

"What's the point?" I fold my arms over my chest. "If you don't want the throne, what does it matter if the queen did kill her husband?"

Luc's eyes burn steadily in the low light.

"I loved my father very much. If I can prove the queen was, in fact, the one who murdered him, I will kill her."

I recoil. "I refuse to be a part of this any longer."

I turn to leave, but Luc traps me, pinning me to the slot machine, the buttons mashing against my backside. His voice goes low, dangerous.

"You don't have a choice."

"Oh yeah?" I spit, thrashing against his hold. "What are you going to do? Kill me?"

"Worse," Luc says, voice so soft it's like a caress. "I'll tell everyone you're a fraud. You'll be ruined, Lisette. And then I'll crush that ring of yours to dust."

He's so close I can taste the air that escapes him in shallow breaths. Can see the way he angles his body, curves it to mine. And that's when I see his bluff. The bluff that was there all along.

"No, you won't."

Something dark flits across Luc's face and he releases me with a jerk. He runs a shaking hand through his shorn hair and when it doesn't meet resistance, he lets it fall, staring at it as if bewildered.

"My father took me to a show on the Noose once," he says, almost absently. "A female performer. Delilah. She could escape from anything."

I remember her. I don't say anything though, just watch him.

"That was the first time I ever saw a magician perform. Of course, I'd seen people use magic for all kinds of practical reasons, but never like that, just for fun."

His voice is wistful.

"It was obvious how much she loved performing. There was this joy—a light to her. She was the most beautiful thing I'd ever seen."

His eyes find mine, hold mine.

"You remind me of her."

He takes a step forward. Instinctively, I pull back and pain scrawls across his features.

"Please, Lisette . . . help me avenge my father. The queen trusts you. This might be my only chance."

The king of the Noose, reduced to begging at the feet of a street performer. Normally, I'd be delighted at the irony, but his desperation, so like my own, freezes me.

"Please."

The word, repeated so softly I can barely hear it, breaks me. I hesitate. His eyes burn so hot, I can almost feel the heat.

"What you did . . . in the theater . . . you brought him back . . . my father. Do you think—that is, could you—"

It's painful to watch him like this and even more painful when I realize what he's trying to ask.

"I can't." The words come out as a whisper. "The dead can only be brought back once."

He nods, turning away before I can see the vastness of his despair, a yawning chasm of grief. A despair I know intimately. Edward's face floats behind my lids as an unexpected wetness floods my eyes, causes me to blink rapidly. Luc leans against one of the machines heavily, as though the weight he carries is suddenly too much to bear.

"I'm sorry." I'm surprised to find I mean it.

Luc turns to me, desperation scrawling across his features. "Then you'll help me?"

I'm torn. On the one hand, I understand Luc more than I ever thought possible. His grief mirrors my own: the loss of someone so dear, it feels like a chunk of my heart has been cut out. I know what it's like to hemorrhage pain, nothing to staunch the bleeding. And I definitely know what it's like to want someone dead more than you want to live.

But a tiny, shameful part of me refuses to jeopardize my own mission. I'm so close to becoming Jester, *so close* to finally sating the unquenchable hunger that resides within me. Not only that, but the queen has done nothing in all the time I've spent with her to arouse suspicion.

Luc watches me and the raw hope on his face is almost enough to undo my resolution. Almost.

"I can't help you."

I leave before I can see him collapse into himself, an entire soul's worth of grief imploding.

The final show is mere weeks away. Like magic, Luc has disappeared from the Noose, leaving rumors and speculation in his wake. Finally, there is nothing in between me and winning Jester. As the queen's favorite, all I have to do is perform tomorrow night, and almost by default, I'll be crowned the winner. Luc was, after all, my only real competition. The only problem is, I can't perform.

I reach for my powers, but they tangle and knot in my blood. Head pounding, I reach further, grasping at the obstinate threads of power and forcing them to comply. The weak outline of a spirit shimmers onstage, so hazy I can't even tell what they look like.

"You're losing your magic."

The spirit I've barely managed to summon disappears at the sound of the voice, leaving me lightheaded. Luc steps from the shadows backstage, watching me sway, arms folded across his broad chest.

"I'm fine."

Doing my best to steady myself, I try to summon another spirit, but my grip on my magic is tenuous at best, and the spirit does not answer the call.

Luc assents. "No doubt you're saving your energy for the final act."

"Will you leave me be? I already told you I have no information for you." Exhaustion and something else—guilt perhaps—have distilled into their purest form: anger.

"Let me heal you."

His voice is gentle, but I am tired of being a pawn in a game I never wanted to play. I shrug him away.

"You know I have nothing to offer in return."

"Won't offer, you mean." Luc's gaze turns shrewd. "You're only hurting yourself, you know."

"So be it," I say, even though part of me wonders if it's true. My hand, blackened and numb, aches for the touch of his magic. With just a word, I could be whole again. I refuse to be used any longer, but what if I could turn the tables, just this once?

Use him, the way he used me?

The memory of his grief, so like my own, surfaces like a dead log but I push it away. Just because I relate to him in one small way does not mean I forgive him for months of betrayal. Nor do I forget that we are competitors, first and foremost—always rivals.

"This is the last time," I tell him, pretending to relent. "I won't be a part of your games any longer."

"As you like." He keeps his expression neutral, but I see something there behind the careful set of his mouth—greed, leaping like a hungry flame. I cast about for something to tell him. If there is anything I've learned performing, it's that a lie is most easily swallowed when coated in truth.

"The queen has a number of poisonous plants," I tell him, voice lowered as though conveying the most precious of secrets. "I've been to her personal greenhouse. Any one of them could have been used to poison the king."

"Interesting . . ." Luc considers the information, turning it over and over like a chunk of gold. What he doesn't realize is that it's fool's gold, nothing more than a shiny rock.

"She even grows devil's tongue." The information slips out of me before I realize its worth. Not that such a tidbit is actually incriminating, when all the queen's plants are merely a pharmacy for her numerous maladies, and the plant in question is used to treat menstrual cramps. But devil's tongue is illegal to grow and I'll be damned in all nine hells if I actually gave Luc something he can use against the queen.

Luc's golden eyes widen, making my heart sink. "That's it!"

"She only uses it for cramps—" I say but it's too late. Luc grabs my face and kisses me so hard I see sparks.

"I've given you what you asked for," I say, shoving him away. I hope he can't see the way my cheeks flame in the dim stage lights. "Now heal me."

Luc doesn't say a word as he heals me. I can see him working over the information like a coyote with a bone.

I've given him nothing of worth, nothing he can use. So why does it feel like I've sold the queen for this?

"Keep up the good work," Luc says, before he leaves. I shake out my newly healed hands, flexing my fingers, when movement out in the empty auditorium catches my attention.

Only it's no longer empty. Seated in the back, eyes glittering, is Yasmin.

"Yasmin!" I call out, but she's gone before I can stop her, disappearing through the back exit. I leap over half-folded chairs, stumble over the tiny steps that lead out of the bowels of the theater. How much did she hear? Worse still, how much did she see? I recall Luc's jubilation, his stolen kiss, and my feet fly ever faster. I burst through the exit, blinking in the unexpected brightness of the Crown lobby, but it's no use.

She's gone.

CHAPTER
29

For once, the high judge has no plan. Other than the gun tucked hastily in his robes, he has nothing.

It is late. The halls of the king's suite are empty, other than a few guards. It's easy to get past them. They know the high judge and let him pass with deferential nods. Witnesses, he thinks, but it matters nothing so long as he accomplishes his designs here tonight. After the king lies in a pool of his own blood, his son's death avenged, the high judge cares not what happens to himself.

Murmuring nonsense about a summons, the high judge pushes open the heavy door to the royal sleeping quarters. It glides open, as velvet and silent as the night itself. He can make out the bulk of his ruler, sleeping deeply under mounds of silk, on a bed big enough to fit the high judge's entire family and all three wives. The king does not so much as stir at the high judge's approach, although he's anything but quiet. It's unsettling, the high judge decides, for a king to sleep so deeply. Although he knows he should be quiet, part of him *wants his son's murderer to be awake when he kills him. For him to suffer the way the high judge has suffered.*

His foot connects with one of the bedposts. The sound rings out through the room like a shot, setting the high judge's pulse racing. Miraculously, the king sleeps on, motionless under all his bedding. Blowing out a breath, massaging his chest, which pains him when his heart races like this, he pulls the blanket slowly back. Bulging eyes greet him, and a mouth frozen in a snarl.

Yelping, the high judge backs away from the bed, apologizing. The king does not answer him, a crimson froth blooming on his lower lip. Dead, the high judge realizes, pushing aside the rest of the blankets, which fall to the floor with a soft thud. Both the king's hands are fisted, the veins on his neck standing out, every muscle taut as though he died fighting. But no wound marks him. It's then the high judge notices the smell in the room, as sweet as the spun sugar he used to enjoy as a child, although there's something unpleasant there too, a rotting smell that makes him think of carcasses, mangled on the side of the road. Covering his mouth with his shirt, the high judge searches for a sign, any indicator of what happened. Mad dog disease perhaps, the high judge thinks, eyeing the bloody froth bubbling on the King's lips. That would certainly explain the rictus of the limbs . . .

"What are you doing?"

Whirling, the high judge turns to face the queen. Dropping into a hasty bow, he struggles to think of a reason why he is here, alone, in front of the dead king.

"The king needs medical assistance at once—"

The queen takes in her husband, still frozen in agony, and the glass in her hand drops to the floor and shatters.

"What have you done?"

The question comes out as a gasp.

"It wasn't me, Your Majesty. I had, er, pressing court issues to discuss with His Majesty. He was like this when I found him—"

"Guards!"

The guards materialize like shadows disengaging from the walls, confused when they see only the queen and the high judge in the room.

"Your king is dead," the queen says to the guards, and the high judge is impressed against his will. No sign of grief mars her delicate features, only a will of iron. The woman was born to lead, he must admit. His ire is not with his queen, although right now she is making a grave mistake . . .

"Seize the traitor."

Her extended hand is like an axe, sentencing him to a death he does not deserve, but the words to defend himself do not come. He barely resists when the guards shackle him and check him for weapons.

"He was carrying a gun, Your Highness."

Bowing, the guard drops the gun into the queen's outstretched hand. She inspects the gun, blue eyes glinting ice, cold and hard.

"Put him under house arrest. We will execute him tomorrow at dawn."

Suddenly, the high judge finds his voice.

"The gun was . . . the king was not shot! Check him!"

The guards ignore him, although their gazes dart to the contorted man crumpled in his bedsheets. If he could just get them to listen . . .

"Her Majesty is not an unjust ruler," he says, pleadingly. "Do not sentence me without fair trial."

The queen considers him, and he wonders at her composure, how she can stay so calm when her husband lies dead beside her, still warm. Her gaze darts to her guards, whose grips have slackened on his manacles.

"Very well," the queen relents as the air whooshes out of him. "I will have the inspector gather evidence here, and tomorrow you will be tried."

"Her Highness is honorable and just, and will rule forever," the high judge murmurs, relieved. The evidence is on his side. He did not murder the king and will be exonerated after the trial.

"Take him back to his home for the night." The queen's jaw is clenched, the only sign of emotion on her otherwise smooth face. "And whatever you do, do not let him use magic."

CHAPTER
30

"Mistress, a summons from the queen."

"Now?"

With only a handful of days left before the final show, the interruption comes as more than an annoyance. Instead of a note, the queen has sent an actual messenger, and not just any messenger, a guard, a lanky boy of nineteen or so, who flushes at the sight of my bare legs.

"It is urgent."

His voice cracks on the final syllable. *Of course it's urgent,* I think, grabbing a robe. When is it ever not urgent? I follow him reluctantly to the elevators. I'm surprised when he does not lead me to the queen's suites but instead takes me down to one of the private conference rooms the queen uses for court business. I don't even have time to feel dread before he bows me in, the door clicking shut behind us.

The queen is arrayed in all her finery, seated upon a makeshift throne. My gaze snags upon her heavy ceremonial armor, the kind she only dons for serious matters. Execution. Treason. Her eyes burn like chips of diamond. I curtsy belatedly, my legs betraying me by wobbling, and tug my robe around me further, flimsy shield that it is from the queen's wrath.

"Lisette Schopfer. Do you or do you not deny affiliating with Natalia Obrist, and her son, Luc Obrist, in conspiring against the Crown?"

Any defense I might have had dries up in my throat like dust. The queen waits like stone, the only indication of her displeasure the staccato tap tap tapping of her tiny, heeled boot. I clear my throat.

"Your Majesty—"

I wait for her to interrupt, rend me with whatever proof she has of my dealings with Luc and Natalia, but she simply waits, both hands gripping the armrests of her high-backed chair. A fire rages in the hearth behind her, even though the room is already hot, so hot, sweat dripping down my spine.

"I have dealings with the former," I say slowly, hoping against all hope she is in a lenient mood today. "But not what you think. I disavowed myself of them both, immediately upon learning their true motives."

The queen's cerulean eyes are dark, almost black. "You lie."

"I do not!"

The words tumble out before I can realize how pointless they are. Her mind was decided before I set foot in this room.

"Here, here is the proof!" I rip my glove off, revealing the twisting black beneath. It's only been a day since Luc healed me last, and already the poison creeps up my palm. It's happening faster, I realize, heart thudding dully.

The queen stares, uncomprehending. Twisting my father's ring, I hold it in front of me.

"Luc discovered that I have magic poisoning and used the fact against me."

My own words sound hollow and juvenile in my ears, a child tattling on a sibling.

"Your Majesty, I wish you no harm, you know this." Desperation clings to my words, souring them. The queen's hand clenches.

"I know nothing of the sort," she hisses, and in an instant, the stone she hides behind has shattered. "It is always the ones closest to me I trust the least."

There is something else there, behind the fury. Pain. I seize on it.

"I am your friend, Your Highness."

The queen laughs, but it is a mirthless sound. "Do you always sell your friends to the highest bidder?"

Without meaning to, I think of Yasmin. No, I want to shout. But the queen is right. I am a liar.

"I have been accused of murder," the queen says, softly, almost absently. "Do you believe I poisoned my husband, Lisette?"

"Of course not!" The words tumble out in a guilty rush. *Poison.* My own careless words, exchanged for a reprieve from my own self-poisoning, have come back to haunt me like a spirit, unbidden.

"Prove it."

The queen's face is a mask once more, as heavy as the armor she wears.

"Anything," I say, dropping to my knees. The queen is silent, no doubt weighing my words against my actions.

"I want you to kill Luc."

The breath catches in my throat. So this is to be my punishment. I wonder if I wouldn't prefer the axe to my own throat instead. The thought of Luc dead at my hand is too much to bear. I want to crumple under the weight of the request, let the marble floors swallow me whole. I can feel the queen's gaze on me, scrutinizing my every facial tic.

"Your Highness—" I manage, but the words catch in my throat, so I clear it. "My queen, of course he deserves to be punished, but *death*?"

I try hard to smother the despair that colors my tone. The queen straightens, fingers tightening against both armrests, knuckles white. "He is guilty of treason and conspiring against the Crown."

There is not enough air in this too-hot room.

"If you successfully manage this, I will pardon your own transgressions, of course," the queen continues, adjusting the golden clasp, shaped like a roving vine, that sits at the base of her throat.

A royal pardon. My whole life I've sought the approval of the Crown and now that it's finally within my grasp, it feels hollow. I should have known the price would be more than even I was willing to pay. And then the queen delivers the final blow:

"And I want you to execute him during the final show."

I stare at her, uncomprehending. "You wish me to murder him publicly?"

For some reason, the act feels more vulgar done this way, his death made into a spectacle. But what else should I have expected in Oasis, where pain is sold as entertainment daily?

"It is for your benefit," the queen says, cold. "Even after everything you have done to me, I still seek to protect you. His death will be nothing more than a tragic accident, at the hands of a fellow performer. You will be forgiven by the Crown, the people, and you will be free to enjoy your new position as Jester."

Jester. There is little more than a week left before the final show, the show where the queen will announce her choice for Jester. Is this really the way I want to win though? As if sensing my thoughts, the queen continues.

"He will die either way, whether by your hand or another's. I hope you are not having second thoughts about defending a traitor."

Luc made his choices, I think. *Do not feel bad because he was caught in his own snare.* I tell myself this, but I'm the one tangled, fought over by the two wolves who set the trap.

I'm afraid to answer, afraid to speak the words that will turn me from traitor to murderer, so I shake my head instead.

"Come to me," the queen says, extending her pale hand. Rings glitter on her slender fingers. "Since you have chosen the path of loyal servant, you may kiss the royal ring."

The edge of the gem cuts my lip. I wonder how many other mouths have breathed lies on this same stone, while swearing fealty.

Her words come as if from a great distance. Fury and a wild desperation pound through my blood, making the world around me shimmer with heat. I long to pounce upon her and wrap my fingers around her delicate swan's neck and throttle her until she's limp and gray.

"Don't look at me like that," she says, grimacing. "Once you have accomplished what I ask, I will repay you with magic of your own."

Although my breath still comes in heaves, her words hit like a drug. Magic of my own. Never again a slave to stolen magic. For that, I would serve this horrible woman. For that, I would kill. For that, I would do anything.

I push Luc far from my mind, already on my knees. The promise of magic bows my neck further still, my lips brushing the exquisite marble floor beneath, the only thing lower than myself.

"Your Highness, as always, I am your humble servant."

I wait in Yasmin's dressing room backstage. I'm furious with her. My thoughts rage in time with the blood pounding through me as I finger a bouquet of long-stemmed roses set by her mirror. There are so many flowers in the room, it's hard to breathe. Dried, live, even an arrangement of fake flowers, adorn every available inch of surface in the lavish suite. I watch the clock count the seconds until her encore is finished.

At 9:04, the door clicks open, right on schedule.

"Hello, Yasmin."

She lets out a squeak, the macaw on her shoulder struggling to maintain its hold. But she quickly regains her composure, expression going cool at the sight of me, seated at her vanity.

"What are you doing here?" she snaps, shutting the door.

"Like you don't know," I retort. After everything we've been through, I can't believe she betrayed me to the queen. All over a misunderstood kiss. Her face remains carefully neutral, arms crossed over her chest.

"I don't suppose you've come to apologize then."

"Apologize?" The word roars out of me, and for a moment, she looks unsettled. Good. Let her see the consequences of betraying me. "You sold me to the queen!"

I expect her to be defensive, hells, I even expect a fight. But what I don't expect is the utter bafflement that crosses her face.

"What are you talking about?"

She almost looks genuine. But she forgets that I'm a performer too, that I see through an act as well as anyone. I forge ahead.

"Don't play stupid. I know it was you!"

"I don't know what you're talking about!"

A stalemate. We stare at each other, chests heaving. The parrot lets out a low clucking sound, shifting its weight from foot to foot.

"You told the queen. About Luc and I," I say, low, angry at the tears that rise unbidden to my eyes. Yasmin's mouth drops at the accusation, speechless.

"You really think I'd do that?" she finally asks, mouth a tight line.

I roll my eyes. "Of course. I know better than anyone how much you hate Luc. I saw you in the audience when . . . I know you overheard us."

"And you assumed my reaction would be to betray you, my closest friend." Her voice is flat, without inflection. Staring at her arms wrapped tightly across her midsection, as if to protect herself from me, I have my first misgivings.

"You hate Luc," I repeat, but I barely convince myself anymore.

"So what if I do? I care about you." She laughs, high and bitter. "But you're too self-absorbed for friendship, aren't you? Too busy scaling the cliffs of your own ambition."

I gape at her, completely disarmed.

All this time, I thought Yasmin's friendship was . . . not an act exactly, but for entertainment. A show. Like everyone else. Gone as soon as the applause fades and the lights dim.

"You know nothing about me," she says when I don't respond. The pain in her eyes adds to my overabundance of guilt. "And you're an even worse friend than I thought. Get out of my dressing room."

"But—"

"Get out!"

<hr/>

The Book of Laws is heavy, the pages brittle. I have not touched it since my father's death. Once, I knew all the laws within. Once, I let myself believe my father would teach me, like he taught my brother. A vindictive pleasure surges through me at the thought of what my father would think of the show I have planned. Of him knowing I used his precious book as part of a magic show. Such nonsense would have been blasphemous to my father.

Flipping idly through the thick pages, the comforting smell of old book emitting with each page turn, I skim through the text half-heartedly.

When a murderer is found guilty, a suitable sentence must be determined . . .

The text is as dry as the book itself, full of old laws and bylaws no one but my father cared about. How I ever hoped to be his apprentice is beyond me. . . .

A scribble, hastily penned in my father's hand stops my page turning. My father did not write in his books, limiting his notes to the stern black notebook he kept on his desk.

Amarantyllus/devil's tongue
highly toxic: muscle spasms, confusion, frothing, hydrophobia,
coughing up blood
sweet-smelling

I stare at the words, which make no sense. My father was a judge, not a botanist. Why would he have any interest in a poisonous plant?

Heart sinking, I scan the page the note was left on. It's mostly useless: dense blocks of information on presenting evidence for defendants. Unless I've inadvertently stumbled across my father's plan to murder the king . . .

I'd never really thought my father guilty. Not even the day they executed him, after a trial so short, we barely got there in time to hear the verdict. I remember Hattie, silently braiding my hair with trembling hands. In the end, it hadn't mattered how I looked, since by the time we got there, my father had already given his defense.

The judge, a hastily appointed substitute for my father, was going over the evidence with a baffled look on his face, shuffling papers repeatedly to hide his inexperience.

"So, on the night of the . . . incident, you were found at the king's bedside, alone and with a weapon."

"A gun," my father interrupted. I could see from the way his hands clenched the stand in front of him that he was afraid, even though his expression was bland, almost nonchalant. "But as your inspector has already pointed out, there was no gun wound."

"Wounds can be healed though . . ." the false judge put in, shuffling the papers again in that maddening way.

"As you all know, I have no healing powers and I was found alone. If you'd let me summon the king, he can tell you himself who murdered him—"

"What were you doing in the king's quarters in the middle of the night?"

The question came not from the judge but the queen, who stood up, hands fisted at her sides.

My father, who always had an answer, merely opened his mouth and shut it again.

"I did not kill the king," he finally answered, but even I knew it wasn't enough, this meager defense from the only man who knew the law better than anyone else. "He was clearly poisoned; the symptoms were the same as—"

"Enough."

The judge peered over his spectacles at the queen, who slammed the table in front of her with two shaking fists in an uncharacteristic bout of emotion.

"He was the only one there the night of the crime, and I will not have him attempting to deceive the courts with trickery."

"I do not attempt to deceive anyone!" My father burst out from the stand. "Everyone knows the dead cannot lie, why won't you let me—"

"You are a judge of the land," the queen snarled. "And if anyone knows how to lead a jury, it is yourself. I will not allow this trial to be tainted by magic. I've heard enough."

All eyes watched the substitute judge, who let out a nervous "aah."

"It's quite clear, is it not?" the queen snapped.

"Of course, of course, Your Majesty." The judge's head bobbed on his neck. "I, er, pronounce this man guilty of murdering the king."

The gavel swung down, sealing my father's fate with a hollow thud. Guards swarmed my father, who had the dazed look of someone who has just been solidly punched in the stomach.

"There was no gunshot wound! The king was poisoned! Check the glass at his bedside!"

It was then my father finally lost his composure. The guards pulled him shouting and pleading from the stand. And then Hattie turned my head from my father, before I could suffer the further disgrace of watching him, a common criminal, being dragged from the room.

Poison.

Sweet-smelling.

The taste of the tea I accidentally brewed the queen, the slick nauseating taste of it on the back of my throat floods my mouth with saliva. What if these notes aren't my father's own murderous plan, but his attempt to solve the crime himself? And if my father didn't kill the king, is it really possible the queen did?

CHAPTER
31

Although there is no point in rehearsing the grim show I have planned, I sit on the empty stage anyway. I stare at the knife given to me by the queen. Running it against my hand, I can smell the poison coating it, even from here: a ghost of sweetness.

For once I do not have to plan my show. It's obvious what I need to do. The silver glints against the blackness of my palms, the blackness that now reaches my shoulders.

Stolen magic will corrupt your soul. Is this what Cillian meant? That I'd be so desperate to keep my magic, I'd murder for it?

"Lisette."

I don't look up as Luc crosses the stage to where I sit. I'm not surprised to see him, even though it's been almost a week since the queen's summons and more than that since I saw him last. After a moment of hesitation, he drops to the stage next to me, long legs folded awkwardly underneath him. He leans back on his hands, letting the stage lights bathe his face in a hazy glow. The spotlight has always loved him, I think resentfully. It limns the strong lines of his jaw and sparkles in his golden hair.

"What do you want?" My voice is flat. I don't look up from the knife, the knife I could kill him with right now.

"I've come to release you from our deal."

The knife slips in my grasp, clattering to the floor.

"Excuse me?"

Luc sucks in a breath, as though the words are physically painful. "If you truly believe the queen is innocent . . . I trust you. You're released from our bargain."

I pick up the knife, still not comprehending. "Just like that?"

Luc takes the knife from my shaking hands and sets it carefully next to me. When did he get so close? And devils, when did I fall prey to his spell? The heat between us shimmers like sun on sand. Hesitating, Luc takes my hands in his, one finger tracing the black veins that fan out like lace all the way to my shoulders. He follows the lines, his touch burning all the way up. Leaning down, his lips brush my exposed shoulder. I shiver despite the heat.

"You're a fool," he says softly. "Is it truly worth all this to you?"

His question tumbles in my mind, and for a moment, I don't know the answer. He turns my face up to his, amber eyes questioning, and finally, here is a question I do know the answer to. My lips part in response and he leans to meet them with lips that taste like gunpowder and honey. And although I've kissed him before, this kiss, without bribery or manipulation to sour the sweetness, is exquisite. How is it that I've never known how badly I wanted this? Wanted him? I kiss him fiercely and with abandon, pulling him by the neck even closer. Gently, he leans me down onto the stage, his hands tangled in my hair. A pain in my back rouses me from the spell of passion, an annoying dig in my spine. The knife, I realize. The knife I'm going to kill Luc with in mere hours.

I freeze. Luc pulls away reluctantly. I stare at the forgotten knife, my own reflection distorted in its mirrored blade.

"Are you all right?"

Luc's question startles me, his obvious concern making the guilt rise in my throat like acid, but it's his earlier question that still tolls in my head. *Is it worth it?*

Only this time, I don't have an answer for him. He must see something in my eyes though, something I can't articulate, because he gets up then, quietly, leaving me alone on the empty stage. I picture the audience filling the seats of the Crown. Applause drowning the pain until I can't remember it any longer. I'm standing, arms outstretched to receive the imaginary accolades.

It's then I realize Luc healed me. Gone are the long black trails marring my hands and arms. I test for my magic, surprised when it responds instantly, evoking a specter of a woman who does not say anything, only watches me with fathomless eyes.

I don't need the queen, I realize. Not if I have Luc. He can heal the corruption, save me from my magic poisoning. But am I willing to give up my dream for him, everything I've sacrificed? Am I willing to give up Jester?

The spirit disappears with a sigh that shudders through me like a winter wind, as the possibilities spiral in front of me.

Is it worth it?

My hand hovers in a fist above the scarred bookshop door, hesitating. Forgoing formality, I reach for the handle instead, letting myself inside with a soft jingle of bells. The sight of Cillian, enveloped in his favorite chair, is like a balm, even if he does scowl when I enter.

"We don't have a lesson today."

I drop into the rose chair, the chair I've come to think of as my own, inhaling the scent of musty books and lavender. Brows knit, Cillian tucks a bookmark into the book open in his lap and stares at me.

"You look like you're on your way to be executed."

I flinch at his choice of words. Not executed, but executioner.

"I'm fine."

The two most false words ever spoken. I can tell Cillian doesn't buy it, but he lets it go. Letting out a resigned sigh, he stands up and cracks his neck.

"Guess I'll put a pot on, then."

"We need to talk."

Cillian eyes me warily but sits again.

"If you're here to ask for my magic again—"

I cut him off. "You can keep your magic. I won't tell your secret."

It's the only gratitude I can give him for everything he's done, meager thanks though it is. Although I'd never tell him, I've grown fond of Cillian during our time together, even if he is crankier than a dowager with bunions. Something about him, something I can't quite name, reminds me of Edward.

Cillian squints at me. Takes off his spectacles and rubs them on his crisp linen shirt. Replaces them. "Excuse me?"

I sigh, hiding a smile. "Your magic is yours, Cillian. I release you from our agreement."

"You mean you're done blackmailing me?"

"Must you be so difficult? Yes, I'm done blackmailing you."

The sigh that gusts out of him is enormous. "Thank all five thousand devils. What changed your mind?"

Guilt. Yasmin. Luc, offering me the same trust. The promise of my own magic, offered with a catch. A chance to be someone other than my father. But all I say is, "I never liked your magic that much anyway. Far too pretentious for me."

I dodge the book he hurls at me, laughing. At least, I haven't ruined everything in my life.

"The final show is tomorrow night . . ." I know Cillian isn't fond of how I use my magic, but I ask anyway, because suddenly, I need at least one person in my life who doesn't hate me. "I'd be honored if you came."

Cillian sniffs loudly, pretending to be very interested in dusting off a book that looks perfectly clean to me. "I suppose I could spare one evening . . . more of the usual theatrical nonsense, I expect?"

"Of course." I hand him the ticket, hiding a smile as he tucks it neatly in his front pocket, patting it once. He sighs again.

"I owned the theater."

He says it as though it is a grave admission, but I have no idea what he's talking about.

"What theater?" I ask, not following.

"The theater, the one I burned down," he says impatiently. "Before, you asked why I did it."

I squint at him. "Why would you burn down your own theater?"

"I got a notice from the queen stating that my theater had been built on royal lands and was therefore property of the Crown." His face is distant. "I put all my tuition money into building that theater. It was going to be spectacular."

"I thought you hated theater."

The look he gives me is thoroughly offended. "Not that awful drivel you call theater. Cinema. Classic film. Art."

"Ah."

"Anyway, once they told me I had thirty days to vacate the premises, I did what had to be done." Cillian shrugs. He's so matter-of-fact, it takes me a moment to process.

"Devils, Cillian!" I say, reeling. "You would've been executed on the spot for going against the Crown like that!"

"I suppose so," he says airily, wiping at the tea ring under his cup. The weight of his confession, of his trust threatens to overwhelm me.

"Thank you. For everything," I say. Cillian pulls a face.

"Don't get sentimental on me now, little blackmailer."

I punch him in the arm. "Don't be late to my show, or I'll burn your bookshop to the ground."

His answering smile is wry. "That's more like it."

It's showtime.

The knife has been whetted with poison, the same poison that killed Luc's father, the king. Fast-acting. Luc won't have time to heal himself once it hits his bloodstream. Death, within minutes. It's a simple blade, to administer such a fate. Dull and practical, not unlike the queen herself. Without fine jewels set in its hilt, bare of decoration or excess, it could be any other blade.

Only, any other blade couldn't kill Luc.

I am the blade, I think, bitterly. The only one close enough to Luc to kill him. The only one who knows enough of his secrets, enough of his magic. And now I'll repay his trust by stabbing him. Funny, only a few weeks ago, I *wanted* to kill him. And now that I've been ordered to, I wish there were any other way.

The queen, or Luc? If it were only a matter of choice, of who I liked better, my decision would be made in an instant. If it were who I trusted, who I cared for, who I loved—

I set the knife down, grim. There is no point in naming those feelings now. Because it's not a matter of who I love more. It was never really even a choice. I've been nothing more than a pawn, all this time, subject to the whims and games of everyone around me. Willing to abase myself to please those who only wanted to use me.

A door opens and then the clicking of boots echoes through my dressing room. I don't need to look up to know it's Raster.

"Tonight's the night," he says, laying a long-stemmed rose on my dressing table. "Are you ready?"

His question burns, ominous. I've never been less ready. But I can't admit that to my seeker.

I smile, don my mask once more. "Of course."

He smiles back, exposing gleaming teeth. "Don't disappoint me."

And then he's gone, leaving me alone with my lies. I'm exhausted, tired of running in circles trying to make everyone else happy.

Tonight, I'm done trying to please. Tonight, this show is not for the queen or Raster or my father or anyone else.

This show is for me.

CHAPTER
32

Luc is not surprised when I take the stage with him for the final time, even though my act is supposed to be after his. I suppose it makes a certain sense to him. After all, the show that won me my fame was the one where I stormed his stage. We've been rivals since the beginning, why not end it that way?

The knife is heavy.

The theater is filled, my first sold-out show. My eyes scan the audience—faceless blurs—but all I see are witnesses. I can just make out the queen beyond the haze of the stage lights.

"Well?" Luc's voice jars me from my thoughts. His grin is lazy; he expected this, and he's ready to play. I don't allow myself to wonder what our final show could've been like if we had finally worked together. Instead, I pull the knife from its sheath, hefting it to rest in my palms. I'm careful not to let its deadly tip so much as scratch the surface of my skin.

"My father was the high judge." My voice rings out, unchallenged. I can't see the audience's reaction, their surprise, but I can feel the tension building, powder in a keg. I pace the stage, circling ever closer to Luc.

"He was accused of murder and treason."

I can see the queen's brows knit. I had not prepared her for my speech, but I hope she allows me this one final liberty.

"Not just any murder either, but that of King Reginald the third of Terraca."

The audience is restless now, shifting, muttering, but I am alive as never before.

"A kingkiller."

The word that has haunted me for so long now falls easily from my lips.

It's nothing more than a skin I've long outgrown. Luc's eyes burn into my own, but for once, he holds his tongue.

"His magic was passed on to me, and in his place I seek the same things he once did. Justice. Peace. Deliverance."

I weigh the knife carefully in my palms. Life and death. Justice and mercy. Innocence and corruption. All rest in the palm of my hand. Perhaps I am more my father's daughter than I ever realized.

"Tonight, I come to deliver justice on behalf of the queen. A terrible crime has been committed. The scales of justice hang unbalanced."

The knife no longer droops, it is light in my hand. I know what must be done.

"This man conspired against the queen and sought to murder her."

I swing the knife, leveling it so it points directly at Luc's heart. There are gasps, muted and hushed. Luc's eyes widen but I've already steeled myself for the betrayal I know I'll find there. To my surprise, it's not betrayal or even hatred I see reflected back, but understanding, oceans of compassion that almost undo me.

Trust.

I stumble, but the wheels have already been set in motion, there is no going back.

"Justice—" I wheeze, lurching toward him. "Must be delivered."

And then I plunge the dagger into his heart.

He goes limp in my arms. Slowly, painfully, bleeding out on the same stage that's tasted his blood so many times before.

"Always . . . figured you'd be the death of me," he manages, smile crooked. The effort costs him, and he spasms, wracked with pain. Tears drip from my lidded eyes, blooming on his collar as I hold him. His pain is my doing and the knowledge burns like hellfire. I cannot blame the queen for this, as much as I long to.

She may have given me the dagger, but I'm the one who plunged it into Luc's heart.

"Please forgive me," I murmur into his hair, the words tasting of salt, as I brush his sweating brow. My tears mingle with his blood—salt and copper. Luc does not answer as the light slowly fades from his amber eyes, his final breath rushing out of him. His end is sudden, too sudden, his lifeless body still warm in my arms. A sob rips out of me, against my will. For a moment, I forget the audience, the stage. There is only Luc and me, bathed in a halo of stage light.

Around me, shouts swell as the audience realizes that this show has no happy ending.

Carefully, I lay Luc's body on the stage, ignoring the blood that stains my hands. The tears, a steady warmth on my cheeks, do not slow. I brush the quietest of kisses on his mouth and rise. Shaking out a white sheet, I drape it carefully over his silent form. I raise both hands, the sight of all that red quieting the audience instantly. They are so easy to entreat, to compel, with the promise of more thrills. It doesn't matter how many lives are exchanged for that pleasure.

I twist at the heavy gold ring on my finger.

"Let us see now, what the dead has to say."

It is easy to summon Luc, easier than any of the others. He comes quickly, outlined in silver and stained in blood. I don't miss sight of the queen's face, shocked, as bloodless as Luc's.

"Has justice been delivered, spirit?"

"Guilty, I was," Luc admits solemnly. "But there is still one more guilty than I. Your father was innocent."

Disbelief, betrayal, fear. All the things I expected to see on Luc's face lie bare on the queen's.

I cross the stage. "Tell me, spirit, for the dead cannot lie. Who killed the king?"

Luc's black eyes consider me, and then he turns to the audience, raising one glowing finger. Like a beacon, it cuts through the crowd, who shrink away from its trajectory.

"The queen."

To my surprise, the queen starts clapping. Loud, echoing applause, the only sound in the otherwise silent theater.

"Quite a show, quite a show! Well done."

The audience glances from Luc to the queen and back again, as though unsure what is real. My heart sinks.

"For a moment, you really had me going," Sonora admits, smile brittle. "Guards!"

The stage is stormed by guards, who drag me to the queen. I don't fight them; I choose instead to focus on Luc. I reach for him, fingers grasping nothing but air and light as the guards drag me away.

I'm thrown in front of the queen. There's a smattering of applause from the audience, who are still unsure if this is part of the show or not.

"Give me your hand."

I do so, hardly aware of what she asks.

My mind is a fog. Her fingers, always so cold, find my father's ring and pry it from my hand. She extricates the gem easily from the setting. With a single deft movement, she crushes the stone under one steel boot, grinding my father's ring and my magic into dust. Onstage, Luc fades in the spotlight to nothing.

"No!"

My fingers scramble uselessly through the sparkling powder. It's gone. After everything I've sacrificed, my magic, my entire magical lineage, *Luc*, my one shot at glory is gone. The queen watches dispassionately. I lift my eyes in agony.

"Why would you—"

"Did you really think I could let your treason go unpunished?"

"At least I'm not a kingkiller," I spit.

At this the queen stops. The fury on her face is naked, exposed. "You dare to accuse me of murdering my husband?"

"I do."

It took me a while to reach the same conclusion as Luc, but once I did, the pieces fell into place easily. The queen's extensive knowledge of the right poison to use on someone capable of healing themselves, the same gift that Luc's father passed on to him. The strange symptoms of the deceased King, the same symptoms caused by devil's tongue, not found naturally in Oasis but grown in abundance in the queen's private greenhouse. The rage of her husband's spirit, directed not at me, the descendent of the supposed kingkiller, but his murderous wife. As they say, the dead cannot lie.

"Kill her."

The words rip from the queen's mouth, and half the guards flounder, unsure who to trust. The queen snarls, a feral sound, and snatches one of the guns from the guards, leveling it at my heart. A shout from my left startles me. A flash of violet. A person stumbling into the theater aisle. Yasmin. She actually came.

"No!"

Pushing past audience members, Yasmin clambers over seats to get to us. Without looking at me, Yasmin wraps her arm through mine protectively. I grasp her hand and squeeze, trying to relay through that one gesture everything I cannot say. My heart warms when she squeezes back.

"Careful, my queen. You've already been accused of one murder."

Like a ghost, Luc drifts up the aisle. His shirt is still drenched in his own blood, his face pale and grim, and the guards scatter at his arrival, convinced they're seeing a dead man. Only I know the truth: the elaborate mirrors hidden backstage to create the illusion of a spirit. The counterfeit dagger I replaced the poison-coated one with before stabbing Luc.

"I offered you everything," the queen snaps, ignoring Luc. Her hand, the one holding the gun, shakes. "And you would give it up for a traitor?"

The empty spot on my ring finger is a reminder of everything I've sacrificed. But for the first time in months, my mind is clear. Decided.

"Don't flatter him, he's arrogant enough. I didn't do it for him," I say.

Luc's mouth twists in a shadow of a smile.

"If not for him, then why? Why would you betray your queen?" Her breath comes in heaves, and I realize then that she's hurt. All the time I wasted trying to impress her, to crack through her stone exterior, never realizing I already had.

"You killed my father!" I cry, disbelieving.

"He was honored to serve the Crown with his death," the queen says haughtily. "As you should have been."

"So you could repay me in the same way?" I ask. My jaw aches, clenched so tight my teeth feel as though they'll shatter.

Kingkiller. That was my father's only reward for giving his life to his queen. I think of my brother, of myself, of everyone caught in the queen's tangled web, the victims of her injured feelings.

"I trusted you." The queen's voice is low, anguished. "Twice, I trusted you."

I cannot hold her gaze. Unlike her, I am not made of stone.

Without my magic, I am powerless to move against the queen, or so she thinks. She forgets that I was powerful before magic, and I am still capable without it. A knife without poison is just as sharp and more easily concealed.

"He is innocent," I nod to Luc, who the guards have bound.

"He is a traitor," the queen responds, signaling to another set of guards, motioning in my direction.

"As are you, my queen."

At my accusation, the remaining audience members scatter like frightened rabbits, scampering up the aisles. Ripping Yasmin's arm from mine, the guards drag her to where they've apprehended Luc. One of the guards lets out a cry as Yasmin, thrashing like a feral cat, bites him.

"Yes," the queen breathes, almost a hiss. "I killed my husband. The bastard cheated on me, humiliated me, and left me powerless and penniless."

A movement behind the queen catches my attention. Emerald eyes blaze from the shadows behind her. Cillian. He moves slowly, unnoticed by the queen or her guard.

"I could not let that flaccid excuse for a king take everything from my daughter." The queen breathes heavily, pale hands trembling. "That is true love, you know. Sacrifice. Would you not do the same?"

Without meaning to, my gaze darts to Luc. He watches me from the arms of the guards, desperation in his eyes.

"Please, Your Majesty," I say, extending my open palms to her. "Let them go. This is between you and me."

I keep my voice pitched low, soothing, the way one would speak to a wild animal. It is easy now, to give up everything. After pleasing the wrong people for so long, I now know what the right ones are worth. More than magic. More than life. I refuse to be like the queen, a fortress against the very people I care for.

The queen does not respond for so long, I'm foolish enough to think perhaps my words meant something to her.

"You are a fool." A click from the gun startles me, and I realize too late she's chambered a round. She raises the gun, aiming dead between my eyes.

"No!" Luc struggles against the guards, but we are woefully outnumbered. I raise my hands slowly. There's a scuffle among the guards as Luc struggles to break free, but he is too far away to reach the queen in time. Next to me, Yasmin tenses.

Before I can so much as react, close my eyes, do *something*, the queen is knocked forcefully to the side, a shot ringing out. We all duck instinctively, but the only impact is a chandelier, which bursts in a symphony of glass, raining on us.

Fire blazes, lighting dark hair and a furious face. Cillian. He grapples with the queen, trying in vain to wrestle the gun away, veins standing out on his forearms. Another burst of flames, and the queen cries out, dropping the gun. Cillian kicks it away from her grasping fingers as I manage to twist both the queen's arms behind her back, rendering her useless. Yasmin grabs the gun, aims it at the queen.

"It's over," Cillian gasps, hands still smoking. The queen snarls, wrenching in my arms, and in her rage, she is strong, stronger than I am. There's a crack as she twists, and in muted horror, I realize the crack was her wrist bone breaking. She slides from my grip, and before anyone can stop her, she rips the gun from the waistband of the nearest guard holding Luc.

There's an awful clicking sound, and for a moment, the seconds drag like eternities. Then, a shot, ringing through the empty theater like applause.

And Cillian drops to the floor.

CHAPTER
33

My scream rings through the now deserted theater. There are no witnesses here but us.

I rush to Cillian's side; he pants, cupping the wound, which flows freely.

"Take my hand," Cillian gasps as I drop to the ground next to him, pulling open his shirt. A gaping hole in his chest shows the entry point of the bullet, his shredded lungs beneath.

"Luc!" I plead, but the queen has Luc now, the mouth of her revolver digging into his temple.

"Let him heal him, please," I beg the queen, but her face is stone once more. "I'll do anything."

"I was never anything to you, was I?" she muses. "Not like these people."

"It's not about you!" I cry, but Cillian tugs at my arm, pulling me to him.

"Listen to me," he says, breathing hard. I can see how much every word costs him. "She's not going to—here, take my hand."

I do as he says, afraid that if I don't, he'll injure himself more. Cillian's eyes flutter shut, and his mouth moves rapidly. I can barely make out the spell that falls from his dying lips.

"Cillian—"

"Quiet!"

His nails bite into me and that's when I feel it. Power, raw and unburdened, flowing into my blood. Pure, untainted magic that burns bright as a flame and chases the remaining corruption from my veins.

Cillian shudders as he is purged of both magic and blood. His dark green eyes find mine. I clutch his hand, wishing I could force life into him the same way he forced magic into me.

"I have upheld my end of the bargain."

Tears burn tracks of salt down my face. I suddenly have all the power I've ever wanted, and yet, I can't make him stay. I am as useless with magic as I am without.

"Don't you dare go," I plead, shaking him. "Take back your magic, I don't want it!"

"Take care of it." His voice is barely audible, his grip on my hand slackening. And like a candle snuffed by the wind, he's gone.

For a moment, all I can hear is my own heart.

Pounding.

I close my eyes. Open them.

"I am the daughter of the high judge," I say, rising from the ground. The blood of Cillian stains my hands. The blood of Luc. The air around us tastes like salt and rust, and something else, something that crackles within me like lightning. The remaining guards scramble, dropping Luc in their haste to flee.

"By this woman's hands, three men have died. Justice demands life for life."

The queen is pale but unafraid, her gun still trained on Luc's skull. "Don't make it four."

Of course she is unafraid. She has never understood who I am. What I am capable of. I summon Cillian's magic easily. It comes when bidden, as warm and familiar as Cillian himself. Flames erupt in both hands, and the queen's eyes widen.

"What—"

"Release him, and I will allow the courts to deal justly with you," I say, coolly, even though the flames in my hands are so hot, sweat beads on my brow.

"As if I am foolish enough to believe that lie."

The flames in my hands are modest, but an inferno is building within me. The queen sees it, the flames of my wrath flickering on her pale face.

"Another illusion?" she sneers, but there is little bite behind her words.

"It is up to you whether or not you want to find out," I say evenly, even though the pain of Cillian's death consumes me faster than the flames.

The queen only screams in response. It is an unearthly sound, the howling of the damned. With a jerk of her hand, the ground beneath us rumbles. Vines, sinuous and writhing, burst from the cracking marble, twining themselves around Luc and Yasmin. Even Cillian is not spared, his lifeless form swallowed up in leaves and thorns.

"Lis—" Luc chokes as the vines plunge into his mouth, strangling his final words. *Not his final words*, I think desperately, grabbing the thick plant wrapped around him with one burning hand. Thorns bite into my flesh, but the plant shrinks from the flames, releasing him onto the floor. The bruises on his neck already stand out, and he's unconscious but otherwise seems fine, his healing already at work. Now, to find Yasmin—

I whirl around. Vines pin Yasmin to the wall. They shoot from her mouth, obscene, squeezing her throat like fat constrictors. Thorns dig into her skin, tear into her clothing. Her eyes are wide with fear. I grab at the vines with fistfuls of flame, but every dead branch grows anew, multiplying faster than I can combat them. Yasmin's eyes roll back into her head as the last of her oxygen is cut off. I drop, helpless. I can't free her without setting them all ablaze, and the effort could very well kill her too. Not only that, but Cillian's magic is unfamiliar and the unrestricted blaze of power too unwieldy.

"Let her go!"

The queen simply watches, blue eyes alight. I have nothing left to offer her, and she knows it. Beneath us, the hotel lets out a groan. The vines have weakened the foundation. She's going to bring us all down with her, I realize. On the ground behind her, Luc's eyelashes flutter.

"I'm giving you one last chance," I call, as pieces of the wall fall to the floor, shattering upon impact. Behind me, Yasmin is still, so still.

Vines snake around my ankles, making me stumble.

"You *used* me," the queen shrieks. "Just like everyone else. But I used you too, did you know that? You were never good enough, not really. I knew who you were all along."

The vines are around my neck now, tightening. Struggling only seems to strengthen their hold, so I relax, let them twine into my hair.

"You'll never be anything more than the daughter of a traitor. A *kingkiller*. A magic-less hack."

The queen's voice is like venom, hissing and curdling. But she's wrong about me. She always has been. I burn with magic.

Take care of it, I hear Cillian whisper, and now the meaning is twofold. And I know exactly what Cillian would do.

"*Terrificus majesticus*," I whisper. The theater ignites.

Now you see it. Now you don't.

Flames devour everything, vines, plush velvet seats, then the queen. Her mouth gapes as the blaze consumes her, skin crackling. She howls, burning to nothing but rage and pain, her very essence. I force the flames still higher, the image of Cillian seared into my mind. She killed him, and now she faces the consequences of those actions. *Justice*, my father's voice whispers like smoke. Execution by fire seems almost merciful after all the pain and death wrought at the queen's hand.

The smell is awful, both sweet and charred. Nausea licks at me as a popping sound fills the theater, and with it comes the sickening realization that it's the queen, the fat on her smoking bones cooking. The vengeance drains from me, replaced by a hollowness. I cannot stand watching the queen suffer any longer, and let the flames consume her then, snuff the rest of her life in an instant.

It is over quickly. I stare at the spot where the queen stood, now nothing but ash.

Still hungry, the fire licks at everything. Everything except us. Miraculously, the fire rages but leaves Luc, Yasmin, Cillian, and me unscathed. Eyes streaming, from smoke or grief or both, I recall Cillian striding from the scene of his arson, untouched by fire. Although the inferno doesn't burn us, clouds of thick black smoke choke the air and the entire hotel is dangerously close to collapse.

A hand grips my arm, startling me.

"We need to get out of here." Luc's voice is smoke choked and hoarse. I can just make out Yasmin through the haze, slung across his back, but I can't tell if she's breathing. My eyes burn, too dry even to cry.

"Cillian—"

Luc's expression is pained. "You'll have to leave him."

I pull away, choking on the thick smoke. Every breath scrapes out of me. "I'm not leaving him!"

Luc protests, but I barrel into the flames. I find Cillian as I left him, curled in on himself. Tears stream from my burning eyes, sudden and fierce. I am hacking now, all that black smoke replacing the air in my lungs. Although Cillian has a solid five inches on me, I grasp him by the shoulders and pull for all I'm worth.

"Come on!"

Luc, like a sentinel through the smoke, waves me forward. I do my best to follow after his hunched figure, pushing past the roiling black clouds. I'm dragging Cillian now, every breath scalding. I can't see where we're going, and I can only pray Luc knows the way out. A chunk of ceiling plaster catches the side of my head, sending a sharp streak of pain shooting through my skull and rendering me momentarily useless.

"Lisette!"

Luc's voice is farther away now, and I can't see him through all the smoke. Around me the hotel burns, all the lavish, over-the-top extravagance the queen hated gone in a roar. It feels impossible to breathe. Ash-infused air scalds my throat, burning me from the inside out. I reach one shaking hand forward, marveling at the way the flames dance over my skin. Next to me, Cillian stares and stares, the flames reflecting in his empty eyes.

"You were wrong, Cillian," I cough. "Magic *is* fun."

But the words are swallowed up, stolen before I can even utter them. There is no oxygen left. The fire mutters, rages, and crackles, alive. I let it wash over me. One word and I'll burn with the rest of the Crown Hotel. I just have to hold on long enough for Luc and Yasmin to make it out.

But I can't. My lips form the spell, the one that will end this, and then I'm dragged away, as the world dissolves into smoke.

CHAPTER
34

I awake, cold. It's a stark contrast, and I shiver against the absence of flame. I'm in an unfamiliar bed, blankets piled on, but still I shiver. I shut my eyes against the sudden remembrance, the pain that burns hotter than any fire.

You can heal some things, but you can't heal everything. Physically, I am fine. No more burns mar my skin, each breath comes easily and clear. But the weight of Cillian's death crushes my heart until it feels like I can't breathe. I keep my eyes jammed shut, afraid to let the world in. Even with my eyelids closed, the tears stream steadily into my pillow.

"I know you're awake."

Luc. His voice is soft, reassuring, holding none of the condescension I've come to associate with him the last few months. I allow the light in, squinting. My eyelids scrape against my raw eyes.

The room is dark, save for the lights of the city and a dying sunset framed by floor-to-ceiling glass. I recognize the room as one of the

Panther suites, obsidian and luxurious. Hovering over me, Luc's brow is furrowed. I'm in his suites, his bed. Somehow, I'm surprised when his fingertips stroke my own; warm and gentle.

Everything hurts. Still, I nod, knowing that if I speak, I'll only cry and that'll be it. An ocean of grief pulls at me, waves of agony that seek a release. The only other option is drowning.

Luc seems to understand.

"Cillian," I manage. My voice is still hoarse, smoke choked.

"I got him out." Luc is quick to assure me. "I went back after. The flames . . . they never even touched him. Or any of us."

His tone is full of wonder. I balk at it. It's not me he should be in awe of. It's Cillian.

"Thank you," I whisper.

Luc's golden eyes are soft. "I could tell he was important to you."

I can't answer him then, the pain in my heart somehow so much sharper than any of my injuries.

"That boy . . . he was your friend?" Luc goes on.

Another nod, although "friend" feels like a highly inadequate word to describe Cillian. Mentor, savior, salty curmudgeon . . . I bite back the tears that threaten to drown me.

Luc grips my hand in his. "I'm sorry."

How does anyone ever heal from grief like this? I wonder. How do we ever go on knowing those we love are lost forever? The thought is a dagger, a slicing reminder.

"Yasmin," I croak, frantic. "How is she?"

Luc grimaces. "She had some nasty wounds. Turns out the vines were venomous."

I struggle to sit up, but Luc pushes me down easily. "She's going to be fine. I just got done healing her an hour ago."

My eyes burn, still irritated and inflamed from the smoke and my own salty tears. "Thank you."

He leans forward, the motion causing his shirt to gape open. In a flash, I remember the dagger I buried in his chest. The light fading from those amber eyes.

My fingers scramble for his chest, pulling open the fabric there, but all that remains of my treachery is a scar, an ugly gash, raw and pink, just where his heart is. I cry out at the sight of it.

"I'm so sorry—"

Luc shakes his head, cutting off my apology. "Pretty bold of you to assume I'd figure out your plan back there."

I grimace. Although carefully planned and executed, none of it had been an illusion. Except, of course, the part where Luc had died in my arms. "You're a stage performer. Thinking on your feet is part of the job."

"I should've known." Luc sighs, but his eyes are fond. "'Stab now, think later' seems to be your motto."

"Yeah, that was a bit of a risk." I sigh, closing my stinging eyes. I'm exhausted, tugged by waves of both physical pain and the freshly gaping hole in my heart.

"You saved us all, back there." Luc's voice is barely a whisper.

My eyes flutter open again. He's looking at me so intensely, I feel like I might combust at any moment.

"Of course I would," I say, confused.

"I didn't know if I was worth it to you," Luc admits, a small smile tugging at his lips. His long lashes lie flush against his cheeks as he studies his feet. It occurs to me then, that underneath all the mystery and intrigue, Luc is nothing more than a boy. "I was under the impression nothing would stand in the way of you being Jester."

Shame heats my cheeks now.

"I almost chose that." My voice is a whisper. Admitting it to Luc feels vulgar, somehow.

"We're all fools about something." The way Luc watches me, it's very obvious what he is a fool for. Magic sparks, warm and tingling, in my stomach. I catch his hand in mine. His fingers are long, warm. Carefully, shyly, I trace his chest. Spidery white marks cover the skin there. Scars, I realize. A thousand scars for the thousand deaths Luc has suffered. I find the most recent one, the one I gave him.

"How did you know?"

Luc watches the path of my finger, somehow knowing exactly what I mean. "I didn't."

I let my hands drop, suddenly ashamed at his trust. "The knife the queen gave me was poisoned."

Luc's expression darkens. "No doubt the same poison she used to kill my father. Nobody knew he had already passed his gift on to me, his bastard son, a full year before he died. I imagine she knew all along who I was, with such a unique gift."

I consider this, recalling the same sickly sweet scent of the knife. How easily I could've killed him. How close I almost came to doing just that. The thought makes me cringe, and Luc wraps a warm hand around my own.

"You didn't choose that," he says quietly. I brush the quietest of kisses on the scar on his chest, breathing in the smell of him, smoky— and just there, a hint of oranges.

"Since I am no longer the queen's fool . . . perhaps I can be yours?"

Luc lets out a chuckle, low in his throat. "Devils knows I've been your fool long enough."

I smile against his chest. Gold eyes serious, Luc lifts my chin, tugging me toward him. I let my fingers glide through his shorn hair tentatively, then rake my fingers through it. Grasping my chin, he drags my face to his, our lips crashing together. The kiss is frantic at first, both of us drowning in our own way, but it softens quickly into something deeper. Something that threatens to burn me alive. Taking his lower lip in mine, I bite, just enough to elicit a groan from him. I let him go, heart stuttering at the flush that paints his jaw.

"And if I decide to stab you again?" I ask softly, teasing. The yearning in his eyes catches my breath. He extends both hands to me, palms up.

"Lisette, you've shot me, stabbed me, and completely stolen the breath from my lungs more times than I can count. Whatever heart I have left is yours to do with as you will."

"You really are a fool," I say fondly, and before he can argue, I cover his mouth with my own.

"For the record, this is a terrible idea," Luc says, as the box in his arms gives a tremendous shudder.

"For the record, I don't care." I knock loudly on Yasmin's dressing-room door, eying the box. Although I'll never admit it to him, I'm grateful Luc offered to carry it.

The door swings open, revealing a costumed Yasmin. Squealing, she wraps me in a warm hug.

"I've been so worried!"

"You've been worried?" I laugh. Compared to her, I came out unscathed. Pulling back, I take her in. Although there are some yellowish bruises on her throat and arms, she looks good. I throw a grateful look at Luc, who is so focused on keeping the box comically far from him, that he doesn't even see.

"Gift for you," he says, shoving the box at Yasmin. Scanning the many holes decorating the top of the box, her grin grows wicked.

"I hope this is what I think it is."

"I know what it is, and I still hope it's somehow changed," Luc says, grimacing. I shove him, chuckling. Yasmin carefully pulls the top of the box off, revealing a heavily furred spider, the size of my hand, crouched in the corner.

"Oh, it's absolutely precious!"

Luc throws me a disgusted look. I stifle a laugh. "It's a female. The trader we bought it from said it would be fully grown within a year and then you can . . . mate it."

I cough over the last part, hoping she doesn't notice. She doesn't. Rubbing the spider's bristly abdomen, she croons to the beast.

"You delicious little thing, I'm going to call you Madam Fluffylegs."

Luc shakes his head. "You have weird friends."

I elbow him. "Don't you have something you need to say?"

"Oh yeah." Letting out a long-suffering sigh, Luc turns to Yasmin. "I'm sorry I killed your spider."

Yasmin raises an eyebrow, as she lets the spider scuttle up her arm. "You're lucky I don't repay the favor."

There's no bite in her tone though, as she nuzzles the giant arachnid.

"You could always have Lisette do it for you," Luc says, nudging me. I smirk.

"True."

Luc eyes the spider with distaste. "Well, we've really got to be going, right, Lis?"

"I'll bring her by for a playdate sometime," Yasmin says, dark eyes dancing.

Luc gags at the thought. "I hate spiders."

"I know," Yasmin says, smiling, and the warmth that blooms in my chest is almost enough to make me forget the one person who could've made this moment perfect.

CHAPTER
35

"So you're the regent until the queen comes of age?"

Luc and I stroll the halls of the Palm, where the entire royal retinue has been transplanted since the fire. It's strange to see servants and guards everywhere, out of place in Natalia's domain. Even Raster fled Oasis, after news of my treachery reached his ears.

"Turns out I have a knack for government. Who knew?" Luc turns a toothy grin on me.

"Why not just claim the throne? You are the true heir, after all."

We both stop, as if following dance steps to music neither of us can hear. Luc swipes a hand through his hair, long again and knotted. His beard is still scruffy, but he has shed his stage clothes for the clothes of a courtier, sleek and polished. He looks like a prince, I realize.

"Too much time in the spotlight." Luc grimaces. "I'll be happy if I never go onstage again. I've always done better in the shadows anyway. Ah, here she is!"

With a squeal, a mess of floppy bows and lace throws itself at Luc. Laughing, he picks up the little queen, who giggles when he tickles her.

"Besides, Queen Sophia has already told me of her plans to pass a law decreeing that everyone who desires shall have a free puppy."

I drop low in a curtsy. "You will make a fine queen one day, Your Highness."

The little girl eyes me, one finger stuck in her rosebud mouth. At only three, and without the influence of her manipulative mother, she could yet grow into a good ruler.

Especially with Luc's guidance.

"You'll be moving up north to the capital then, I suppose," I say, surprised at the way my heart twinges at the thought. Luc's mouth tightens as he reluctantly nods. I let my gaze slide to the tiles so he won't see the tears blurring my vision. "Of course. Perhaps you'll visit?"

"I doubt it," he says, and my heart drops further still. "Oasis isn't the best place for children, unfortunately."

"Right," I say. His place is with his half sister now.

"But—"

I jerk my head up.

"Technically, you did win the position of Jester."

He says it significantly, as though it means something. I stare at him, uncomprehending. After everything that's happened, I'd forgotten about Jester. The whole competition feels like a joke, now that the queen is dead.

"Devils knows I could use the entertainment, surrounded by all those dour aristocrats." Luc's eyes twinkle. "I'll even let you stab a few for fun."

Queen Sophia's eyes widen and Luc laughs at her shock.

"Only joking, sweet."

Jester to the prince regent. My family's good name restored. Everything I ever wanted, but somehow it doesn't feel right. Like I cheated, somehow. Sensing my hesitation, Luc passes Queen Sophia to her nursemaid.

"Lis—"

"He wouldn't have wanted it," I say, staring at my hands, which although sooty, bear no trace of the black lines that poisoned my blood only a week ago. Cillian's magic, freely given, has eradicated my magic poisoning for good.

Luc cocks his head. "Who?"

"Cillian. My mentor." I squeeze my eyes shut against the memory of Cillian swooning onto the lush gold carpets, soaked with his blood. "He hated the pomp of Oasis . . . and believed magic should be used for noble purposes."

Although it's painful not performing, it's the least I can do to honor his memory and his magic.

"Ah." Luc steps closer, and I have a sudden longing to muss his hair, pull each carefully placed strand from its place of order. "I suppose Oasis does have a lot of . . . pomp."

I appreciate that he doesn't dismiss my words, even though they spill out, illogical and messy.

Brushing my hair from my face, he studies me closely. "Do you believe what you do is noble?"

I think of the joy from the audience when a trick goes right. The wonder. For even just a moment, I can make them feel magic.

My voice is barely a whisper. "Sometimes."

"Speaking as someone completely biased—" Luc grins at the smile he's teased from me "—your show is unlike anything I've ever seen. You're not just talented, you're passionate. And you make the audience feel something. That's more than I can say for most of the spectacle that is Oasis."

I nod. I want to believe he's right, that performing isn't purely selfish, that Cillian would want his magic used that way, but I just can't.

Luc bites his lip. "Listen, Lisette . . . I can't speak for Cillian. But he gave you his magic knowing what you'd use it for. And that makes me believe you somehow managed to convince him that what you do is worthwhile. But in the end, only you can decide how to use what he's given you."

With a gentle kiss to the cheek, he leaves me then, his words still echoing in my head.

CHAPTER
36

I brush off the sandstone gravestone. The engraving is simple. His name. The span of his life, too short. For a while, I was torn on what image best represented Cillian. A flame, for his magic? That seemed wrong somehow. I finally settled on an open book, with a quote from Cillian himself underneath:

A good book and a strong cup of tea
the most underrated magic in life.

"I'm leaving."

I whisper the words, even though I'm alone in the little church cemetery. It's a very different resting place from the one my father was buried in.

After things died down in the court, I had my father exhumed. His ruined body lies, shrouded, next to Cillian's in front of me. His stone is as somber as he was: only his full name and the dates of his birth and death remain to mark his life. Better to be remembered for nothing than to be remembered as a traitor.

I wonder what Cillian would think of me leaving Oasis, following the one person I swore to hate my whole life. Out of habit, I twist at the spot on my finger where my father's ring used to sit. I'd give anything to have his magic again, to bring back Cillian, just for a moment. To ask him if I'm wrong to go with Luc, to keep performing.

On a whim, I grasp for the magic, reaching deep for Cillian, wherever he is now. No spirit swirls into being, no apparition of Cillian to scold sense into me.

Only fire answers, the gentle flicker reflected on the stone in front of me. The cheery flames remind me of him, somehow. I touch my fingers to the edges of the shrouds, the flames nibbling at first, then eager, devouring the bodies beneath. Ash is caught on the air, as both my father and Cillian are finally freed from their mortal frames. I watch until my eyes burn, until tears stream down my cheeks, watering the graves beneath.

"Am I late?"

The voice startles me, soft and melodic. A woman stands, hesitant, hands clasped in front of her. Her hair is auburn and wild, freckles spattered across her nose, but her sparkling emerald eyes are almost an exact match for Cillian's. Beside her is a girl, perhaps a year older than me, her dark, unruly curls a longer version of Cillian's.

My throat tightens.

"You must be Mirian." Cillian's mother. The woman nods, gaze trailing the smoke. It wasn't easy to track down the busy scholar. I'd assumed my many letters would remain unanswered.

"I'm Tova," the girl says, her smile sad. "Cillian's younger sister."

"I'm Lisette," I say, extending a hand, which she grips. "I'm glad you came."

"I hadn't heard from Cillian in years," Mirian admits, turning away from the pyre, fists clenched. "I assumed he was just too busy at the academy. And then when I received your letter . . . I . . ."

Whatever else she was going to say is swallowed up in a sob. The same feeling of uselessness I've felt every day since watching Cillian die threatens to overwhelm me.

"I'm so sorry." My whispered apology seems to waft away with the smoke, but Mirian nods, swiping at her eyes. Shame bubbles up inside me, as hot as acid. "He saved my life."

"Foolish boy," she says fondly, shaking her head. "To think I would've cared about the academy . . . I should have written him. Something . . . I thought there'd be more time . . ."

She dabs absently at her eyes with the hem of her sleeve. Tova wraps her arm through her mother's, leaning her head against her arm, her own eyes sparkling.

"He gave me his magic." The words tumble out of me, the only comfort I can offer these suffering women. "I want to give it back to you."

Both Tova and Mirian look at me, their green eyes wide.

"Why would you do that?" Mirian asks.

"It's yours. He would have wanted that," I say, even though my hands clench at the thought of losing Cillian's magic. My magic.

For a long time, Mirian doesn't answer, standing before the pyre, tracing the smoke with her fingers. She is silent for a long moment before facing me.

"I do not want it."

"Then *you* take it." I turn to Tova, desperate. "He told me you were his favorite, surely he would have wanted his magic to go to you—"

Tova doesn't let me finish, her many curls bouncing as she shakes her head. "I'm training to be a shrine maiden. We are not allowed to possess magic."

"What about your other sisters, perhaps one of them—"

I falter. Mirian regards me, face serene.

"He gave his magic to you, did he not?"

I struggle to find the right words. "He was dying, he didn't have a choice—"

"Of course he did," she says, studying me with an expression so like Cillian's, my heart squeezes. "He could have kept his magic when he died. But he chose to pass it on to you."

"But—"

Mirian raises a finger, and the argument dies on my lips.

"I have no doubt you'll make him proud."

We watch the smoke in silence for a while longer, before the two women turn to leave.

"Before you go—" My voice shatters the silence. Both women face me, eyebrows raised, as I hand Tova a bundle wrapped in one of Cillian's old coats.

"What's this?" she asks, tugging back the fabric to reveal gold eyes glowing from a ball of gray fur. "Oh!"

"This is George," I say, rubbing the surly cat behind one ear. "He was your brother's dearest companion here in Oasis. I know Cillian would want you to have him."

"Oh," she repeats, one tentative hand reaching to stroke the cat's head. George's eyes slit at her touch, rumbles emanating from his chest. When she looks up again, her eyes are filled with tears. "I'll take care of him."

Still stroking the cat, Tova and Mirian pick their way past the many headstones littering the cemetery.

"Thank you," I call, although there is no way they can possibly understand everything I've infused in those two words. They seem to though. A gentle smile gracing Mirian's lips and a raised hand from Tova, and then they're gone too.

It's then I know what Cillian would've wanted, the right path for this new magic.

Wiping at my wet eyes, no doubt smearing red dust across my face, I stand up, placing a hand in farewell on the stone.

"I promise I'll use it well." My words float into the evening air, to the stars that dot the vast sky above me. "Perhaps I'll even find a theater to burn in your name."

I leave them then, my father and Cillian, the two stones leaning toward each other like old friends.

I twirl the knife of the king, making my way across the crowded dining room to where the Sulian ambassador sits, large drumsticks clenched in both meaty hands. Luc watches but does not try to stop me, not even when I stab the knife into the wood of the finely carved table, directly above the ambassador's groin. I don't miss his flinch.

"All this talk of war bores me. Shall we play a game?"

The little queen was tucked in bed hours before the international guests arrived to threaten her fragile reign. The ambassador, a man named Kappi, sneers at me, wiping chicken grease from his blubbery lips.

"What is the prince regent's mistress doing at a formal *peace* council?"

"Jester," I correct, using the knife to parry his next bite to the floor before it reaches his lips. He slams a fistful of meat and bone to the table with a crash.

"A fool's a fool."

"Perhaps so," I acknowledge, picking my fingernails with the knife before hopping nimbly on top of the table. "But no one knows a fool better than a fool."

His bushy eyebrows pull together, a storm cloud threatening to unleash. "Your Highness, I beg you, control your *clown*."

Luc shrugs, sipping his wine. "I'm afraid I have less control over her than you do."

I throw him a low bow, not missing the curve of his lips behind the goblet.

"Come now, it's so tense in here. Let's play a game."

Kappi's men eye each other, muttering. They look close to declaring war right here in the dining hall.

"I'll even let you go first." I hand the knife to Kappi, hilt first. He takes it eagerly, looking as if he's tempted to sink it into my thigh.

"Now, the game is simple enough for even you to understand."

Kappi scowls, clenching the knife the same way he clenched his drumsticks.

"The first person to kill the prince regent with this knife is the new king of Terraca," I begin, waving grandly at Luc.

"Now wait a minute—" Luc stands, but I wave him away. He takes his seat reluctantly, and I can tell from the way he drums his fingers that he's nervous.

"Now this is a game I can get behind," Kappi says, flexing his fingers. "I am excellent with a blade. I hope you are good at dancing, *Highness.*"

Luc throws me a look, but I shake my head, focused on Kappi, who stands up with a grunt. He switches the knife to his right hand, and judging from the easy way his fingers grasp it, he's not lying about his skill with a blade. Leveling it at Luc's heart, he pulls back the knife, ready to throw.

"Of course there are rules," I interject, right before he can release the blade. Kappi lets out an exasperated noise.

"Get on with it then."

I tick them off on my fingers. "First, you only get three chances. Second, you must stand across the room, in the doorway."

"I imagine you'll have me close my eyes next," Kappi grumbles.

I throw him a sparkling smile. "Not a bad idea, but no. Third, the hit must be fatal. Just hitting the prince regent isn't enough—you must kill him to win the throne."

"All right, all right. Anything else?" Kappi asks, cracking his neck, eager to begin.

I consider. "Just one thing. If you lose, and lose you will, you must leave the kingdom and never threaten Queen Sophia's rule ever again."

Kappi stares at me hard, before breaking into a smile that reveals cracked teeth. "Very well, little clown. Let's play the game already."

I jump off the table, taking a spot far enough away to dodge any wayward throws but close enough to keep an eye on Luc.

Luc plucks off his crown, letting it fall to the table with an ominous clatter.

"Perhaps I *should* try to control my clown better," he mutters, flexing his fingers. I throw him a wide smile in return. His eyes project a warning—*you'd better know what you're doing.* All this time, and still he never learns.

"Make sure to aim it just so—" I adjust Kappi's grip, so the knife is level.

Kappi yanks his arm away from mine. "I know what I'm about, wench."

Biting back a million different retorts, I give Kappi his space. He lifts the knife. Lowers it again.

"I want his word that the throne is mine if I hit him."

I groan. "His death isn't word enough?"

But Kappi is as stubborn as a desert mule. "I'm not falling for any tricks."

We'll see about that.

"Very well," Luc says, holding a fist to his chest. "I swear on the magic that flows through my blood that the crown is yours if you succeed in killing me."

Kappi licks his lips greedily, apparently satisfied, and gives a mocking bow. "All right, princeling. Let's play."

Weighing the knife, he shifts his stance, letting his right foot slide forward. His arm glides in a deadly arc, releasing the knife. I suck in a breath, but his aim is a hairsbreadth off and the blade hits the wall next to Luc's temple with a ringing sound. A mere inch to the left and Kappi would be trying on the crown right now.

"Practice throw," Kappi rumbles, as his men chuckle. I toss him the knife, trying to keep my expression light, amused.

"Two throws left."

"Yeah, yeah." Rolling his massive neck, Kappi alters his stance, letting the knife go with such force I can hear it. And this time, I know Kappi won't need the extra throw. Sure enough, the knife buries itself in Luc's chest with a thwack that makes me cringe. Eyes wide, Luc drops to his knees, trying to staunch the blood that escapes him, but it's too late.

A death shot.

He falls forward onto the blade, facedown.

"Check him." Calm, even though he just slaughtered the prince regent, Kappi watches as one of his men rolls Luc over, filthy fingers feeling for a pulse.

"Dead," the man affirms, letting Luc slide to the floor. Kappi makes his way to the crown, inspecting it with a practiced eye.

"A little small, but it'll do, I suppose."

I swallow back my anger, working to keep my placid expression. It must not work, because Kappi's attention turns from the crown to me.

"What's wrong, little clown? Did your game not go the way you hoped?"

The laughter of his men echoes off the stone walls. I say nothing as he places the crown on his head, the gold glinting amid his greasy hair. Instead, I summon my magic. I think of Cillian every time I do, somehow knowing even without him saying so that he'd be proud of the way

I've chosen to use it. After all, what's more noble than protecting those you love? The crown blazes, flames gobbling at Kappi's oily hair eagerly. With a roar, he swats at the inferno on his head.

"I'm afraid you didn't follow the rules, Lord Kappi," I call over the sound of his men attempting to beat the fire out with a matted bearskin rug. Finally, one of them manages to dislodge the crown with an overenthusiastic swing. It clinks across the room and rolls to a stop in front of a pair of snakeskin boots. Although the crown is no doubt white-hot, slender fingers reach for it, replacing it where it belongs, on a bed of golden hair.

Kappi glares at me, a few tufts of hair still smoking. "You cheated."

"I believe the rules were that I must be fatally wounded," a mild voice puts in. Kappi stumbles backward at the sight of Luc, drenched in blood, pale but still very much alive. "So I would argue that it's you who cheated."

Luc tosses the knife, still coated in his own blood, at Kappi's feet. With one hand fisted in his chest to staunch the warm blood turning rusty on the gold of his royal suit, Luc looks like an apparition. The stuff of nightmares.

Kappi drops in a hasty bow, sweat on his upper lip, and the rest of his men follow suit. "Please, Your Majesty . . . we will honor our oath and leave in peace."

Luc flicks a careless hand at them. "Go."

They scrabble over each other in their rush, darting frightened looks over their shoulders as they do so. As soon as they're gone, Luc drops the facade, collapsing in a heap into a chair.

"Devils, girl. I sometimes think you enjoy watching me die."

I smother a smile. "I'll get your tinctures."

"Ah-ah." He wags a finger at me, eyes burning despite the pain he must be in. "You of all people should know what I really need in order to heal."

"Of course, Majesty. 'The kiss of a pure maiden,' correct?" I scan the room. "I'm afraid Margarite just left."

"Come here, you insufferable thing," Luc growls, tugging me to him. His lips find mine, hungry, and suddenly, I'm all out of tricks. Always at his mercy. Pulling away, Luc caresses my cheek, watching me with a fondness that seems to melt me from the inside out. Tucking a lock of my hair behind my ear, Luc winces as the movement tugs at his still-healing wound.

"Isn't there a way to avert war that doesn't involve me getting stabbed though?"

I shrug. "I'll look into it."

"You're the worst Jester ever, you know that?"

I can't help the laugh that bursts from me. "I am nothing but a paid fool, Your Highness."

Luc's eyes are soft as he studies me, drinking me in. "And I am your fool, always."

Is it worth it?

This time when Luc pulls me to him, I realize I finally know the answer to Cillian's question.

THE END

ACKNOWLEDGMENTS

I always thought writing a book was a lone wolf endeavor until I actually wrote one myself. And realized it takes a whole pack! So many wonderful people made this book what it is today, and although I'm certain I'll forget a few, I'll do my best.

First off, I have to thank my first readers, my betas and critique partners: Haleigh Wenger, who is one of my best writing friends and most trusted critique partners, ily! You make my books better, and that's why you're my first reader. The ladies of the Slack writing club who took the time to read and offer feedback; Sam Stewart, my feral fairy friend who offers writing advice worth its weight in diamonds; Maria Farb, whose gentle, but sharp eye caught many mistakes; and Claire Hill, whose fantasy writing skills are unmatched. My dear mentor and friend, Katrina Emmel, who helped me level up as a writer more than anyone else— sending you ALL the chai tea and hugs. To Kes Trester, who saved my query and first ten with her eagle eyes and kindness. My sister, Hailee, who excitedly reads anything I throw at her and whose advice I trust almost more than anyone else's. My niece, Addie, who is totally my hype girl and who I have no doubt will be a killer author herself one day. My sisters-in-law, Kendra, Brittany, and Kerianne, as well as my friends, Carey and Adrian, who all read this story and offered amazing advice early on. I'm lucky to have family and friends who love to read!

I'm extremely lucky to have been blessed with supportive parents. Mom and Dad, thank you for paying for many, many college creative writing classes, reading every silly story I threw your way, and for believing in me. I still smile when I think about how you guys thought my story was good enough to be a movie. I love you.

Thanks to my husband who laughed at me when I told him you needed a degree to write a book. I could not have written this book (or any of them) without you. You have pulled me out of so many slumps and celebrated this whole journey with me, ups and downs. Thanks for all the rejection chocolate and all the nights spent watching the boys so I could write. I'll never be able to say it enough—I love you.

To my boys, Eivin, JD, and Leif, who are super patient with a mama whose head is oftentimes full of plot and character. Thanks for being such good nappers so I could steal an hour or two a day to write. You guys are my joy.

Of course, this book never would have seen the light of day without the enthusiasm and passion of my rockstar agent, Colleen Oefelein. Thank you a million times for believing in both me and my story. There is nothing that can compare with having an agent who is your fiercest advocate as well as a dear friend. I'm lucky enough to have both and more in Colleen. I look forward to selling many more books with you, my friend.

Forever grateful to the entire CamCat team who made all my author dreams a reality. What a wonderful group of people! Sue Arroyo, who runs CamCat with grace and aplomb and still took the time to make me feel like a welcome part of the team; my cover editor, Maryann Appel, who designed an absolutely stunning cover; and Helga Schier, who does so much behind the scenes. And my editors! Bridget McFadden, my editor, served up some seriously helpful edits and took this book to another level. You were a wonderful advocate for this book from start to finish, and I couldn't ask for a better editor. My copyeditor, Ellen Leach, who caught the fact that I burned down a hotel and then had that same hotel reappear in the next chapter—God bless your sharp eyes!

And to anyone else who might've slipped my brain, thank you. I'm sorry I have the brain of an eighty-year-old goldfish.

Lastly, thank you, my reader, for picking up this book. I wrote it for you.

ABOUT THE AUTHOR

Brielle D. Porter decided to become a writer after a well-meaning elementary school teacher told her she had a gift for it. Stolen moments under the covers reading anything from Harry Potter to William Goldman solidified the desire to one day tell stories herself. *Jester* is her debut novel.

Brielle lives with her husband and three sons on a lavender farm in Northern Idaho. When she's not writing, she can be found running and beekeeping. Brielle is so passionate about her hobbies that you should only ask her about them if you have plenty of time to spare.

If you've enjoyed
Jester by Brielle D. Porter,
you'll enjoy
Sara Hosey's *Imagining Elsewhere*.

CHAPTER
1

Moments after she met Candi Clifton for the first time, Astrid Friedman-Smith experienced a sinking feeling of recognition. She knew karma when it came around to bite her in the ass.

It was on that very first day at her new school that Astrid found herself flying—literally flying—across the cafeteria and then falling face down on the polished linoleum while her classmates laughed and threw milk cartons and french fries at her.

She knew she deserved it, especially because her own poor choices had been one of the main reasons she was at this new school in the first place.

It was the fall of 1988 when they moved from Queens to Elsewhere, New York, in part because Astrid had a not-so-insignificant problem with bullying and harassing other students. A problem so big, in fact, that it had made the New York area tabloid newspapers, which ran third- and fourth-page headlines like, "High Performing High Schoolers Get an A+ in Cruelty" and "Out on Her Ass-Trid: Lead Bully Expelled From Prep School."[1]

Astrid had lived in Elsewhere for a full two weeks before that first day in the cafeteria and she'd still believed the move had been punishment enough. This was partly because, before the move, when Astrid had looked up Elsewhere in the World Book Encyclopedia,[2] all she was able to discover was that it was a small, economically-depressed community where the high taxes were matched only by a startlingly high suicide rate. *Some real small-town values right there,* Astrid had thought. She'd imagined that if she could simply survive her senior year at Elsewhere High, she'd be fine. She'd had no idea that surviving Elsewhere might actually be a challenge.

She'd heard of Candi before she'd met her—and even seen a picture of her. For some inexplicable reason, there was a lurid painting of a twelve-year-old Candi hanging up in the public library. From what Astrid had gathered, this Candi girl, despite only being in high school, ran the town of the Elsewhere.

This made no sense to Astrid, but then again, there were lots of things about her new town that she hadn't been able to fully comprehend. How it was possible, for example, that the town simply "didn't have cable" and barely got network television stations?[3] Or why was it that everyone was so scrawny? (And not in a fashionable New York way; they were unhealthy, sunken-eyed and sallow-looking). And why, at least if the classes Astrid had attended that first day were any indication,

---

[1] But we'll get to that.

[2] The hard copies of Wikipedia. Big books in an alphabetical set, they covered lots of topics, but were sort of limited. For example, there was no entry for anything really "contemporary" and there was no good sex stuff, much to the dismay of many middle schoolers.

[3] Once upon a time, if you had a good antenna on the top of your house, your television was able to "stream" (not what we called it) 7 or 8 stations. *And that was it.*

did no one seem all that concerned with attendance, academics, or really anything close to scholarly rigor at Elsewhere High?

Astrid couldn't ask these questions though, because, up until the day she met Candi, no one was willing to actually speak to her. All of her overtures of friendship had been met with either blank indifference, nervous giggling, or wide-eyed, outright fear.

That all changed the day she met Candi.

Astrid was sitting at one end of a long table, empty except for a cute, nerdy kid alone at the other end, who was immersed in a D&D rulebook.[4] Astrid was—strategically—sensorially-cocooned: The Cure blasting on her headphones, eyes glued to her blue binder, on which she was putting the finishing touches on an elaborate rendering of the words "THE SUGARCUBES," and chewing on the turkey sandwich she'd just bought and then customized (removing the turkey and putting chips in its place).

She had almost forgotten herself, munching away, when a strange sensation overtook her—it was as though someone had thrown a big down comforter over the entire cafeteria. She looked up to see that everyone was talking differently, standing differently. They had an unconvincing nonchalance about them, as though a camera crew had entered the room and they were trying to "act natural."

And then, there she was. Candi.

She wore a white cinch-belt over a skin-tight pink dress, layered pink-and-white socks and white ked sneakers, and dozens of bracelets on each arm. Her voluminous blonde hair, which framed her face like a lion's mane, added several inches to her height. She walked like a runway model, drawing each knee up before shooting her pointed foot forward, like an archer drawing an arrow. Lift, shoot, lift, shoot.

---

[4] Don't ask Astrid how she knew what it was. She wouldn't want to talk about it.

Other students parted to let her pass. She was flanked with a girl on each side, who walked just a bit behind her, reminding Astrid of the v-shaped formation birds flew in.

Frozen mid-chew, Astrid wondered if they had planned the entrance. It felt like something out of a John Hughes movie.[5] Perhaps the music still streaming into Astrid's ears helped, giving the trio's dramatic march a soundtrack.

As it became clear the girls were headed toward Astrid, Astrid's tablemate quickly put the rulebook in his pocket and scurried away.

Astrid longed to follow him but was pinned in place as Candi, with a flip of her magnificent hair, rested her gaze on Astrid's face.

Awkwardly, Astrid put down the pen she was gripping and, despite her churning stomach, forced a hopeful smile. Astrid, who had been popular, really popular, at her old school, thought maybe this would be her chance, her introduction into the upper echelons of Elsewhere society.

She willed herself to play it cool.

Or at least cool-ish.

Candi crossed her arms and regarded her coldly.

Astrid stopped smiling.

---

[5] John Hughes made a bunch of '80s movies that, for many of us, really capture the '80s teen experience. Be warned, though, like a lot of '80s pop culture, they're totally racist and sexist.

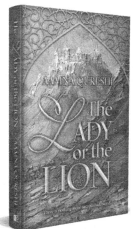